"Does nothing ever ruffle your calm, Verity? Or do you insist on producing *sensible* advice under all circumstances?" Will demanded, irritation suddenly overcoming the tattered remnants of good manners.

"Would you rather something did ruffle me?" She paused, one hand on the door frame, arrested in the act of tossing her wrecked hat inside, and smiled at him. It was not reassuring. "I have no intention of not being sensible, or of pretending to be less intelligent than I am, even if you would prefer me to produce some tears and flutter my handkerchief. I have no idea how to have a fit of the vapors, if that is what you are expecting, Will."

It might be easier if she did succumb to nerves, he admitted to himself. Then he could rely on his own judgment without having to give due consideration to her, undoubtedly reasonable, objections. That smile—genuine, amused, warm. He had no idea she could smile like that.

Author Note

Where the inspiration for a novel comes from always varies for me—sometimes a character arrives in my imagination, sometimes a pair of lovers or sometimes a scene or a place.

With Will and Verity's story, I saw Verity in her excavation, clutching a skull, and a handsome gentleman crashing down in front of her—but who they were and how they had arrived in this situation, I had no idea. So I let them talk and gradually they began to reveal themselves to me. Will is a duke bearing a crushing load of responsibility and with an upbringing that had almost—but not quite—suppressed his wicked sense of humor. Verity is a bishop's daughter with an independent streak and a secret that make her a most unsuitable match for a very proper duke.

But...an attraction that they won't admit to, a shared sense of the ridiculous and the wicked schemes of a brood of unruly children keep throwing the two together.

Will and Verity took over and told me their story—and I hope you enjoy discovering it as much as I did writing it.

LOUISE ALLEN

Least Likely to Marry a Duke

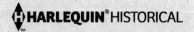

HARLEQUIN®HISTORICAL

Recycling programs
for this product may
not exist in your area.

ISBN-13: 978-1-335-63503-7

Least Likely to Marry a Duke

Copyright © 2019 by Melanie Hilton

Printed in U.S.A.

Louise Allen loves immersing herself in history. She finds landscapes and places evoke the past powerfully. Venice, Burgundy and the Greek islands are favorite destinations. Louise lives on the Norfolk coast and spends her spare time gardening, researching family history or traveling in search of inspiration. Visit her at louiseallenregency.co.uk, @louiseregency and janeaustenslondon.com.

Books by Louise Allen

Harlequin Historical

Marrying His Cinderella Countess
The Earl's Practical Marriage
A Lady in Need of an Heir
Convenient Christmas Brides
"The Viscount's Yuletide Betrothal"
Least Likely to Marry a Duke

The Herriard Family

Forbidden Jewel of India
Tarnished Amongst the Ton
Surrender to the Marquess

Lords of Disgrace

His Housekeeper's Christmas Wish
His Christmas Countess
The Many Sins of Cris de Feaux
The Unexpected Marriage of Gabriel Stone

Visit the Author Profile page
at Harlequin.com for more titles.

To Chris, Dickie, Robbie and Darren,
who built me my wonderful library and study.

Chapter One

Great Staning, Dorset—May 1st, 1814

William Xavier Cosmo de Whitham Calthorpe, Fourth Duke of Aylsham—William to his recently deceased grandfather, Will in his own head and Your Grace to the rest of the world—strode up the gentle slope of the far boundary of his new home and relaxed into the calming certainty that all was as it should be.

There was the slight matter of the turmoil he had left behind in the house, but he would do battle with that later, when he returned for breakfast. Patience and the application of benevolent discipline was all that was required. A lot of patience.

Now he was doing what any responsible landowner did first thing in the morning—he was walking his estate, learning its strengths and weaknesses and needs so that he could be a good landlord. He was the Duke now and he knew his duty, whether it was to the undisciplined brood of half-siblings who were currently making domestic life hideous or the hundreds of tenants and the numerous estates that were now his responsibility.

Oulton Castle, twenty miles away, was the true seat of the Dukes of Aylsham, but although, naturally, it was in a state of perfect repair and management, it was completely unsuitable for the large and lively family he had just acquired. This manor, Stane Hall, had been in the hands of excellent tenants for years, but with its improved drainage, its unoccupied Dower House and its complete absence of lethal moat, towering medieval walls and displays of ancient weaponry it was a far safer home for now. He could only be thankful that the tenant had been ready to retire to Worthing and had needed no persuasion to leave.

Will pushed thoughts of problems away to focus on what he was doing. This was the seventh day he had been in residence and the first morning he had been able to spare to inspect the land. Ahead must be the northernmost point of the boundary.

He checked the map he had folded into his pocket. Sure enough, the six low irregular bumps that lay before him like a string of half-buried beads were shown with stylised hatching and labelled *'Ancient Tumuli (Druidic).'* The low morning sun cast long shadows from their bases and the boundary line was shown on the map as running along the crest of the chain. There was no sign of a fence.

That was not good. Fences were of the utmost importance to a perfectly managed estate and he intended Stane Hall to be perfect. Dukes did not accept second-best, either in their staff, their surroundings or themselves. That had been one of the first lessons his grandfather had taught him when the third Duke had plucked Will out of the miserable chaos that life had become with his father, the now deceased and always erratic George, Marquess of Bromhill.

The old Duke's first attempts at training the perfect heir had all gone for nothing the moment his son, the newly widowed George, set eyes on the lovely Miss Claudia Edwards, writer and passionate educational theorist. A life made notorious by the couple's eccentricity had ended with the Marquess's plunge to his death from a rooftop, where he had been putting into practice the theory that a gentleman should be able to perform any task he might ask of others, including manual labour.

Three months later Will was still struggling to feel anything but deep irritation that his father, whom he had hardly known, had failed to grasp the simple fact that he had an obligation to provide employment for as many local people as possible, not replace his own roof tiles at the expense of a skilled craftsman. Will rather suspected that the realisation that he could now hand the title safely to his grandson had enabled the old Duke to finally give up the fight against a debilitating heart condition.

The loss of his grandfather was one for which he was not yet ready to forgive his father. Will had been Marquess of Bromhill for only five weeks when he found himself Duke of Aylsham. That was only eleven—no, twelve weeks ago, he corrected himself. Three months and the pain inside for the grandfather he had lived with for fourteen years had not subsided. But while dukes might observe all the outward shows of mourning, they did not speak of loss and loneliness and certainly not of their fear of finding themselves inadequate to the role they had to fill, Will told himself. He wondered if the old man had felt like this when he had inherited the title. Grandfather would never have admitted it, he thought ruefully.

Will had absorbed all his predecessor's lessons and

he intended to be every inch as perfect a nobleman as the third Duke. That would be easier with the right wife at his side, he knew. The old man had been firm on the importance of not marrying an unsuitable woman and that rule was underlined in Will's mental list of priorities, as if his father's example was not warning enough.

Suitable meant well bred, handsome, fertile and brought up to the highest standards of deportment. A pleasant disposition, an adequate level of education and reasonable intelligence were, of course, desirable. Unconventional ideas and eccentricity were impossible, as demonstrated by his stepmother, who, despite perfectly understandable displays of grief for her recent loss, absolutely refused to observe any of the mourning customs suitable to her sex and station in life.

Will brought his mind back from the problem of his stepmother and the prospect of the Marriage Mart—which could not be contemplated for the next forty weeks of mourning, unfortunately—and reapplied it to the matter of boundary fences. He could have brought his estate manager with him on this walk, but he preferred to make his own judgements first, not allow his staff to gloss over shortcomings or try to distract him from problems.

Brooding unproductively on the past had brought him to the foot of the largest tumulus. Naturally, he had come out dressed appropriately for the rigours of the countryside, and well broken-in boots and his second-oldest pair of breeches were entirely suitable for scrambling up hillocks.

His boots slid on the rabbit-cropped grass as he reached the top, turning as he climbed to face back the way he had come. From here the view over his park was a fine one with the distant glint of water from the lake, a group of grazing fallow deer and mature trees in picturesque coppices. The warming air brought green scents, a hint of hedgerow blossoms, the rumour of the dung hill awaiting spreading in a nearby field.

Was the house visible from here? He shifted back a step to change the angle and the ground vanished from beneath him, pitching him down into the mound in a shower of earth and stones.

Will landed with a painful thud on his tail bone. Dirt and pebbles rained down on his bare head and his low-crowned beaver hat rolled away over beaten earth to the knees of the young woman crouched in front of him. The young woman with a loose plait of rich toffee-coloured hair over one shoulder, wide brown eyes—and a human skull clutched to her midriff. At which point something bit him sharply on the left buttock.

There was very little warning, only a long shadow falling across her as a body crashed down into her excavation slicing into the mound. Verity lunged forward, grabbed at the skull and rocked back on her heels as the man landed in front of her with a grunt, one short, sharp Anglo-Saxon expletive and a loud rattle of stones.

Silence. It was neither a thunderbolt nor a fallen angel facing her, either of which might have been easier to deal with. The dust settled, leaving her staring at a fair-haired man, blue eyes narrowed against the light, mouth set with either discomfort or fury. Very likely both. He was dressed in expensive, simple and utterly appropriate country clothing, now filthy.

Utterly appropriate. I know who you are. Oh, no...

His handsome face contorted in a wince of pain

and she realised why. As social disasters went, this ranked high.

'Sir, I fear you may be sitting on a tooth.'

Not the correct form of address, but as we have not been introduced...

Those blue eyes narrowed a little further as he shifted on to his right hip, reached underneath his coat-tails and produced a human jawbone. '*A* tooth? Singular?' he enquired. Then his gaze shifted to what she was cradling against her bosom. 'Madam, you appear to be holding a skull. A human skull.'

'Yes,' Verity agreed.

Presumably he was being sarcastic with the *appear*. It could hardly be mistaken for anything else.

'I am and it is. Is the jawbone undamaged? I mean, are you unhurt?' There was no really ladylike way of asking a duke if his left buttock had been wounded by an Ancient Briton. It was absolutely out of the question to snatch the jaw from him to check that it was intact. *The bone, that is.*

'I am sure it is nothing serious, madam. I apologise for my language earlier.' It would be much easier to deal with this if he had shown the anger he must be feeling. Or even moaned in acknowledgement of the pain. As it was, the conversation might as well be happening at Almack's. The Duke shifted his long legs as though to stand.

'No!' She took a breath and moderated the volume. 'Please stay exactly where you are or you will damage the sides. Just allow me to move everything.' Verity placed the skull carefully in the box of hay she had prepared for it and held out her hand for the jaw. When that was safe she moved back, gathered her skirts around her ankles and stood up.

The Duke, being a gentleman, had averted his gaze. He was probably too cross to consider ogling her in any case. Verity ignored the urge to see exactly what would provoke him into behaving improperly and waited while he rose to his feet in an enviably effortless and controlled manner.

He is the youngest Duke, not yet thirty, and he has no vices to mar that fine figure.

Her cousin Roderick had told her about the man who was now Duke of Aylsham. His reputation had been built up over many years of being merely the impeccable Lord Calthorpe and apparently the man was a byword for acting with absolute propriety under all circumstances.

They call him Lord Appropriate.

Roddy had written that about eighteen months ago, in the course of one of his chatty, gossip-filled letters.

Of course his father the Marquess, is eccentric, to put it very kindly, and his stepmother is a notorious bluestocking, so it was probably a relief to be rescued by his grandfather, who took him to live with him when Calthorpe was a boy.

The old Duke is the stiffest stickler for what is due to his position that you may imagine, but, even so, Calthorpe appears to have gone to extremes to conform. One day he will be the starchiest duke in the kingdom. He has even managed a duel with perfect correctness—a lady was insulted, he issued a challenge, deloped, shook hands with the

*other man even though he did not delope, merely
missed, and refused to gossip afterwards.
Inhuman, I call it.*

It seemed she was responsible for shaking an entirely
improper oath out of the man, in addition to ruining
his lovely but tastefully well-worn clothes, scraping his
expensive boots and biting, by proxy, his perfect ducal
backside.

*And it probably is perfect, judging by how fit he
seems. Those thighs...*

At least he was capable of standing and nothing appeared to be broken. Verity told herself to wait until
after the Duke had gone before she fussed over her careful excavation through the tumulus. 'You are probably
wondering what I am doing?' she said. The very way
he was *not* looking at her outfit of a plain skirt, laced
boots and tweed jacket conveyed perfectly his shock at
seeing a gentlewoman so attired. Goodness knew where
her straw hat had gone.

'I was surprised to find my Druidical monument bi-
sected, I must confess,' he said, perfectly courteous, but
without a hint of a smile. 'I was even more surprised to
discover that it was being filleted by a lady.'

Verity opened her mouth, shut it again, taken aback
by just how much she wanted to shake the man. He
was polite. He was, not to put too fine a point on it, a
supremely decorative example of his sex. But all she
wanted was to shock another swear word out of him, or
a smile, or an admission by so much as a flicker of an
eyelid that he had glanced at her ankles as she stood up.
His manner was perfectly correct, but she could tell, as
clearly as if he had said so, that he thoroughly disap-

proved of her and thought her occupation bizarre and unseemly.

Oh, the horror of it! A female engaged in an intellectual pursuit involving engaging her brain and getting her hands dirty! Civilisation as he knows it will probably come to an end at any moment.

'I am sorry to contradict you, sir, but it is not your monument, it is *our* monument. I have been most careful to excavate a section through this side of it only. *My* side. I am not convinced it has any connection at all with the Druids and I am most certainly not *filleting* it. This is a precise excavation conducted according to the most modern antiquarian principles. I can lend you the relevant papers on the subject if you are interested.' She smiled, the kind of winsome, ladylike smile she had once reserved for tea parties at the Bishop's Palace before Papa retired. The Duke was an intelligent man, she was sure. He would recognise a lightly disguised snarl when he saw one.

The contrast between her words and the smile made him narrow his eyes, presumably in displeasure. 'Your side? This land belongs to you?'

Verity pointed to the one remaining post sticking out of the crown of the mound, twelve carefully measured inches back from the edge of her cut. 'That is the remains of your fence.'

His lips tightened. Did he think that was an implied rebuke about the state of his boundaries? 'I fear I should have introduced myself earlier.' He removed his gloves, produced a vast and spotless white linen handkerchief, wiped his hands free of the dirt that had penetrated despite them and held out the right one to her. 'I am Aylsham.'

'I had guessed as much, Your Grace.' Verity swiped her hand over her skirt and took his. 'I am Miss Wingate.' She retrieved her fingers rather abruptly. 'My father is the Bishop of Elmham—the retired Bishop, that is. The current incumbent's country seat is nearer the county boundary, but the Old Palace actually belongs to Papa. He bought it from the Church Commissioners when he was recovering from his stroke. They thought it too antiquated for present times, but we are very fond of it.'

She was talking too much and recognising why was no help. This was an attractive man—even if he was a judgemental aristocrat—and he had her at a disadvantage. She was partly responsible for his accident, she was looking a fright and under these circumstances she had no idea how to behave with him.

'Miss Wingate. I was intending to give myself the pleasure of calling on your father tomorrow. If his health permits, of course?'

Why am I cross? Verity asked herself as she explained that the afternoon was the best time for her father and that, naturally, he would be delighted to meet the Duke. *Because I care what he thinks*, she answered. *And that is infuriating.* Just because he had broad shoulders and a firm chin and blue eyes and looked as though his smile—if he ever produced one—would be delicious, there was no reason to fawn over the man. She spent her life ensuring that, as far as it was within her power, men did not get fawned upon to the disadvantage of women. Once had been quite enough in her experience.

Now the Duke was looking around him. A small furrow appeared between straight brows two shades darker than his hair. 'You are alone, Miss Wingate? I cannot see your maid or your labourers.'

'My groom will be collecting me at eight.' She glanced up to the east, noting the position of the sun. 'It must almost be that now. If you will excuse me, I will secure my excavation.' The skull was the most important thing, of course, but she had to make sure that the descent of one long-limbed male had not disturbed or damaged anything else.

'May I assist?'

'No,' she said sharply. 'I mean, no, thank you, Your Grace. If you could just stand over here, clear of the cut surfaces and the floor? Yes, there, perfect.'

Stop it, she scolded herself as she picked up the brush and tidied up the fallen pebbles and earth. *He is not perfect, merely a well-formed gentleman. And do not pretend you were not examining the rear view just now. You knew perfectly well the tails of his coat would disguise any sign of damage done by that jawbone.*

The Duke had broad shoulders and a trim waist to go with those long legs. It was maddening—surely *something* had to be imperfect? Other than his manner, of course. Who would need an ice house when they had the Duke of Aylsham to hand, ready to cast a chill over any situation?

The sound of wheels on gravel heralded the arrival of Tom with the pony and trap. He pulled up well clear of the excavation as he had been taught and came over, hat in hand. 'Good morning, sir. Miss Wingate, are you ready?'

'This is the Duke of Aylsham, Tom, and, yes, I am ready. Please put the tools in the back and then this box, very carefully.'

* * *

Will watched the retreating vehicle, picked up his hat and flicked the worst of the soil off it with his handkerchief. Both hat and handkerchief appeared ruined to him, but Notley, his valet, would no doubt work his magic on them, along with the scuffed boots, scarred gloves and soiled coat.

He made his way around the mound to the gap between it and the next, smaller, tumulus. For some reason he wanted to have his feet on his own land before he thought about that little episode.

What a hoyden Miss Wingate was, not at all what a prelate's daughter should be. Will lengthened his stride along the headland, making for the point where a hedge and track cut back towards the house. Dressed like a working woman, no hat, no gloves, hair coming undone on her shoulders, grubbing about on hands and knees in the earth—and handling a human skull as though it was a pudding basin. Outrageous. *And* she had been laughing at him because of where that confounded jawbone had attacked him, he could tell, even though she had kept her face perfectly straight. There had been a devilish twinkle of amusement in her eyes. They were a rather attractive brown...

The unfortunate Bishop must be sick indeed if he was allowing his daughter to carry on in such a manner, Will concluded as he reached the track. In no way was such an occupation fit for a gentlewoman. Even his stepmother drew the line at grubbing about in earth for old bones. It was most unfortunate, because there was no way in which he could prevent his half-sisters from making her thoroughly unsuitable acquaintance, given that they were now neighbours. He could hardly snub a bishop.

How old was she? Twenty-three or four? Those dark eyes, that hair, like golden toffee streaked through with rich brown, those long legs and the elegant curves as she had risen to her feet... Her feet had been encased in boots more fitted for an under-gardener, but the flash of ankle he had glimpsed had been slender and rounded.

Stop it, Will, his conscience admonished as he climbed over a stile. *She is clearly going to be an embarrassment as a neighbour and you have no business thinking about women at the moment in any case. Not for another forty weeks.*

This mourning was a confounded nuisance. It was all very right and proper, of course. And he sincerely and deeply grieved for the loss of his grandfather, but he desperately needed help with his brood of half-siblings and a wife would be perfect for that. A wife with nerves of steel and a rigorous sense of duty, he added to his mental list of requirements. But no lady who was suitable to be the wife of a duke would consider flouting convention and being wooed and wed before the mourning period of a year was over.

And now he had gone half the distance he had intended to cover that morning and the encounter with Miss Wingate had made him forget to record points about the land as he went. Will climbed the next stile, sat down on the far step and got out his notebook.

Blockage in the west ditch, the fence across the tumuli...

A warm, mocking brown gaze... *Mocking.* She thought that entire episode was amusing, the confounded chit.

* * *

'Good morning, Papa. Good morning Mr Hoskins, Larling.' Verity caught sight of herself in the long mirror as she entered her father's bedchamber on the stroke of half past nine and gave her reflection a nod of approval. She had bathed, changed, breakfasted and organised the events of the early morning into a suitably edited version in her head and now, looking the perfect model of a senior clergyman's daughter, was ready to keep her father company while he breakfasted.

Her father smiled his lopsided smile, the Reverend Mr Hoskins jumped to his feet and mumbled a greeting in return and Larling, the valet, placed the breakfast tray on the bedside table.

A savage brain seizure almost two years before had left her father unsteady on his feet, liable to tire rapidly and with virtually no comprehensible speech. It had, mercifully, not affected his very considerable intellect. James Wingate was still a formidable scholar of the early church in Britain and was continuing his work with the assistance of his Chaplain and secretary, Christopher Hoskins.

Trial and error had helped the household establish a strict routine. Verity rose at dawn, had a cup of coffee, put an apple in her pocket and went off to her excavations for two hours, returning to bathe and take breakfast. At nine thirty her father broke his fast, in bed, while she entertained him with the results of her morning's excavating and plans for the day.

When he rose the Bishop would retire to his study with Hoskins and they would work, communicating in their own manner, until luncheon at twelve thirty. Then her father would rest for two hours and either resume his researches until four or receive callers.

Which left Verity the afternoon free, provided there were no visitors and the cares of housekeeping did not entangle her for more than the morning. And today there was nothing to detain her. The threat of a descent by the Duke tomorrow she would worry about when it happened.

Her father finished his porridge and lifted an eyebrow, her cue to recount events so far.

'I have succeeded in removing the skull intact, Papa. I can see no sign of anything buried with the body, but then, the rest of the skeleton is not visible, being under the far side of the mound. I will clean it and take measurements and then I can rebury it and fill in the cut. You recall that I have already made sketches of the exposed interior of the mound.'

He nodded, smiling his approval, encouraging her to continue. The only problem was, nothing else had happened at the excavation other than her unexpected visitor.

'The Duke was out walking and…er…dropped in to see what I was doing.'

'The Duke of Aylsham?' Mr Hoskins asked, quite as though the neighbourhood was replete with a selection of dukes to choose from.

'Yes. He was perfectly civil and expressed a desire to call tomorrow, Papa. I said we would be happy to receive him.'

Her father's hands moved in the rapid signs that only his Chaplain was able to decipher at speed. 'Does he appear to be intellectually inclined?' Mr Hoskins asked.

'I have no idea, I'm afraid. He seemed intelligent,

although whether he has intellectual leanings I could not judge. He does not seem to know anything of antiquarian matters.'

And he certainly does not appear to believe in women using their brains.

The Chaplain was translating again. 'I look forward to meeting him. His grandfather was a man of great powers—I have high hopes of our new neighbour.'

Verity told herself to be glad. The stimulus would be good for Papa, the presence of the ducal household would be excellent for the local economy and she should not be selfish. What did it matter if the man thought her an eccentric hoyden or blamed her for the teeth marks on his posterior? His opinion, good or bad, was a matter of supreme indifference to her. She had better things to think about, surely, than a pair of chilly blue eyes.

Chapter Two

The breakfast room closely resembled a menagerie after all the cage doors had been opened. Will strode to the head of the table and nodded to Peplow, the butler, who pulled back the heavy carved chair, tilted it, then let it go with a thud.

The sound was enough to attract the attention of the other occupants of the room. Silence fell. Six heads turned in his direction, four footmen kept their gazes firmly fixed on the opposite wall. After the first two days they had learned not to flinch too obviously.

'Good morning, Althea, Araminta, Alicia. Good morning, Basil, Bertrand, Benjamin. Gentlemen, your sisters are waiting for you to seat them.' He remained standing while his half-sisters took their places with varying degrees of elegance, then sat, with a nod of permission to the boys which coincided with their own scramble to sit. 'Basil, it is your turn to say grace, I believe.'

Basil, fourteen and possibly the world's least devout boy, lurched to his feet again and looked around wildly for inspiration. 'Er… Thank you, God, for kedgeree for breakfast. Amen.' He sat down again with a grin of relief.

Will told himself that he should probably be grateful that the thanks had been addressed to the deity and not to Beelzebub and nodded to the butler to begin service. He had rapidly discovered that a breakfast where everyone helped themselves from the buffet was a recipe for chaos.

'Boys, napkins. Benjamin, pass your sister the butter, she should not have to ask twice. Althea, Araminta, Basil, tomorrow afternoon you will accompany me to call on our neighbour, the Bishop of Elmham. Please inform Miss Preston and Mr Catford that you will be absent from your lessons.'

'A bishop?' Althea wrinkled her very pretty nose. 'That sounds dull.'

'Bishop Wingate has retired due to ill health. He is, however, a notable scholar and, I should not have to point out, it would not matter if he was as dull as ditch water, it would still be our duty to call upon our neighbour as a matter of courtesy. You address a bishop as *my lord*.'

The rest of the meal was an obstacle course through instructions on etiquette, a lecture on the absolute necessity to do things out of duty which might not give one pleasure, the privileges and responsibilities of rank and the discovery that Basil had a mouse in his pocket.

As the screams and tantrums occasioned by the discovery, capture and banishment of the mouse subsided, Will wondered whether he was doomed to a stomach ulcer by the time he was thirty and mentally prepared himself for the horrors of the daily meeting with the children's tutor and governess.

It was too much to expect that a few weeks could undo the damage of a childhood where the only rule their doting and deluded parents had imposed was to do exactly as one wished, the moment one thought of it and without any pause for reflection. That way, his stepmother had explained, the natural genius of each child would unfurl tenderly, like the petals of a flower. They would learn what they needed to know as, and when, they felt the necessity.

The only small mercy was that they were not illiterate, he thought, doggedly finishing his ham and eggs. The desire to read completely unsuitable books had driven all of them to master their letters and then, when they wanted to compose their own stories, to learn to write. Mathematics, however, was apparently a closed book to all of them and as for basic etiquette, that was an alien concept he was painfully—for all concerned—imposing on them.

I need a wife, he thought again.

He could teach the boys to be gentlemen, but his sisters needed more than a governess. They had their mother, of course. Lady Bromhill was living in the Dower House, writing another tract on the natural education of children, no doubt, and holding forth at length to anyone who would listen on the iniquity of imposing rules of mourning on women. Her grief was deep and genuine, Will fully acknowledged, but her methods of expressing it were outrageous. He lived in daily anticipation that she would scandalise the neighbourhood by appearing in a crimson gown or emulate the women of Classical societies by rending her clothing and beating her bare bosom while wailing in Ancient Greek.

Will shuddered. It was unfortunate that his siblings

would be exposed to another unconventional female to-morrow when they called on the Bishop, because the last thing that they needed was the example of more shocking behaviour. He mentally squared his shoulders; his grandfather had shown him all too clearly that being a duke was no easy undertaking but, somehow, he had not expected that raising a delinquent family would be part of his duties. For the thousandth time he reminded himself that they had recently lost their father, that their lives had been turned upside down as much as his had, that he must temper discipline with kindness.

Verity surveyed the sunny room at the front of the house with muted satisfaction, given that she was about to act as hostess to the Disapproving Duke. The Chinese drawing room was the smaller of the two reception rooms and, being next to the library, was the most convenient and comfortable for her father. He was seated in a deep leather armchair, discussing the morning's newspapers with Mr Hoskins, who was reading out articles which Papa would then comment on by sign language.

They had reached the reports from the House of Lords which always prompted vehement gestures when Bosham, their butler, announced, 'His Grace the Duke of Aylsham, Lady Althea Calthorpe, Lady Araminta Calthorpe, Lord Basil Calthorpe, my lord.'

Verity did a rapid assessment of the ages of the juvenile party and sent Bosham a meaningful look. He nodded and departed, hopefully to warn the kitchen that more than Oolong tea and dainty cakes would be needed.

'Miss Wingate, Your Grace,' Mr Hoskins said, taking on himself the introductions that her father could not make.

The Duke blinked, stared and then had himself under control almost before she realised how surprised he was at her appearance. Verity produced a smile and saw a gleam of something very like approval in those blue eyes.

I am just the same woman as the one who shocked you yesterday, she thought crossly. *I am wearing a suitably modest and pretty afternoon gown, my hair is just where it should be and I have powdered away the evidence of a touch of sun on my nose. So now you approve of me, do you? But I do not crave your good opinion, Your Grace.*

He shook hands with her, went across to her father and waited a barely perceptible moment to be sure a handshake was going to be returned before offering his hand.

Mr Hoskins bowed. 'My lord welcomes you to the Old Palace, Your Grace. I am Christopher Hoskins, chaplain and secretary to the Bishop.'

The Duke was not too top-lofty to shake hands with Mr Hoskins as well, which pleased Verity. He turned to beckon forward the youngsters. 'Bishop, Miss Wingate, Reverend Hoskins, may I introduce my brother and sisters? The three younger ones have remained at home.'

They were a handsome family, Verity thought, but their manner was strangely stilted, as though they were performing by rote, not going through a familiar and routine courtesy. Were they afraid of their brother? She had an unpleasant suspicion that perhaps they were. He probably would not even have to administer corporal punishment to cow them—one look from those bleak blue eyes was enough for a sensitive child, she was sure.

The Duke took a seat by her father and Verity gathered

the younger Calthorpes to her on two sofas set at right angles around the tea table. 'They will bring in refreshments shortly,' she said, smiling in the face of their poorly concealed examination of herself and the room. 'Now, do tell me about yourselves. You have other brothers and sisters, I believe?'

The oldest, Althea, she recalled, said, 'Oh, yes, there are six of us. I am sixteen, Araminta and Basil here are twins and they are fourteen, then Alicia is thirteen, Bertrand is ten and Benjamin is nine.'

'And you live with your brother and your mama? I would like to meet her, but I am sure she does not feel like visits just at the moment. I was so grieved to hear about your poor father and, of course, your grandfather.'

'We didn't know the old Duke. He and Mama and Papa did not get on,' Basil confided. 'We live with William now and Mama lives in the Dower House because William is our guardian and he says we are little savages and need civilising and Mama considers civilisation stunts natural creativity. We miss Papa and Mama is sad. But Will doesn't care, he just makes us learn the stupidest things, like arithmetic and Latin. And we have to *behave*. All the time,' he added darkly.

'We have to learn *deportment* and sewing and the use of the globes,' Araminta added. 'The girls, that is. The boys don't have to sew or balance books on their heads.'

That did not sound too tyrannical—a typical aristocratic education, in fact. 'Arithmetic is very useful,' Verity offered. 'It will help you manage your allowances, for example, and make sure you are not cheated in shops.'

That appeared to strike home with the girls, but Basil seemed unconvinced. 'There is lots of money. Too much to worry about. And Mama and Papa never made us do anything we didn't want to. Mama says mourning is an outdated convention intended to oppress women and that we should be sad about Papa just how we want and not go about draped in black. She would like you to visit, I'm sure.' He grimaced. 'I think mourning is meant to oppress boys as well. Papa wouldn't want us not to enjoy ourselves. It doesn't mean we don't miss him, because we do.'

'It is only right and natural that you miss our father.' The deep voice behind her made Verity jump. 'But society has its conventions which are part of what makes us civilised. And you want to be civilised, do you not?'

'Yes, William,' three voices chorused. The three faces looked unconvinced.

He is turning them into little puppets, Verity thought, studying the young people's expressions. 'Would you like to go out into the gardens?'

They jumped to their feet, earning a hiss of displeasure from behind her. Verity stood, too, and turned to face the Duke. He towered over her. *Too close, too large and too sure of himself.*

'Such a lovely afternoon, don't you think, Your Grace?'

'Delightful,' he agreed smoothly. 'And I would very much enjoy seeing the gardens.'

I did not mean you, too. Stay in here and be pompous. But she could hardly say that.

'This way.' She led them to the glazed doors opening on to the terrace and, of course, he got there first to open them for her. His cologne was a subdued hint of Spanish leather. *Very masculine and restrained. How appropriate.*

'Thank you so much.'

The Old Palace had once been a fifteenth-century fortified house with four wings which made a square around a large inner courtyard. As the country became less unsettled under Henry VII, the Bishop at the time had demolished one wing, opening the courtyard out to the south and leaving a U-shaped building. Under Henry VIII, the scars of the demolition were disguised by two fanciful towers at each end of the U and finally, under James I, a garden was created where the courtyard had been.

Now, in the sunny May weather, the early roses were coming into flower, bees buzzed in what would soon be billows of lavender and rosemary and water trickled from the central fountain.

'This is delightful. The colours are most harmonious.'

Finally, she thought. *Something you approve of.*

'Yes, is it not charming? It is generally regarded as a most romantic garden.'

'Romantic.' He sounded as though he had never heard the word before. 'I was thinking that it was well planned.'

Verity shot him an exasperated look, stumbled on the top step and was caught around the waist and set firmly on her feet again before she could blink. The Duke removed his hands, leaving the impression of size, warmth and strength.

'Thank you.' It was most disconcerting, that easy physicality with that very restrained behaviour. Disturbing, somehow…

The youngsters had vanished down one of the pathways. The Duke turned from frowning over that as Mr Hoskins helped her father to his seat just outside the doors.

'My lord would be delighted if you would care to explore the garden, Your Grace,' Mr Hoskins said.

Her father was regarding her with a particularly bland expression that aroused Verity's suspicions. *What are you up to, Papa?*

Then she saw his gaze was flickering from her to the Duke and back and understood.

Oh, no, Papa. We have had the conversation about matchmaking before—and the fact that this one is a duke makes absolutely no difference whatsoever.

But he was a guest and common courtesy must be observed at all costs. 'Do allow me to show you the fountain, Your Grace. It was created to a design of my late mother's, although she never saw it completed.'

He offered his arm as was proper and she placed her fingertips on it as they began to stroll along the central path. Was it simply the fact that he was a duke that created this strange aura of power that he carried with him? Or was it just that he was a tall, broad-shouldered man approaching his prime? Or perhaps it was simply this ridiculous awareness she had of him, a potent combination of physical attraction and dislike.

Her friend Melissa Taverner would doubtless say it was because Verity was suppressing her natural animal instincts and she should indulge in some flirtation, or even kissing, in order to give them free rein. But then Melissa would probably find the Duke's stepmother a sister spirit, with equally advanced notions about 'natural' behaviour. Verity did not want to revert to nature. She had given in to those instincts once before—and discovered them seriously flawed—and now she simply wanted to have control over every aspect of her own life.

As they approached the central pool she chatted brightly about plants and garden design without receiving any response beyond polite murmurs. Then the Duke said, abruptly, 'Did you lose your mother recently, Miss Wingate?'

'When I was ten. It was a short illness of a few months. She was gone almost before anyone realised how serious it was.' There was something about the quality of his silence that prompted her to add, 'You were young when you lost your own mother, I believe?'

'I was nine. Eighteen years ago. I hardly knew her.' Perhaps he thought that sounded harsh because he added, 'Do you recall your mother clearly?'

'I remember her face—but that is easy, her portrait hangs in the dining room. I can recall her voice—it was gentle and sweet. I do not think I ever heard her raise it. Her hands were soft.' Verity caught herself before her voice wobbled. 'She was very pious and a very...*traditional* wife, I think.'

Not very intelligent, I suspect. No intellectual to match Papa. But a good woman. One who was loved. One who created a happy home.

'Are you pious and traditional, Miss Wingate?'

Startled, she glanced up, and caught a flicker of something unexpected in the heavy blue gaze. Amusement? Warmth? *Sarcasm, probably.* 'Pious? I hope I am a faithful churchwoman, but I lay no claim to piety. You know already that I am not *traditional*, Your Grace. But as I am not married, who knows whether I would be such a wife as my mother was.'

They had reached the fountain and she moved away from him to sit on the stone rim of the pool. She trailed her hand in the cool water and waited until the fish rose, as they always did, to nibble hopefully at her fingers. In the distance the laughter and calls from the young people told her that they had found the maze and over that happy sound drifted the first rippling bars of a piano sonata.

'Who is the pianist? They are very skilled.' The Duke propped his cane against the stone and stood beside her, too much on his dignity, she supposed, to perch on the fountain rim and risk the spray. He looked up and his gaze sharpened on the eastern tower.

'She is a friend of mine. There is no pianoforte in her house and so she uses mine to practise.' The others would be up there, too, in the Demoiselles' Tower as Mr Hoskins, with one of his unexpected flights of fancy, called her private turret. Lucy playing; Melissa, fingers inky, working on her latest novel; Prue with her nose in a Greek grammar; and Jane painting the view, or her friends at work. The door at the top of the decorative external stairway that encircled the tower was firmly closed, thank goodness.

'That is very generous of you. Your friend makes good use of the opportunity.' He paused so long that Verity looked up to see him frowning in the direction of the catcalls and laughter. 'Excuse me if I am jumping to conclusions, but if the fact that she does not own her own pianoforte means that her financial circumstances are a trifle restricted, might she be interested in teaching my sisters?'

There was no pianoforte in Lucy's home because her parents, who could perfectly well have afforded one in every room, considered music, other than church music, to be decadent and probably sinful. Most things were sinful, according to Mr and Mrs Lambert, especially anything that gave pleasure. Verity sometimes wondered how Lucy and her four brothers were ever conceived. Miserably, probably. She had learned to play at school, from which she had been removed when her parents discovered that three of the pupils were the illegitimate daughters of an earl. When they realised that Lucy had been practising on the old piano in the church vestry she had bruises on the palms of her hands for days and now they had no idea she was still playing.

'I am afraid not. It is not lack of funds, it is her mama's sensitivity to any loud noise that prevents Lucy from playing at home.' *Loud sounds including laughter.* 'It is a good pianoforte, but I am an indifferent player, so I am delighted that she puts it to such good use.'

'No doubt you are proficient at other musical instruments. The harp, perhaps? Or you sing, I have no doubt.' The question seemed automatic, as though he took it for granted that she was merely being coy.

'No, I play no musical instruments, Your Grace, and my singing is of the kind better heard at a distance.'

Like bagpipes—ideally with several intervening glens.

'You are too modest, I am sure, Miss Wingate.' He was still frowning in the direction of the maze, she noted. *And finding it impossible to believe that I do not have the full set of desirable ladylike attributes.* The Duke's opinion of her must be sinking lower with every discovery about her true nature. *Excellent. I will seem so very ineligible that he will not even recognise Papa's hopes of throwing us together.*

'I do not indulge in false modesty, Your Grace. I am aware of my strengths and abilities and quite clear about my weaknesses.' That earned her a very penetrating look. Perhaps young ladies were not supposed to discuss weaknesses. Now that she thought of it, there was a possible double entendre there. Or was she sensitive about it because her worst weakness had most definitely not been the kind of thing one discussed in polite society? 'Shall we walk to the maze and see whether your sisters and brother have discovered the way to its heart?'

'Most certainly.' He offered his arm again as she stood, the frown lines between his brows relaxing as they moved to a safer topic. 'Is it a complex pattern?'

'Very, Your Grace.' It was quite trying, being so comprehensively disapproved of. How difficult for him, but, of course, he could not ignore the attention due to a bishop living in the neighbourhood. Verity found a bland smile from somewhere. 'The summer house in the centre is very charming, but it rarely receives visitors, the maze is so devious.' She did not look up at her tower as they passed it. She doubted very much if her friends had interrupted their work to come to the windows, but they might have been distracted by the children and she had no desire to explain her 'reading circle' to the Duke if he saw a collection of female faces looking down at him.

'And here is the entrance. It is a very ancient maze, Tudor, my father believes, judging by the thick trunks of the yews in the hedges. I can hear the young people and it does not sound as though they have reached the centre yet.'

'One can normally hear them all too clearly, Miss Wingate,' the Duke said drily. But there was a hint of affection there, a touch of amusement in the deep voice, and Verity felt a sudden, unwilling, twinge of liking.

He does love them after all, she thought. *Perhaps*

*there is a warm heart under that starchy exterior, even
if it is only for his badly behaved siblings.*

'Their mama believes in a very liberal approach to
child-rearing, I understand?'

'"Each child, if left to his or her own devices and not
bound by the chains of convention and artificial disci-
plines, will unfurl as a perfect flower." That is a direct
quote, Miss Wingate. I have yet to discover what bloom
Basil is destined to be. A bramble, perhaps. Or deadly
nightshade.'

'I am sure the theory is well meant,' Verity ventured.

*Of all the dangerous ideas! Children need security
and boundaries and an education that will open their
eyes to the delights of the world, as well as preparing
them for its pains and duties.*

'Now that, Miss Wingate, is damning with faint
praise.' This time the amusement was plain to hear.

*Goodness. The man has a sense of humour. How un-
expected. And how admirable that he can smile about
the task he has before him.* 'I agree that it is wrong to
suppress joy in a child, or to warp their natural character. The knack, I suppose, is to allow the flowers to
continue blooming, but to ensure they are fitted for the
soil in which they must continue to grow,' she suggested.
'If I might stretch the horticultural simile somewhat.'

'Exactly that, Miss Wingate. I have three sisters and
three brothers. The girls must make good marriages and
the boys must find occupation suited to their rank and
talents. They cannot simply run wild their entire lives.
We will get there, I am certain, but to be quite frank
with you, it will be an uphill road.'

'Basil, you beast! You said you could find the centre *easily* and now we are lost and you have no idea *at all* how to get out and we will starve in here and our bleached bones will be found in a hundred years!' The shrill voice came from just behind the nearest stretch of yew hedge.

The Duke sighed. 'It seems I have a long way to go yet.'

Chapter Three

'Lady Araminta,' Verity called. 'Stay where you are, keep talking and your brother and I will come and find you.' She lowered her voice and smiled up at the Duke, suddenly at ease with him. 'I assume Lady Araminta enjoys Gothic novels.'

'Apparently, yes. I must speak to her governess about that. Bleached bones, indeed.' Was it her imagination or was there the smallest hint of a smile on those severe lips?

And I really ought to stop finding excuses to study his mouth. Looks are not everything. Looks are no way to judge anyone. And he means to censor innocent, if fanciful, novels, just because she is a girl.

'Here is the entrance.' She led the Duke under the arch of yew and into the shadows of the maze. She knew the way to reach the centre, but where had Araminta got to?

'It is very gloomy in here.' The voice was still close. Araminta had clearly calmed down somewhat and now she was beginning to sound peevish.

Second left—it looks wider, it would have attracted her. Now right and right again and—

'There you are, Lady Araminta. Now, follow me and we will soon be at the centre.'

The girl beamed at her. 'Thank you! Will, do you know the key to the maze?'

'No. I am relying upon Miss Wingate, otherwise I would be as lost as you are.'

'I thought you knew everything.' The wicked look she slanted her brother made Verity want to laugh. The girl had nice, natural manners and a sense of humour that was attractive.

'All mazes are different,' the Duke said. 'I know that much about them.'

They had regained the entrance and now Verity could count in her head. *First, then second, then third, then second, then fourth, then fifth...*

'Help!' That was Althea. They saw her the moment she spoke, standing with her back to them. 'Oh, there you are.' She turned as her sister called her name and fell in behind them with a sigh of relief. 'Basil, the little wretch, has found the centre. He has been mocking me for five minutes at least.'

'He'll be sorry,' Araminta assured her.

And four, then five, then six.

'Here we are.' They stepped out into a sunlit circle with a tiny thatched building in its centre.

Basil was perched on a bench on the miniature veranda, swinging his legs. 'What took you so long?'

His sisters regarded him with loathing. 'How did you get here so fast?' Althea demanded.

'Look at his knees. He crawled through the bottom of the hedges,' his twin said. 'You beast, that's cheating.'

'I got here first, that's what counts,' Basil said with a smirk. 'I used my intelligence.'

'And you appear to have ruined a pair of perfectly good pantaloons in the process,' the Duke said sharply. 'Besides abandoning your sisters and failing to stand up when ladies appear. The cost of the trousers will be taken from your allowance. You may now apologise to Miss Wingate for your poor manners and will escort your sisters safely back out of the maze by the conventional paths.'

'I'm sorry, Miss Wingate. But I don't know the way out.' Basil was on his feet now, brushing ineffectually at his knees.

'I marked it,' Althea said. 'I tore a scrap of paper from my notebook and dropped it at every turn.'

'Very clever, Althea.' The Duke gave her an approving nod and received a brilliant smile in return. 'But pick up all the paper as you go.'

They filed out obediently, then there was a yelp from Basil and the sound of running feet.

Verity suppressed a snort of laughter and sat down on the bench. 'I suspect your sisters are taking their revenge on Lord Basil. Shall we sit for a moment? That will allow them to get clear of the maze, then you will not have to see anything requiring a reproof.'

'They must feel I spend my entire time reproving them.' The Duke sat down heavily on the veranda steps.

'You love them and want the best for them. And they know that.'

'Do you believe so?' For a moment she thought he was going to lean back against the supporting post, but he recollected himself in time. Doubtless sitting on the steps was quite casual enough for his dignity.

'That you love them? That is obvious.' And, surprisingly, she realised it was true. 'That they know it I can tell from the way they respond to you. They do not sulk or send you unpleasant looks when your back is turned. Are the younger three as intelligent as these?'

'They are bright,' he agreed, as though reassuring himself. 'And, yes, the others are as intelligent. They all were,' the Duke added, his voice so soft that she thought he was speaking to himself.

Verity guessed she had not been intended to hear those last three words, but she answered the pain in his voice anyway. 'There were others?'

'Just one. My eldest half-sister, Arabella. She would be seventeen this year. She died just before my grandfather took me to live with him.'

'An illness?' He had fallen silent. Verity suspected he wanted to talk, but was simply unused to speaking to anyone about such an emotional subject. Or perhaps did not think such revelations *proper.*

'It was a virulent fever. It is not something that we speak of in case it distresses the children.'

You cannot admit that it distresses you, *of course.*

'You may be assured that I do not repeat confidences, Your Grace,' she said as she got to her feet. 'Perhaps we should be making our way back.'

'Indeed. We should return to the sunshine or you will become chilled,' he said as they began to wind their way back to the entrance.

The Duke seemed happier reverting to his starched-up self, she thought. A pity—she had almost liked the man who had confessed to his anxieties over his siblings, had allowed a little humour to touch him.

'Is the Bishop fit enough to travel a short distance?' he asked as they emerged into the sunshine and Verity waved across the garden to where her father sat with

Mr Hoskins. 'Might I hope he will be able to return my call? I would be pleased to entertain him at Stane Hall.'

'On a good day, certainly. He usually drives to church every Sunday and the Hall is only a short distance beyond that. His health is not entirely predictable, however. I would not want to commit him to any specific day long in advance.'

'You must be congratulated on your daughterly devotion in keeping house for your father. His indisposition, coming as it did, I believe, at a time when you must have been making your come-out, would have been most difficult for you.'

Verity opened her mouth and closed it again with a snap. Dukes, presumably, thought themselves as entitled as archbishops to make pompous personal observations. A lack of response, she hoped, would choke him off.

'It is an uplifting example of daughterly duty and devotion to see you sacrificing your own hopes of marriage in this way,' he continued, finally finding something about her he approved of, it seemed.

Apparently silence was not a strong enough hint. 'I had no particular *hopes*, as you put it, at the time of my father's seizure and I am most certainly not sacrificing anything.' By the time her father had suffered his stroke her heart had been broken, her hopes betrayed. 'So many women are yoked in marriage and lose all their freedoms by it. I fully intend to retain mine, Your Grace.' Her head told her that marriage was too great a gamble and she had proved to herself that her judgement of men was so faulty that she could not trust her heart.

'Do I understand that you do not approve of marriage?' The Duke's tone now was as frosty as she had made hers.

'It seems to me an excellent way of perpetuating the human race in an orderly manner. It provides for the civilised upbringing of children and shelters the elderly. It certainly contributes greatly to the comfort of men. It is unfortunate that all of this is so often achieved by the sacrifices of the woman concerned.'

'Sacrifices? A lady is protected and maintained by marriage. Her status is usually enhanced.'

'And in return a woman loses all freedom, all control of her own money and lands, all autonomy. She becomes utterly subject to the wishes and whims of her husband. I love my father, and will always care for him, but beyond that, I live my life as an independent woman, Your Grace.'

'None of us is independent, Miss Wingate. Freedom is an illusion. Ladies are restricted by their natural delicacy, gentlemen by their duties and obligations.'

'Some of us have more freedom than others, it is true,' she said.

Natural delicacy, my hat! The temptation to say something very indelicate indeed was great, but she controlled it.

'A duke has a great deal, a married woman very little. I have the privilege of birth and prosperity and I am fully aware that if I were the daughter of an agricultural labourer or a weaver as disabled as my father is now, my life would hold very little freedom. My *delicacy*, as you put it, would have to be disregarded. I am fortunate and I do not intend to throw away that good fortune simply because social pressure dictates that I should be married.'

The words, *And who would be foolish enough to ask you, with that attitude?* were almost audible, she thought. The Duke closed his lips on them. That clearly caused him a struggle because it was a moment before he spoke. 'I trust that you find the freedoms are worth the sacrifice, Miss Wingate. I see that the children have extricated themselves from the maze. I must bid the Bishop good day and remove them before they disturb his peace any further. Thank you for a most delightful afternoon.'

Liar, Verity thought, as she walked with him towards her father's seat. *He thoroughly disapproves of me and he is clearly regretting those indiscreet confidences in the maze. He never intended to make them so he will like me the less for that.*

She kept a smile on her lips as she showed the party out, but it took several minutes pacing up and down the hallway before she could recover it sufficiently to go out to her father. It was a shock to find herself so upset at the unspoken disapproval. She did not like the man, so why should it matter what he thought of her?

'What did you think of our new neighbour, Papa?' She exchanged a quick glance with the Chaplain over the Bishop's head and he nodded encouragingly. Her father was not overtired, it seemed.

'A fine figure of a man,' Mr Hoskins translated as her father's hands moved. 'A considerable asset to the neighbourhood. He has suffered two bereavements in a short time and finds himself with many responsibilities in addition to acquiring the care of six younger siblings. I feel confident that he will rise to the challenge.'

Her father nodded and mouthed, *Most impressed.*

'And what do you think, Mr Hoskins?' It was too easy to forget that the man had opinions and a voice of his own and she always tried to bring him into the conversation in his own right.

'His Grace's reputation does not lie. He seems a perfect paradigm of what a nobleman should be. One cannot envy him the responsibility of so many brothers and sisters as well as having to assume the burden of his great rank at so young an age.'

'He must be twenty-seven and he behaves as though he is fifty-seven,' she muttered.

Her father was speaking again. 'Charming children. Intelligent and lively.'

'Yes.' She could agree with that. A pity their half-brother did not have the natural charm to match theirs—or his own looks and breeding.

'There will be quite a fluttering in the dovecotes when all the hopeful mamas in the district realise what an eligible bachelor has landed in our midst,' Mr Hoskins said, then bit his lip and gave her father an apologetic look. 'Most frivolous of me to consider such a thing. And, of course, the poor man is in mourning.'

Her father chuckled and moved his hands slowly enough for Verity to translate. 'He will not be in mourning forever and there is nothing to stop him looking in the meantime. You never know, he might find a young lady he likes in the neighbourhood.'

'Papa, *really.*' There was a twinkle in his eyes as he looked at her.

You are not going to try matchmaking on my behalf. Not with that *man. Or any man.*

But of course there was no danger of the Duke taking an interest in her, however much her father might wish it. She had shocked him with her outspoken views on marriage on top of demonstrating that she was an antiquarian hoyden who attacked upstanding aristocrats with mouldering skulls. Miss Verity Wingate was the last woman the Duke of Aylsham would want as a wife.

* * *

'I like her, she has a nice smile and she isn't stuffy. Are you going to marry her, Will?' Basil sat on the carriage seat opposite him and cocked his head to one side like a particularly nosy, and somewhat scruffy, sparrow.

'Do not refer to a lady as *her*, Basil. And do not ask intrusive personal questions. I am most certainly not going to marry Miss Wingate.'

Beside him his sisters sighed loudly. 'But why not?' Araminta demanded. 'Miss Wingate is nice. And pretty *and* she is right next door, which is very convenient.'

'Do I need to remind you that we are all in mourning? I cannot consider courtship until a year has passed from my grandfather's death.' He could well believe that they had no clear concept of the formalities of mourning because they did not even have the colour of their clothing to remind them. Their mother had put her foot down and refused point-blank to allow her daughters to be dressed in black, or even grey or lilac, on the grounds that it would depress their spirits. Will had pointed out that their spirits were *supposed* to be depressed during the mourning period and she had told him that he was cold and unfeeling.

On the other hand, the children were mourning their father in their own ways, he supposed. Sometimes he came across the girls with suspiciously red eyes and Basil's more outrageous feats might be a way of distracting himself from painful memories. He had an uneasy suspicion that their upbringing had given them a different, more natural, way of dealing with their emotions than was suitable for him.

'How stuffy of you, Will,' Althea said. 'Being sad about Papa doesn't alter the fact that you need a wife because of us. I overheard Miss Preston tell Mr Catford that your life would be so much easier if you had a duchess.'

'Eavesdropping is unbecoming to a person of gentility, Althea,' Will said automatically. Miss Preston was quite correct: life would be much easier with a wife by his side. *And in my bed*, a wicked little voice whispered in the back of his mind, prompting his imagination to present him with an image of Miss Wingate rising naked and dripping from the fountain pool. 'We will not mention the subject again.'

And you can stop it, he snarled at his own imagination as he crossed his legs. *She is a hoyden, a bluestocking, an unnatural female opposed to marriage. Utterly unsuitable.*

It was bad enough having his stepmother inhabiting the Dower House and infecting the children with her madcap ideas. An unconventional duchess was the last thing he needed.

'And the Bishop is nice, too,' Araminta pronounced. 'I like him. He's got kind eyes and he talks with his hands and I'm sure he enjoys having visitors. I shall call on him again.'

'He will come to us if he is well enough.' Will tried not to contemplate his siblings descending uninvited and unsupervised on the Old Palace in order to observe the Bishop, or to try to enliven his routine. 'It is not proper to call again until one has received a return visit. Now, tell me what you each learned in your last lesson.'

That, as he might have expected, was greeted by a collective heavy sigh. Will refrained from joining in and reminded himself that no one had ever said that being a duke was easy.

'Will,' Basil piped up. 'What have you done with your cane?'

* * *

'Who was that man and all those children?' Melissa demanded as Verity closed the door and leaned back against it.

'There were only three of them and they are sixteen and fourteen so hardly children, although I agree, they do manage to inhabit the space of about twelve.' She pushed away from the door and went to flop, in an unladylike manner, into the nearest chair. An hour of the Duke was more than enough. 'I am sorry if you were disturbed.'

'We weren't,' Melissa assured her. 'I was pacing up and down seeking inspiration for a truly horrid haunting and saw them out of the window. We had heard the young people earlier, of course, but who is ever disturbed by the sound of happiness?'

'Very true.' Prue peered over the top of her Greek grammar. She was lying full length on a bench, propped up on one elbow and naked except for a strategic length of muslin. 'But you look exhausted, Verity. Come and sit down and have a drink. Bosham brought us some lemonade earlier, before we'd started.'

As far as the staff and anyone else was concerned— including, most especially, the parents of her friends— they came to the Old Palace three times a week to form a reading circle.

If their parents assumed this was a group studying religious tracts, sermons and uplifting works while sewing for the poor, then that, Verity considered, was entirely due to their own imaginations. No one had ever exactly described the nature of their meetings and they certainly all read at some point during those afternoons. Lucy Lambert read music, Melissa Taverner read over her work so far because she did not dare take it home with her, Prudence Scott read textbooks and Jane Newnham, the artist among them, read books on the theory of perspective and colour or the lives of great painters. At the moment she was creating a set of studies of Greek muses, using her friends as models. Verity could not recall which muse represented literature, but Prue and her grammar book made a good enough representation.

Verity flitted between antiquarian papers, Gothic novels, her large embroidery stand where she was creating a tapestry of the fall of Lucifer in vivid colour, books on gardening and a wide drawing table where she was plotting the results of her excavations on the mounds. At the moment the skull perched on top of her notes like a bizarre paperweight, staring blankly at Prue's exposed curves.

The tower chamber was situated over her ground-floor sitting room and bedchamber and the maids came in once a week to clean. When they did all traces of her friends' work was locked safely away in cupboards.

There would, as Melissa said, be hell to pay if her father, the local squire, discovered she was reading novels, let alone writing them. He was set and determined on marrying her off well. The other parents were as determined to present perfect, conformable, young ladies to the Marriage Mart and were growing increasingly impatient as their daughters—all aged twenty-three—remained unwed and perilously close to being on the shelf.

When the Wingates had settled permanently at the Old Palace, Verity had made friends fast, but it had taken a month or so before she discovered the secret yearnings and ambitions of the four who became closest to

her. Giving them a safe sanctuary to exercise their interests and talents fitted in well with the way she was
living her own life, but she worried about what would
happen to them. Sooner or later their parents were going
to insist on arranging marriages and, unlike her, clearly
remaining unwed to care for her father, the others had
no excuse and would have to obey.

What her friends needed were liberal-minded gentlemen who would fall in love with them for their own sake,
but where they were to find them in the limited society
of rural Dorset, she had no idea. What would happen
was that their fathers would decide on the most advan-
tageous match among the gentry of the county and put
pressure their daughters until they agreed.

And the problem was, they would all give in eventually, even if they did manage to hold out against the
worst of the crop.

Then it struck her—none of the local gentry offered
the slightest competition to a duke. No hopeful mama
was going to settle for a mere esquire or baronet, or even
the heir of a retired nabob or admiral, if there was the
faintest chance her daughter might catch the eye of one
of the foremost noblemen in the land.

She looked round at her friends and saw they were all
waiting, with various degrees of patience, for her to tell
them who the man with the children had been.

'That man was the Duke of Aylsham,' she announced.
'He would thoroughly disapprove of us, but he is going
to buy us almost a year of freedom.'

Chapter Four

'That was the *Duke*? Do you mean he is staying?' Lucy was the first to gather her wits. She lifted her hands from the keyboard where she had been quietly improvising. 'Mama said that she had heard that he had come to settle his stepmother at the Dower House and would be going back to Oulton Castle.'

'No. Lady Bromhill is certainly living at the Dower House but the Duke has moved into Stane Hall with his six half-brothers and -sisters and, I believe, intends to stay, at least for the mourning period.'

'Oh.' Melissa's face fell. 'I had forgotten that the family is in mourning. I had been imagining balls and parties... Mama will be devastated when she finds he will be here, but not socialising. I cannot understand how his presence is going to be of any help to us.'

'But do you not see? Every mother of a daughter of marriageable age will look twice at any other candidate for her hand because, until the Duke *does* become available, there is always the faint hope that she might be the one to catch his eye. And it will be almost a year before he is out of mourning and can begin openly courting.

The man is such a stickler for proper form that nothing is going to make him choose a bride before then, even if he falls passionately in love.' And the thought of the Duke of Aylsham doing anything passionately sent a shiver down her spine, even as her mind told her that he would never demonstrate an unbecoming show of enthusiasm, even when making love.

'But that is marvellous. All we have to do is go home and tell our parents the good news—and then obediently fall in with every plan they come up with for encountering the Duke or his family,' Jane said with a gurgle of laughter. 'We will throw ourselves into it—and it is certain to provoke our mothers into a positive *orgy* of shopping.'

'That's— *Aargh!*' At Melissa's scream Lucy dropped her music scores, Jane stabbed her brush into the white paint and Prue sat bolt upright, sending her draperies sliding to the floor.

'What is it?' Verity demanded, then gave a started gasp of her own as a large, very hairy, black spider scuttled across the boards and vanished under a bookcase. 'Goodness, that gave me a fright. I do hate the ones with the knobbly knees. Are you all right, Melissa? I know you do not like the things.'

'Ghastly creatures,' Melissa said with a shudder. 'Do you think it has gone?'

Only as far as the back of the bookcase, Verity thought.

'I am sure it will not come back with us here now. And I will have a word with the maids about cleaning more—'

The door on to the outer staircase that circled the tower banged open, thudded against the wall and sent a vase toppling from the nearest bookshelf. Melissa darted forward and caught it, collided with the man who burst through the opening and sat down with a thump on the edge of the *chaise*.

For a second everyone froze. *Like Grandmother's Footsteps*, Verity thought wildly before she realised that the intruder was the Duke and that he was staring at Prue's completely exposed bosom, which was, as Prue herself sometimes lamented, her most outstanding feature.

Everyone moved at once. The Duke spun round to face the bookcases, Prue ran for the door to the internal staircase and Verity, Melissa, Jane and Lucy came together to stand shoulder to shoulder, a wall of indignant femininity between their friend and this man.

As the door closed behind Prue, Melissa pushed the vase into Lucy's hands. 'I will take her clothes down.' She scooped them up and left.

'I apologise,' the Duke said, his back still turned to them, his voice stiff with suppressed emotion.

Outrage, Verity guessed. He would not like being put in the wrong like this. Or being made to look ridiculous. A gentleman bursting into a room of young ladies to save them from danger was heroic. To rescue them from a spider, farcical.

'I realised that I had left my cane behind and I was searching for it in the garden when I heard a scream. I thought a lady was being assaulted in some way.' He removed his hat.

'Only by a very large spider,' Verity said drily. 'But, naturally, we appreciate your, er, gallant defence.' She moved Jane's easel to face the wall. 'You may turn around again, Your Grace.'

'Ladies.' His bow was a masterpiece.

Verity was not sure how it was possible to bow sarcastically, but she was certain that was what this was. It was just too perfectly judged to be anything else. 'May I present Miss Lambert and Miss Newnham.'

They curtsied and he bowed again as Melissa came back. She rolled her eyes at Verity, then turned and swept into a graceful obeisance.

'And Miss Taverner. Ladies, this is the Duke of Aylsham.'

And don't you dare ask who Prue is, she thought.

But of course he did not. 'My apologies for interrupting you, ladies. Good day to you.' He resumed his hat, left by the door through which he had entered and closed it, very gently, behind him.

'Hell's bells,' Melissa said faintly. 'What a very beautiful, very frightening man.'

'How is Prue?'

'Resigning herself to imminent ruin. I told her a duke would be too much a gentleman to ever refer to the matter.'

'He has gone.' Prue came in, dressed, but pale-faced. 'I saw him from your bedchamber window, Verity. Will someone help me with my hair?' She held out her hand, shaking so much that half the pins she was holding fell to the floor.

'I will.' Lucy pressed her down into a chair and began to put up the brown curls. 'He will not say anything, we are sure—far too much the gentleman.'

'And it would lower him in his own estimation to gossip,' Verity added, patting her friend's shoulder in an attempt at consolation. 'He is an absolute pattern book of proper behaviour. You will be quite safe, Prue, don't worry.'

'But I will be sure to meet him,' she wailed. 'And he will recognise me and I will just sink through the floor, I know I will. Even if he says nothing, Mama will guess something is amiss if I blush scarlet whenever I see him.'

'I doubt he was looking at your face,' Melissa said, with a significant glance at Prue's bosom which was positively heaving with emotion. 'You must just brazen it out, Prue. Tell your mama that you are knocked all of a heap by his rank and looks and your overwhelming urge to be worthy of him. Besides, he is in mourning, so you are unlikely to encounter him often.'

'I suppose so.' Prue began to look slightly less ill.

The clock struck four. There was a faint shriek from Lucy, who began to bundle up her sheet music while the others tidied their work away into the cupboard.

'Leave it, hurry down,' Verity urged. 'Prue, blow your nose. And take some tracts with you, everyone.' A pile of tub-thumping religious tracts had been sent to her father by a well-meaning curate. Papa, having scanned one, pronounced it badly written, inaccurate and guaranteed to make heathens of the most devout churchgoer. Verity had saved them as props for her 'reading group,' who went off downstairs, bonnets and gloves in place, each clutching a leaflet. 'And the book for next week is *Pilgrim's Progress*,' she called after them.

'But we all read that ages ago,' Melissa stopped at the head of the stairs to protest.

'Exactly. Which means we don't need to talk about it again, but you know all about it if your parents ask what we have been studying.'

She found she was feeling a trifle shaky so she sat down to set a few more stitches in her tapestry. She hadn't finally committed herself to the design of the fallen angel himself—perhaps she could incorporate a few of the Duke's features. Verity began to unpick the black of the angel's eyes. Blue would be more arresting... He was, after all, as handsome as the Devil, if probably rather less cheerful, he had fallen to earth at her feet and he had the power to torment them all now.

Even before the move to Stane Hall Will had learned it was no use offering a place in the carriage to his step-mother on Sundays. Claudia always announced her intention of worshipping the deity—or deities, she was not prepared to commit herself—by communing with nature, which seemed to him to be an excellent excuse for prolonged country rambles accompanied by a picnic basket.

Her children had discovered, to their dismay, that now that they lived with him, a church service, sedate reading and educational pastimes replaced Sundays spent careering around the woods and streams. They had learned not to mope too visibly when Will put his foot down over an issue, but even so, it was a sulky and cramped carriage party that set out for morning service the second Sunday after their visit to the Old Palace and the first when they had attended church.

'Basil, if you have so much to say for yourself you may undertake the reading of the second lesson in my stead,' Will threatened. It was enough to silence his brother, who had been grumbling about having to take young Benjamin on his knees. 'And, yes, we will take two carriages when the weather is bad or Miss Preston and Mr Catford prefer not to walk. But it makes more work for the staff on a day of rest when we should be as considerate as possible.'

At least they all trooped down the path to the church door in an orderly manner. The Verger was waiting to escort them to the Stane Hall pew, right at the front of the chancel. He ushered them in with a merciful lack of bowing and scraping. Will guessed this was because in his opinion the parishioners rated a duke rather lower than their resident Bishop. The high panelled walls of the Hall's pew cut off their view of the one on the other side of the aisle, in the prime position right under the pulpit, but the Bishop's coat of arms was on the door. It had a complex design on the shield, crowned with a mitre and with crossed croziers behind.

All he could see of the occupants was the top of a bald pate edged with greying brown hair, a dark head that must be the Chaplain and the crown of a brown-straw bonnet with a flash of ochre ribbon. Miss Wingate had accompanied her father. At least her rebellion did not extend to churchgoing.

Will brought his gaze back to the interior of his own large pew. The tutor and governess were already there and, under their supervision, the youngsters were at least sitting quietly as they found their places in the prayer books. He sent up a brief prayer of his own for a short and well-delivered sermon and told himself that he was not remotely interested in the presence or otherwise of unbecomingly outspoken bluestockings. He could only offer thanks to whichever merciful spirit looked after well-meaning dukes for the fact that it was not Miss Wingate who had been posing nude when he burst into that tower of outrageous females. With the exception

of the one who had fled, there had not been a blush between them, which was shocking.

His prayers were answered with an intelligent sermon, although as it was on the theme of 'The Stranger
in Our Midst' he could almost feel the collective gaze
of the congregation boring into his back. The Verger
came and opened the Bishop's pew door first, which was
telling. Dukes outranked bishops, but not, it seemed in
Great Staning.

When he reached the door—the Verger bowed them
solemnly out of their pew next—Will saw why the
Bishop had precedence. He was seated in a carved chair
by the side of the Vicar, who was waiting to speak to
his parishioners as they filed out. Mr Hoskins was at
his elbow and Miss Wingate stood a little apart, talking
to a lady he guessed was Mrs Trent, the Vicar's wife.

'My lord. Mr Hoskins. Mr Trent.' It was the first time
the family had attended church in this parish, although
the Vicar had called the week they arrived. 'An admirable sermon, Vicar, I congratulate you. May I introduce
my family?' He gestured his siblings forward and tried
not to be surprised when they lined up obediently and
performed neat bows and curtsies. Their teachers were
clearly doing an excellent job, which reminded him to
introduce them, too.

'But we are holding up the rest of the congregation.'
He led his small flock over to bid good morning to Mrs
Trent, who was still talking to Miss Wingate. 'Ma'am.
Miss Wingate.' Mrs Trent beamed and replied and
promptly began to make a fuss of the children.

Miss Wingate favoured him with a slight bow. He
assumed her frosty manner was due to embarrassment
which was surprising; he had not thought she had suf-

ficient sensibility to feel any. 'Your Grace. Good day. Mrs Trent, I will make certain the gardeners send down those flowers in plenty of time for next Sunday.' Then she was gone with a whisk of deep green skirts, leaving the tantalising scent of wisteria blossom behind her.

Mrs Trent straightened from speaking to Benjamin and Will saw her eyes widen as she looked beyond him. He half-turned to find that, far from filing out of the church after they had shaken the Vicar's hand, the congregation was still milling about inside. Or, rather, that part of it composed of matrons with daughters in attendance was. He recognised Miss Lambert, Miss Newnham and Miss Taverner from the tower and he rather suspected, from the fact that she was the only person not looking in his direction, that the unnamed naked model was the young woman in the blue bonnet half-hidden behind a pillar.

'Oh, dear,' Mrs Trent murmured. 'I am afraid you must expect a certain amount of interest from the parishioners, Your Grace.'

'So I see. As we are in mourning I will not be entertaining on any scale, nor attending balls or parties,' Will said. 'I hope I may rely on you to depress any hopes that the Manor will be hosting any social events, as would normally be the case.'

'Of course. I am sure there will be ample opportunities for you to meet anyone of consequence in the area without any fear of…er…'

'Raising expectations?' he asked with a smile that felt somewhat twisted. It had not occurred to him that he would be hunted, which was foolish of him. In truth, it was how he felt at that moment, with a flock of young ladies in what looked like their finest day dresses and best bonnets all focused on him. He was hardly likely to find a duchess in a sleepy Dorset parish, but that would not depress the hopes of the parents of marriageable daughters, he knew. Unmarried dukes under the age of sixty were gold dust on the Marriage Mart. In a way Miss Wingate's hostility was a refreshing relief.

'While my father lived I was at a remove from the succession,' he confided, low-voiced. 'The title appears to have excited rather more interest than I have been used to.'

Mrs Trent produced an unexpectedly wicked smile. 'My advice is not to run, Your Grace—that only excites them to chase. Think of kittens and a ball of wool. Now, if you will excuse me, I will see what I can do to rescue my poor husband from the throng.'

'I suspect I can help matters simply by leaving. Good day, ma'am. Come along, everyone.' He shepherded his small flock out, with the tutor and governess bringing up the rear to catch the stragglers. Will bowed to left and right, exchanged greetings and kept on walking, trying not to imagine himself as a ball of wool. Somehow this was not quite how he had imagined life as a duke would be. There was considerably less of ermine-trimmed robes and speeches in the House of Lords and rather more worrying about drainage ditches and the lack of application to their Classics lessons on behalf of his small brothers.

And dukes really should not stride down church paths as though they had a pack of petticoat-clad hounds on their tail. Will could not help but think gloomily that his grandfather would have managed things better, but he could not bring himself to administer icy snubs as the old man would have done. Nor did it help his temper to observe Miss Wingate at the lych gate speaking to what, he assumed, must be the driver of the Bishop's carriage.

She gave him a cool nod, waved cheerfully to the rest of his party as they passed and then directed a look brim-full of mischief and amusement at the path behind him. Clearly, he was being followed by the flotilla of hope-ful matrons, their daughters around them like so many frigates, their husbands in tow.

Must stop mixing metaphors. Kittens, hounds and now battleships...

Will did not make the mistake of looking over his shoulder. When they reached his carriage he saw they were boxed in by the Bishop's coach behind and a clus-ter of gigs, barouches and dog carts in front.

As the footman swung open the door Will saw the reflection of the pursuers behind him in the window glass. 'Basil, sit up with the coachman. Miss Preston, Mr Catford, please take seats in the carriage, should you wish. I intend to walk.'

He strode off without a backwards glance, ignor-ing Basil's crow of triumph at being allowed up on the box. There was a stile ahead and a field of cattle on the other side of the fence. No lady was going to pursue him through that, not in her best churchgoing shoes. A strategic retreat, that was what this was. A gentleman could, with propriety, take a dignified country walk on a Sunday morning after church, he told himself. And he would take care to instruct the coachman to have the carriage free and clear to drive off immediately on the next occasion they attended St Mathew's.

The herd scattered away as he walked diagonally across the pasture and Will tried to bring the map of the parish to mind and to work out whose field this was.

His or the Bishop's? Or perhaps it was part of the Vicar's glebe lands. No, those lay to the south. There was a gate on the far side and he went through, closing it firmly on the cows who were following him with the usual curiosity of their kind. Beyond, a track meandered away and then cut left through a copse of trees, the green shade and faint damp smell soothing after his earlier irritation. He was heading in the right direction, he thought, glancing up at the sun filtering through the branches, although he could not recall this patch of woodland.

Will emerged after ten minutes, not on to another field as he expected, but into a wide clearing with a pond in the centre. A tree had fallen parallel to the edge and he sat down on it, taking in the clumps of rushes, the lily pads, the dart and hover of dragonflies. It was a lovely spot, crying out for a small summer house for picnics. If it was his he would see about having one built. Nothing intrusive, not some Classical temple, just a simple shelter, he thought, leaning back on the stump of the tree that formed a convenient support.

It was warm now, or perhaps he was overheated after his impulsive escape from the churchyard.

Ridiculous, running from a pack of women. You should learn how to depress pretention with a cool stare, Will told himself.

He closed his eyes against the sun dazzle on the water.

And that smile on Miss Wingate's face as she watched... She found it amusing, the wicked creature... She has a dimple when she smiles... I wonder whether she ever models for her friend. She...

It was very wrong to find amusement in the Duke's discomfiture, Verity told herself as the carriage finally extricated itself from the tangle of vehicles at the church gate. Her father's hands moved, catching her attention, and she focused on what he was saying.

'What are you smiling about, my dear?' he signed slowly. 'Something has amused you?'

'Nothing in particular, Papa.' *And that is a fib, on a Sunday, too.* 'Such a lovely day, isn't it? Would you like to take luncheon in the garden?'

'I think so, yes. I will have a short rest first.'

'And I will take a walk.' Essentially she wanted to get away from the Old Palace so she could laugh in private over the hunting of the Duke. At least she could acquit him of being rude to anyone. An aristocrat of high rank could turn and wither the pretensions of the local gentry with just a few well-chosen words, or even a look, and it was to his credit that he had not yielded to the temptation to hit back. And not by a flicker of an eyelash had he revealed that he had met her friends before or had identified poor Prue.

Really, the Duke of Aylsham might be a very pleasant gentleman if he was not so starched-up and conscious of his position, she concluded ten minutes later as she made her way out of the gardens and into the water meadows.

He was certainly a very fine specimen of manhood to look at, which was not a thought she should be entertaining on a Sunday.

You see, William Calthorpe, you are leading me astray. Fibs and warm thoughts on the Sabbath indeed!

She would call him William in her head, she decided. Too much dwelling on his title would make him assume an importance in her mind he did not deserve. But it was a long time since she had felt the slightest flicker of interest when she looked at a man and the feeling was not, to her surprise, unpleasant.

The ground under her feet gave a warning squelch, a reminder of last week's rain, but the woodland walk would be dry underfoot and there was the hope that she might spot the peregrine falcon that she had strictly forbidden the keepers to shoot.

Her favourite log was a good spot to sit and the sunlight would be on the clearing at this time of day. If she stayed quite still for a few moments she could see what came down to the pond to drink and Verity walked quietly into the glade to avoid frightening any wild creature.

There. A movement behind the trees, a roe deer coming to the water. With her eyes on the animal Verity edged sideways towards her usual perch. She could just see the tree trunk out of the corner of her eye. Almost there, almost. Still watching the shy deer emerging from the fringe of bushes, she sat down, very, very slowly.

'Hmff?' The surface under her was not wood, it was fabric with a warm body inside it. The body sat up, precipitating her on to the turf. The deer fled back into the woods and Verity looked up into the furious face of His Grace the Duke of Aylsham. *William.* She almost said it out loud. He had been lying along the trunk and must, she supposed, have been asleep.

'What the devil?' He had himself under control in a breath, swung his feet down and stood up. 'I apologise for my language, Miss Wingate. But what—'

'What the devil was I doing?' she enquired as she took his hand and allowed herself to be hauled up. It was not very ladylike. She should not care, but it was galling to keep meeting him when she was sprawled on the ground. 'I did not see you. I had my eyes on a deer that was coming down to drink and I was edging towards the tree trunk to sit down.' Verity brushed the dried leaves and moss off her skirt and wondered what had possessed her to go for a walk in her Sunday best.

He was fuming, she guessed, although the only outward evidence was a slight flaring of his nostrils and the tightening of his lips. She added a mental rebuke to herself for allowing her gaze to linger on his finely sculpted nose and the sensual curve of his lower lip. It was a very bad mistake to equate good looks with a pleasant character and William Calthorpe appeared to combine outward perfection with a starchy, judgemental interior.

'I trust I did not hurt you?' She was not quite certain exactly where on that long body she had sat. She had already been the cause of an injury to his posterior. It hadn't been his legs this time, he did not appear to be winded, so it was probably not his stomach, which left…

I will not think about that. I will not look at the area concerned.

He was not writhing in agony, which was the usual result of hitting a man where it hurt most, as one of her governesses had explained and she had later discovered for herself, so it could not have been too bad.

'This is a most pleasant spot,' he said with the air of a man determined to make polite conversation against great odds. 'I was trying to work out whether it is my or your father's land.'

'Papa's.' She felt ridiculously flustered because she was beginning to suspect that the tension emanating from him was not anger, or embarrassment alone, but quite a different emotion altogether. One that she was experiencing, too, to judge by the fluttering in the pit of her stomach and the unsteadiness of her breath. 'Yours begins on the far southern edge of the copse.' She flapped a hand in the general direction.

Why on earth did she have to keep encountering him in situations that put her at a disadvantage? Clutching a skull at the bottom of an excavation, hosting a female party including one naked model—and now sitting on him.

'Oh.' He looked around.

Anything rather than risk making eye contact with her, Verity suspected. Or perhaps her dishevelled appearance offended him. *Good.*

'A pity, I was planning to build a small summer house here.'

'I doubt Papa would wish to sell.' She realised that she was edging away, poised for flight before she did something obvious like licking her lips or twirling her hair or, for goodness' sake, batting her eyelashes.

'Look out!'

She glanced round, then down at the edge of the pond crumbling under her heel. She flailed her arms wildly and was seized by the wrist, then tugged forward to land against William's chest with a thud that knocked the air from her lungs.

'Oh,' she said inanely. 'You seem to keep rescuing me.'

Only this time he did not let her go. His arms were around her and she was clutching at his lapels and they were pressed together, her head tilted back, his down, so their breath mingled. *How did that happen?* She could see his individual eyelashes and the pale lines at the corners of his eyes where he had screwed them up against the light, or in laughter. His pupils were wide, dark and Verity found herself unable to tear her gaze from them.

Fallen angel... I would like to fall with you... No, stop it. You know where that leads.

'Miss Wingate.' The Duke lowered his head further until their noses were almost touching. She felt his voice rumbling in his chest where they were pressed together. 'Do you by any chance want to kiss me as much as I want to kiss you?'

'I... *Yes.*'

Oh... What had happened to the starched-up, perfectly proper man? What had happened to her, for that matter? And then she stopped wondering and simply kissed him back. His mouth was warm and firm and, when she pressed against him, he licked between her lips, startling a moan of pleasure from her.

Verity came to herself to find they were sitting side by side on the log, her head on his shoulder, his arms around her. 'Your Grace...'

'I think after that you had better call me Will.' His voice was curiously husky, as though he was experiencing some strong emotion, not simply the aftereffects of a kiss.

'Will?'

'Yes, Verity?'

A duke—*this Duke*—was asking her to call him by his first name. This Duke—Will—had just kissed her and she had kissed him back. So, what did that mean? That she was dreaming? That she had completely lost her grip on reality?

'Will,' Verity murmured. She liked his name on her lips. She liked sitting like this pressed against his big, hard body. Verity raised her hand and touched his cheek.

As though her touch had shaken him back to reality Will shifted away, the sensual smile gone from his lips. 'What am I thinking of?' he said as he took his hands from her waist and stood up. 'That was appalling. I must apologise for...for what has just occurred.'

Appalling? 'Apologise? Why?' Apparently she could form at least two words, if not a rational sentence.

'Because, clearly, that was a mistake. A most serious error of judgement.'

Chapter Five

'An error of judgement?' Verity demanded. 'Us kissing each other—'

'Me kissing you.'

'Oh, never mind who kissed who… *Whom*. Oh, bother it! You are saying that kiss was a serious error of judgement? Why, exactly?' All the warmth and delightfully fluttered feelings were becoming another kind of heat altogether. Anger. But of course, she should have known better. This sort of thing never ended well.

'A gentleman does not go around kissing young ladies like you.' Will had found his hat and gloves from beside the tree trunk and was putting them on, very precisely.

'And what, exactly, is a woman like me?'

One who goes romping through the woods on a Sunday without a chaperon, presumably. One who so far forgets herself that she kisses a man she does not like. At least last time I had the excuse of being in love with the man, even if I was idiotically deluded about him.

'A young *lady*, like you. You were thrown off balance by almost falling into the pond. I took advantage of your alarm. And so I apologise, it was unconscionable.'

'It was a perfectly pleasant kiss, that is what it was. *All* it was.' Verity shot to her feet with rather more force than elegance. 'No one took advantage of anyone. I am not some green girl who has no idea what a man is about, no idea what a kiss is—or how to say *no*. I wanted to kiss you, you wanted to kiss me. We kissed. It was an adequate kiss. There is no cause to be ungracious about it. *Will.*'

'Adequate? *Ungracious?* Have you *no* sense of propriety, Miss Wingate?'

'I was Verity a moment ago and I really think we have moved beyond questions of propriety.'

'We had both taken leave of our senses a moment ago.'

'I must certainly have done so.' Her wretched hat had slid down and over one ear. She jerked it back. 'I had assumed I could walk on my father's land without being insulted.'

'I have apologised for that kiss.' Colour flared across Will's cheekbones. 'It was very wrong of me, but no insult was intended.'

'And I have said there was no call to apologise for it. I refer to your inability to recognise that I am a thinking adult who can make her own decisions. Now *that* is an insult. Good day to you, *Your Grace.*'

It felt good to walk away without looking back. Verity even managed it without tripping over any fallen branches or catching her skirts on the brambles. *Insufferable man.* He had asked, she had assented and kissed him back. So why did he then have to act as though she was a little ninny who did not know her own mind?

Although to be honest, Verity thought as she arrived, panting slightly, at the edge of the coppice, she must have been out of her mind to have wanted to kiss the Duke.

Will. I wanted to kiss Will. But why? Just because he is good-looking?

How humiliating if that were the case. Was she deluding herself that there was more to the man than the face that he showed the world, that the glimpses of a lonely, confused child, of a man with a deeply buried sense of humour, were actually the real Will Calthorpe?

She slowed down a little to cross the meadow, then climbed the steps set into the side of the ha-ha, at which point she discovered that she had no energy to go any further and sat down on the lawn—never mind about the grass stains—and stared out towards the distant line of burial mounds to carry on trying to fathom what had just happened.

I do not like the Duke, but I think I might like Will.

But why? And why did she still want to kiss him, even after that humiliating reaction? It had been a more than adequate kiss. It had been a very nice kiss, whatever she had thrown at him just now, but it had not been so spectacular that she had entirely lost her wits. It was surely not because of his rank. She could acquit herself of being as shallow as that. Besides, the sight of a duke was not enough to cause that sensual little shiver or the fluttering low in her belly—it was the man behind the title who caused that.

A cock pheasant strutted down the slope of the lawn, saw her and struck a pose, lifting his tail and fluffing out his wing feathers.

Another handsome male. Is that all it is? I have fallen for broad shoulders and thick blond hair and chiselled cheekbones. And that mouth, of course...

Oh, that mouth—and what she sensed that the man could do with it if he ever let himself go without inhibition.

Goodness, that would make her as bad as any heedless male—excited by looks and without any discrimination about the inner person. And the inner person in this case was starched-up, over-conscious of his rank and power and the last man on earth who would make a good husband for a woman who wanted independence and freedom.

Husband? Verity sat up with a jerk and the pheasant flew away with a squawk of alarm. *Have I taken leave of my senses completely? One kiss and I am thinking of marriage?*

It would be a life sentence of stultifying propriety chained to a man for whom being the perfect Duke appeared to be all important. He would want numerous perfectly proper offspring, too.

Verity thought about children—her own children—now and again with a pleasant yearning ache and a vision of laughing, happy little figures. Certainly the dream had not included producing an heir and a spare to order and bringing up little girls to make perfect, dutiful marriages. Once she'd had daydreams of a charming rectory with roses around the door, children playing on the lawn and a handsome rector crafting an intelligent and humane sermon in the study while she was occupied with whatever the much-loved wives of handsome and intelligent rectors did to pass their day perfectly.

Impatient with her own thoughts, she scrambled to her feet and walked back to the gardens.

You were foolish and young then and you flatter yourself now, she thought, her sense of humour returning as she shook the dried grass stems out of her skirts. *It*

*takes two to make a marriage and whatever makes you
believe, Verity Wingate, that he even thinks of you once
you are out of his sight?*

An unexpected armful of woman was enough to make
any man want to snatch a kiss, she knew that perfectly
well. There was no importance to be attached to the sensual urges of the average male and it would be a mistake
to imagine that a duke, however perfect, was immune
to those same desires.

What had he been thinking, to kiss the Bishop's outrageous daughter? Will strode through the woods, striking
out with the sole desire to reach the edge and find some
landmark to orientate by so he could remove himself
from the area as quickly as possible. He had not been
thinking at all, of course. He had been reacting to the arrival in his arms of a warm, soft, curvaceous armful of
young woman who apparently, in that moment, wanted
to kiss him as much as he wanted to kiss her.

And very good it had been, too, whatever insult-
ingly lukewarm adjectives she had used to describe it.
Verity—*Miss Wingate*, he corrected himself—was obviously the chaste young lady one would expect, but she
had been kissed before and she was more than willing
to kiss in return. He ran his tongue over his lower lip. It
still held the impression of hers, he could still taste her
and the sweet, subtle scent of wisteria seemed to hang
in the air around him, however fast he walked.

But he should not be kissing young women he had
no intention of courting. He should not be kissing *any*
respectable young woman for almost a year, although
it was beginning to dawn on him that twelve months
of celibacy was not going to be easy. In fact, with the

memory of Verity Wingate in his arms, his body was forcefully reminding him that it would be very difficult indeed. He had glimpsed the considerable charms of her friend in all their glory the other day and had hardly felt a flicker of interest, but Miss Wingate appeared to have an inconveniently inflammatory effect on him.

Hell. Which meant that he was either going to have to grit his teeth and put up with it, on top of everything else he had to contend with, or he must spend some time in London setting up a mistress. When his father died and it had become clear that he was going to have to spend all his time, and energies, on the affairs of the dukedom, he had parted amicably enough from his last *chère amie.* It had taken considerable diplomacy, and some very nice diamonds, to achieve the amiable parting: no courtesan walks away from an *affaire* with a duke willingly.

But now… He supposed he could return to Cynthia. But she had doubtless found another protector already and if she had not, then by showing interest he might be raising expectations of a longer-term relationship than he wanted. Once he was married that would be that, he was firmly resolved. It might well be that he would be making a marriage of convenience with the most suitable partner, but that did not mean he could, or would, ignore his vows.

And there was the Hall ahead of him. Will lengthened his stride and stuffed all thoughts of mistresses, and amorous activity generally, into the locked mental cupboard where they belonged when he was in his own home surrounded by his young brothers and sisters.

It took him another twenty minutes to reach his front door, by which time he had recovered his composure, had mentally bullied his body into submission and discovered that he had neither the energy nor the will to dragoon his family into attending evensong.

'Unless anyone wishes to accompany Miss Preston?' he enquired over luncheon. The governess beamed approval at him and six pairs of eyes regarded him with varying degrees of horror, scorn and disbelief. 'No? You amaze me. Miss Preston, the carriage is at your disposal. Benjamin, kindly pass me the cold chicken.'

'When is Miss Wingate coming to visit us?' Basil demanded, regrettably through a mouthful of bread and butter. Will glared, he swallowed. 'And the Bishop. We like the Bishop. And Mr Hoskins. He told us all about the creepiest tombstone with skulls and bones on it in the churchyard. I bet he knows ghost stories. He might even get the Vicar to let us into the crypt.' He shuddered at the delicious horror of it.

'No doubt they will call when the Bishop is feeling well enough.'

And if Verity Wingate is speaking to me again.

Will could not understand what the attraction of the Bishop was for these six unruly children. 'And you are not visiting a crypt. It will be dirty, most unhygienic and it would give you nightmares.'

'Can't we invite them to spend the day, then the Bishop would be able to rest between journeys?' Althea asked. 'The weather is lovely and he enjoys gardens so he would like ours, even if we haven't got a maze.'

'But we do have a lake,' Araminta said. 'He hasn't, so he might like that. And the Bishop can tell you what you have to do to grow a maze, Will. We ought to have one, but it takes ages and ages to grow, as much as twenty years, I expect, so you'll be ancient and decrepit by the time it is a proper one. But we will enjoy it,' she added, as though in consolation.

'Thank you,' Will said drily, contemplating the prospect of being decrepit before he was fifty. 'The Bishop is a very worthy and learned man, but I had not expected you to like him so much.'

'He smiles a lot with his eyes and he tells jokes with his hands and Mr Hoskins translates them. We want them to teach us how to talk with our hands.'

'Oh, yes?' So they could get up to more trouble in secret, presumably.

'Then we would be much quieter and not disturb you,' ten-year-old Bertrand announced with a wide-eyed earnestness that would fool no one, let alone an older brother.

The Bishop and the Chaplain could only be a good influence on the children, of course, and if Will managed to interest his siblings in projects like the design and construction of a maze, then that might be a useful bridge to earning their confidence.

'I shall write and invite them to spend the day on Wednesday,' Will said. 'But you must promise not to plague the Bishop.'

'Of course,' they assured him earnestly. 'We never plague *anyone*.'

'A letter from Stane Hall, Papa?' Verity took the sheet of paper that Mr Hoskins passed her. 'An invitation to spend the day?'

Her father nodded, smiled and made encouraging gestures.

'You would like to accept? Would it not be rather tiring? Oh, I see. The Duke proposes setting aside a ground-floor bedchamber for you to rest. How very considerate.'

Drat the man. I really do not want to discover any good points in his favour.

She read the rest of the letter.

> *Our garden is looking at its best, although nothing to compare with yours at the Old Palace, of course. The children are most anxious that I plant a maze at Stane Hall—before I am too decrepit to appreciate it, they say—and I would find your advice on the correct position, design, et cetera, most welcome...*

At least Will had an acceptable reason for asking them, other than to subject her to his disapproval—or his kisses—at close quarters, Verity thought irritably.

I must stop being cross with him. It will turn me into a sour old maid and produce unbecoming wrinkles.

She should simply ignore him except for the exchange of social niceties. That would restore their relationship to its proper balance and stop her having lurid dreams. Her father would enjoy the proposed outing and he seemed to like the unruly brood of young people. It would be selfish to show any reluctance just to save herself some embarrassment. 'It sounds delightful, Papa. Shall I write and accept?'

It was Monday. She had cleaned, measured and drawn the skull from the burial mound on Saturday and reburied it carefully early that morning and now the excavation could be refilled with earth, the turf laid back. Within a few months, no one would know the ground had been disturbed.

It had been an interesting project, although it had revealed no objects other than the skull. But perhaps that was because she could only investigate one side. Or perhaps the people who buried the body did not leave offerings with their dead. She jotted a note to think about it. Was that normal for a pre-Christian burial?

If she had an entire mound to work on she could have a trench cut right across it. Verity spread butter on her toast and wondered if Will might agree to letting her try with the smallest one on their shared boundary. It might be worth biting her tongue on Wednesday, smiling at him and cajoling the wretched man to see if he could be persuaded to cooperate.

All in the interests of science, she told herself. And nothing to do with seeing if she could soften Will's intense blue gaze. *Will.* It was dangerous to think of him by his given name, but tempting, in the privacy of her head.

Besides, intriguing though he could be, she was immune to any serious attraction men might hold. She was quite safe.

'I am afraid that you have completely seduced Mr Hoskins with your library, Your Grace.' Verity took a seat on the terrace after settling her father in the calm comfort of the bedchamber set aside for him, the tranquillity enhanced by what she suspected had been dire threats from their brother to the Calthorpe children about what would happen if they disturbed him.

It ought to have been thoroughly awkward, meeting Will again after that kiss and the way they had parted afterwards, but it seemed that ducal decorum allowed him to carry on as though nothing had happened, to ignore it out of existence. Verity gave a mental shrug and endeavoured to achieve the same lofty disregard of awkwardness.

'Surely it cannot be superior in any way to the library at the Old Palace.'

Will leaned one hip against the balustrade, looking, Verity thought, as though he was posing for a portrait by Thomas Lawrence—perhaps *The Duke of Aylsham Surveys His Acres.* Or *Portrait of a Dashing but Dutiful Duke.*

'Possibly not, but it is in what appears to be a delightful state of disorder, which is like catnip for Mr Hoskins. He will probably be asking for permission to help you sort it all out and catalogue it, unless you are intending to employ a librarian.'

'I suppose I ought to do so.' Will frowned. 'There is an archivist and librarian at Oulton Castle, of course, but he is fully occupied. Perhaps Mr Hoskins would oblige me by assessing the library and advising me on who I should employ here.' There was a short silence.

Verity resisted the temptation to fill it with chit-chat and waited, studying his face until he smiled. She found herself smiling back with the uncomfortably guilty suspicion that Will knew perfectly well that she was exerting herself to be pleasant in order to gain some concession from him. And then, as they continued to look at each other with that dawning warmth, the equally uncomfortable thought occurred to her that most of her hostility to him was because she was attracted by him and that made her cross with herself and then cross with him.

As if he could help being tall and broad-shouldered and handsome and the possessor of blue eyes that were startlingly expressive when he let his guard down. A ridiculous image struck her of Will standing in front of the mirror every morning and choosing to wear the broad shoulders instead of the narrow, stooping ones, or the elegantly straight nose instead of the snub one—just to torment impressionable females. Verity laughed out loud.

'Miss Wingate?'

Surely that wasn't answering humour in his eyes?

When it is genuine he hardly curves his lips at all, just that quirk at the corners which produces the smallest of dimples. When he is being merely polite, both sides of his mouth lift. Interesting... And so very attractive.

Chapter Six

'I am so sorry, just some foolish thought that amused me,' Verity said.

But Will's smile was back to the cool, polite version. 'My estate manager informs me that your men have begun to refill your excavations at the Druidic mound.'

'Yes, I have reburied the skull now that I have drawn and measured it and the gardeners will replace the soil and turf.' What sort of mood was Will in? He was so difficult to read. 'There will be nothing to show for the digging after a month or so. I did wonder whether you might consider allowing me to cut a trench right through the middle of the smallest mound, including your half.'

Will nodded at Basil, who appeared around the corner of the terrace, then looked pained when the boy sat down on the steps at Verity's feet, leaving damp footprints on the lichen-covered stone. 'To what purpose?' he asked. At least he was not frowning at her.

'For the scientific purpose of examining the entire structure and, if there is a burial, seeing it in its entirety. It would not cause your staff any work and it would be restored and returfed afterwards, of course. It would not intrude on to agricultural land.'

I'm prattling, and he knows that. Be quiet and do not sound so eager.

Verity tried smiling and received a polite lift of Will's lips in return. 'Oh, and anything of any value would belong to whoever owned the half it was found in.'

'You are going to dig up a mound and find treasure? And we can share it?' Basil's eyes were round with excitement. 'But what if it was between the two halves? What if there is the fabulous treasure of some king or warrior under there?' he asked earnestly. 'A gilded sword right in the middle, or a heap of gold coins?'

'I am sure we will negotiate in a civilised manner over any hoard of gems and gold that we discover,' Verity said with a smile for his enthusiasm. 'I will show you all how to excavate and keep records if you want to join in and dig.'

'Oh, yes, and the girls are really interested, too,' Basil began.

'No,' Will said sharply. 'They are not going to grub about in the earth like navvies.'

'Are you, by any chance, teasing me, Your Grace?' But she very much doubted that he was. 'I do not *grub about* and I trust my resemblance to a canal labourer is non-existent.'

'Basil, go and find your brothers and sisters. Miss Wingate and I are having a private conversation.'

There was something in his tone that even Basil recognised as an order. He got up and left, dragging his feet, but not daring to answer back.

'Miss Wingate, while not wishing to denigrate your pastime, I venture to suggest that it is not one which would be considered suitable for a young lady who is a member of the *ton*. Your role caring for your father does remove you from society to a great extent, so this eccentricity is not widely observed, the reason I am sure that your father gives his permission for you to indulge in it, but I—'

'Pastime? Indulgence?' Verity demanded. 'I am engaged in serious scientific discovery, following the latest methods of excavation and meticulously recording the results—'

'Which, of course, will never be published. But that is beside the point. I have no intention of seeing my sisters burrowing in the dirt for human remains like so many scavengers on a waste heap.'

She discovered that her mouth was open with sheer incredulity and closed it with a snap, took a deep breath—but he was still talking.

'They have been exposed all their lives to their mother's wild theories of what is suitable for young ladies and I can only be thankful I have them in my care while I may do something to reverse the damage. I will not have you—'

'You mean that it was fortunate that your father fell off a roof?' Will looked outraged and she knew she had gone too far, but it was too late to stop now. 'I am sure the poor man would be appalled to discover that his daughters are being brought up to have no ideas of their own, to have their natural intelligence stifled.' She drew a breath, then saw who had appeared at the bottom of the lawn. 'Oh, look,' she said, hastily finding a smile. 'Here come the rest of your brothers and sisters.'

Like a relieving force of cavalry...

'It is a good thing that you despise matrimony so comprehensively, Miss Wingate, because no gentleman in his right mind would offer for you,' Will said, low-voiced, although the words stung even so. The colour was high over his cheekbones, his blue eyes dark with anger. She saw him close his eyes for a second, force a smile on to his lips and turn towards the approaching group and only hoped that she had her own expression as well under control. Whatever the arrogant lump of manhood next to her thought, she was not so much of a hoyden as to throw a flowerpot at him, even if that was what her fingers itched to do.

The young people had been dressed up and on their best behaviour for the visitors, but they had become louder and untidier as the visit progressed, only to be removed by governess and tutor before luncheon and returned, braids tightened, necks red from scrubbing, clothes suspiciously neat. Now they came up the lawn at a run, jostled their way up the steps on to the terrace and stood in a row, beaming at her.

'Miss Wingate, did you know we have got a lake? A really big one, with an island in the middle?'

Verity agreed that, yes, she did know about the lake, although she had never seen it. 'And an island, too? How lovely.' She sounded positively inane, she thought, trying not to overcompensate for the anger steaming inside her.

'And it's got one of those bumps like the ones Will said you were digging up because they're full of skulls and treasure,' Basil said.

'I'm sure your brother never said they were full of skulls, Lord Basil. I only found one and no treasure.' Then what he had said hit her. 'There is a burial mound on the island in the lake? Are you quite certain?'

'I think so. It is just like the littlest one on the bound-ary line,' Basil said, ignoring his elder brother's ominous throat-clearing. 'We went and had a look at them in case we could find skulls, too, but Will said we mustn't dig and there weren't any bones to be seen on our side anyway. We didn't know about treasure then.' The care with which he did not look at his brother had her suspecting some holes would be appearing now, whatever Will said. 'But the small one is just like the one in the lake.'

'How do you know about the island?' their brother demanded.

'We took the boat out when we found it, of course. Found the boat, I mean,' Araminta said. 'Then we saw the island, so of course we had to explore it.'

'What boat?'

So his voice drops in tone and becomes very much quieter when he is angry with anyone, not just me.

It still made her shiver, even though his attention was now completely on the boy.

'Er… The one in the boathouse,' Basil said, scuffling his feet and looking so innocent that he had to be guilty of something. 'It wasn't properly shut up, we hardly had to break the lock or anything. And the boat was floating and there wasn't any water inside it.'

The deep breath that Will took made his nostrils flare in an interesting manner, Verity observed, desperately trying for some mental balance.

It does not matter what he thinks of me. It does not matter what he says to me. I do not care about his opinion. He is just an arrogant male.

It did her self-esteem no good at all to discover that she was feeling decidedly shaky.

'You broke into the boat shed, you presumed to be able to judge the condition of a boat and you took it out on a lake, the hazards of which you know nothing about?' Will demanded. 'Which of your brothers and sisters did you take with you?'

'All of us. It was a bit of a squeeze, but not much water came in and Benjamin baled it out with his cap.'

'We can all swim,' Benjamin piped up. 'And the cap dried, sort of. And Mr Otterley said the tenant who used to be here went out on the lake a lot.'

'The head gardener knew you were taking the boat out without permission?'

'Well, he might have thought you had said we could...' Araminta said, twirling the ends of her ringlets and gazing vaguely off into the distance.

'None of us fell in. Much,' Basil said.

His expression was so earnest that Verity almost smiled, but what he had said earlier could not be ignored. 'It could be a burial mound, Lord Basil, although I have never heard of one in a lake like that. Or it might be something of even more interest. They have artificial islands in Scotland called crannogs which seem to have been made by early man, but I have never heard of them in England.' She made herself glance at Will, who was regarding her with what looked like barely controlled exasperation. 'I do not suppose...'

'You wish to visit the island, Miss Wingate?'

'I would very much appreciate it, Your Grace. Perhaps one of your grounds staff might row me.' The anger was like acid in her stomach and it was an effort to keep it from showing in her voice. Whatever he might think of her, she was not going to argue with him here.

His manners were too good to permit him to look anything but delighted at the idea before the children. 'Shall we go now? I must check the boat first, of course.' He turned to his siblings. 'No, you may not come. Miss

Wingate does not want to listen to your arguments over who can fit in the boat and who must stay behind. Please inform Peplow and Mr Hoskins of our whereabouts.'

They walked in silence down the slope of the lawn. Will stopped abruptly and gestured to the left where the lake came into view, curving away around the slope of the wooded hillside.

Someone had to break this silence and either apologise or pretend that the sudden eruption of anger and dislike between them had never happened. She was a lady, whatever he might think of her getting her hands dirty and using her brain, and she was not going to allow him to push her into behaving any other way. 'My goodness, but it is so much larger than I imagined,' she said brightly. From the corner of her eye she could see Will glance at her, but she pressed on. 'How very picturesque it is.' Verity stopped, pretending to shade her eyes and admire the view so she did not have to look at him. 'Is it natural? I cannot see an island.'

Will cleared his throat. 'The River Stane runs through the valley and apparently there was originally a series of large ponds with boggy areas between. A dam was built in 1760, where the valley narrows between two outcrops, and they allowed the valley to flood. The island is out of sight around that headland and I have not had time to go and look at it from the shore, and certainly not from a boat,' he added grimly. Then, as though he could not manage to maintain the stilted tone he added, 'I shudder to think what Basil considers is safe, the wretched thing is probably full of rot.' It seemed they were going to pretend that nothing had happened.

With a turn of the path they could see the boathouse, a charming wooden structure clearly designed to be an eye-catcher in the landscape. The door, when Will tried it, was held closed with a length of string and the lock no longer worked.

'They did say they had *hardly* broken the lock,' Verity murmured, surreptitiously kicking a few splinters of wood away into the nettles.

Will narrowed his eyes at her. 'I suppose you find the brats amusing,' he said as he swung the door open. 'Stay here, the floor may be rotten.'

'I find your brothers and sisters charming and intelligent,' Verity retorted, following close behind and ignoring the muffled snort from Will. 'And admirably unstuffy.'

'I suppose I may know how to take that,' he observed as they looked around the shadowy interior.

'I am certain you may.' She counted to ten, then forced herself to say, 'I mean that they are a breath of fresh air.' *Go on, offer an olive branch.* 'I apologise if you took it any other way.'

'Indeed? That is very gracious of you under the circumstances.'

'I want to get to that island,' Verity retorted, good intentions evaporating. 'And if we are to spend the afternoon in the boathouse quarrelling, I doubt I will achieve that.'

'If we are to reach the island, this appears to be the only available boat,' Will said, ignoring the latter part of her remark. He studied the large rowing boat bobbing at the end of its mooring line. 'It looks dry enough. I will take it out into the open so I can check it over more closely. Perhaps you could join me outside?'

I think I have just been reprimanded for unladylike behaviour again, Verity thought as she let herself out into the sunshine again. *If I push him into the lake I wonder if I will be able to row...*

It was a very tempting fantasy.

There was the sound of faint splashing and the boat appeared from the end of the boathouse, Will rowing with what, to her ignorant gaze, seemed considerable skill. He had not, of course, removed either coat or hat.

'It appears to be perfectly sound. Are you able to step in from that flat rock to your right, Miss Wingate?'

Verity balanced, teetered, told herself not to be feeble about being trapped in a small vessel with a man who had made it very clear that he despised her and managed to step into the boat without wetting either her feet or her hem. She sat down as quickly as possible and gathered her skirts around her legs. 'There is nothing to steer with.'

'I do that with the oars,' he said, digging them in for the first stoke.

'Backwards?'

'Yes. You direct me and I look over my shoulder from time to time.'

'Oh. I see. Do you not feel you would be able to row more comfortably if you were to remove your hat and coat? Oh, really, do not poker up at me like that. We have established that I am unfit to call myself a gentlewoman and, I assure you, I have seen a gentleman in shirtsleeves before without fainting.'

Will gave her the look that she was beginning to realise meant that he could think of nothing polite to say, but he laid his hat on the bottom of the boat behind him. 'I really do not think—'

Verity held out her hand. 'You are not required to. I

will fold your coat carefully over my knees so it does not get creased or splashed.'

Oh, dear, now I've mentioned knees. How shocking of me.

She produced a smirk that she hoped conveyed sarcasm and gazed innocently back into suspicious blue eyes.

There was a momentary tussle of wills, then the ducal raiment was removed, not without difficulty. The boat rocked alarmingly. Verity took the coat, folded it meticulously and waited until Will had begun rowing again before she looked up.

Well. Goodness. If she had admired his figure when he was fully dressed, then the sight of the thin linen shirt blown back against working muscles was enough to make her mouth go dry.

Flustered, she looked down at the coat, fussed over its arrangement and, as Will took a slightly different angle across the water and the breeze caught them, inhaled a heady mixture of fine woollen cloth warm from his body and a spicy cologne. The boat rocked and she held the sides with a gasp of alarm.

'Are you all right, Miss Wingate?'

No! 'Yes, perfectly, thank you. I am becoming used to the motion of the boat, that is all. I have no experience of being on water.'

'You are nervous? There is no need to be.'

'Not at all. Although I cannot swim.' And now they seemed a very long way out and there was a current against which Will had to row hard—the dammed river, she supposed. If anyone fell in here it would be a long way to shore for a swimmer—and probably a long way down for someone who was not.

'There will be no need to worry about that.' Her admission seemed to have cheered him up. Presumably he disapproved of females swimming. 'I have no intention of capsizing this boat and, even if I did, I can swim and would rescue you.'

Probably he swims as well as he rows, Verity thought.

And now she had to contend with her imagination conjuring up visions of the naked wet Duke.

Chapter Seven

Verity made herself focus on why she was here, sitting on a hard, narrow wooden bench in the middle of a cold, deep lake with a man who disapproved of her so completely. *The naked, wet,* disagreeable *Duke,* she reminded herself, hoping that the colour she could feel in her cheeks looked like the effects of the breeze and not wicked thoughts. 'I can see the island.' She pointed over Will's shoulder and he glanced behind to check his course.

'It does not look as though it could be artificial,' she said, squinting against the sunlight reflected off the little wavelets. 'It is a long way out and the water must be far too deep there.'

'Can you see a burial mound?'

Verity shook her head, craning to look past his broad shoulders at the land looming closer. 'No. But there are trees and bushes covering all that I can see, so there may be something hidden there.'

'It must have been a small hill before the river was dammed. Perhaps a watchtower was built there and the children mistook its ruins,' Will offered with scrupulous politeness, as though to counter any disappointment.

The ideal host, she thought, refusing to be charmed. Her friends would be agog to hear that what had passed between her and the Duke of Aylsham. They were meeting this afternoon in the tower room as usual, quite at home there, following their interests freely, companionably silent or engaged in spirited discussion, as the mood took them. Prue might even have recovered enough to agree to disrobe so Jane could finish her picture. All of them, presumably, behaving in a way unfitting to a gentlewoman, unfitting for a gentleman's wife.

They had been delighted to hear about the invitation to visit Stane Hall, convinced that the news of such sociability would make their parents even more determined to pursue the Duke instead of seeking out other, unwelcome suitors for them.

'What are you thinking about to put that smile on your lips, Miss Wingate? If it is something you are prepared to share, that is.'

'I was thinking about my friends, about their companionship and their talents.'

Wishing we could inhabit that tower together, doing what we choose with our lives...

'You find that there is society enough in the area to supply you with many congenial friends, Miss Wingate?'

'Indeed, yes. Of course, plain Miss Wingate need not be as choosy as a duke about the company she keeps. The respectable and the worthy are in ample supply in the district, I can assure you.'

'You think me guilty of snobbery?' One oar dipped, caught and splashed his sleeve with water. The fine linen, wet, became transparent, moulding the lines of his forearm in graphic detail.

'Not at all, you simply know your own worth, Your Grace, as I am sure all dukes do.'

'You do not like me, Miss Wingate.' This time the oars cut cleanly through the surface.

'I am aware that you do not approve of me, Your Grace. You have made that perfectly plain. If it comes to it, I do not approve of you—I prefer gentlemen to have more flexibility, more tolerance. But beyond that it would be foolish of me to go, considering that I am in a perilous situation and entirely at your mercy.'

He smiled tightly, almost surprising her into smiling back. 'You will not trick me into repeating my hasty and intemperate words.'

Nor will you withdraw them, she thought. *Or apologise.*

'I greatly admire the manner in which you support your father—your care and tact. I would have to be blind not to admire your looks and foolish to neglect your intelligence and spirit. I cannot approve of unconventional females—I am sure you can comprehend why—and I will do all in my power to ensure that my sisters are raised according to the strictest principles of behaviour for young ladies. However, I can assure you I will not drop you into the lake in consequence of that.'

'Thank you.' It was difficult to find anything to say in answer to that comprehensive, cool, unyielding assessment.

Damned with faint praise, indeed.

'And my siblings all like you, which has to count in your favour, I believe.'

Goodness, he is going to become positively pleasant in a minute.

'I like them, too. They are charming. Oh, look, we are almost there.'

Will looked back over this shoulder, changed direction sharply before they ran into a bank of rushes and paddled slowly around the island. 'That looks like a beach we could land on.'

The keel of the little boat ground into the gentle slope of the pebbled shore and he put the oars in, vaulted over the prow on to the tiny crescent of land and dragged it a little further up. 'Give me your hand and you can jump down without getting your feet wet.'

Verity stood up uncertainly, told herself not to dither—it did not matter if she looked less than elegant and she could hardly sink in six inches of water even if she did slip—and managed to transfer from boat to pebbles with what she thought was admirable grace. Will's firm grip certainly helped. She freed her hand the moment she was safe on shore. He was very easy to hold on to and she had to keep reminding herself that this was the man who so much disapproved of her that he would forget his perfect manners to tell her so.

'It looks very overgrown,' she said dubiously, looking round them as he tied the boat to a sapling with a rope that had been coiled in the bows. It was clearly a natural island, with rock showing through the grass here and there. The trees were tall, the undergrowth thick. She pointed. 'There is a path of sorts.'

'Made by my brothers and sisters, no doubt. There will not be any wildlife here with such large feet.' He looked around. 'Would you care to sit on that bank there and I will investigate? With this growth of bushes you might harm your shoes or gown.'

'And let you have all the fun of exploration? Certainly not. I shall follow in your steps.'

To her surprise Will did not order her to remain where

she was—not that she would have obeyed him if he had. Perhaps he assumed that after a few minutes she would give up and return to the beach. It was hot work. There were midges, brambles and, for such an apparently tiny island, it was impossible to see more than a few yards in any direction.

After about ten minutes Verity sat down with a thump on a boulder on the opposite shore to the one on which they had landed. 'If there is a burial mound on this island then the only place it can be is over there.' She pointed to a cluster of small trees. 'We have looked everywhere else. I am beginning to wonder what on earth the children saw that made them think there was anything man-made here at all.'

'And I am wondering exactly what retribution is due if this proves to be a practical joke,' Will said grimly, waving away midges from in front of his nose. He had neglected to put back either hat or coat, his shirtsleeves had snagged on brambles and there was a trace of sunburn on the bridge of his nose. 'Let us see what is over there and then…'

'A hut.' Verity peered through the branches. 'How very charming—it is just like a fairy house in an old tale, or a hermit's cell.'

'This is not a fairy tale, nor a Gothic romance, come to that,' Will said repressively. Verity pulled a face at his back. 'It might have been a summer house at one time, I suppose. Not a very interesting design, but it looks quite well built and seems to be in reasonable repair.' They walked up to the front door of the little cottage. 'It can only have one room, but there is a chimney.' Will pointed upwards, but Verity was already pushing at the door.

'It is unlocked and— Oh.' The door swung open on

to a stone-floored room with a hearth taking up almost the whole of one side. There was a window by the door and a rustic table and bench in the centre. Against the wall was a rough bedframe. 'But—Will, look. Someone is living here.' She heard his name on her lips too late to call it back.

'Let me see.' He walked in, ducking under the low lintel, turning slowly on his heel to survey the small space. 'There is a straw tick on the bed and a blanket. Food on the table. Fresh food.' He turned, his expression furious. 'Hell and damnation! Verity, wait here. I have to get back to the boat. *Now*.'

Those confounded children. Worse words came to him as he ran, crashing through brambles, leaping fallen branches. Those devious little brats.

'Oh, Miss Wingate, there's a burial mound...'

A throwaway line certain to snare someone they knew was passionate about such things. And they knew, too, that if a guest expressed an interest in seeing something, then he had no option but to try to oblige them. Only one boat in the boathouse? Like *hell* that was probable. If he hadn't been seething with resentment at Verity Wingate for provoking him into not just losing his temper, but being unforgivably rude to lady, a guest—

A branch snapped back, hit him in the face and sent him crashing into a patch of stinging nettles. This time Will didn't even attempt to control his language. He got up, spat out dead leaves and oaths, ignored the itching wheals rising on his hands and Verity Wingate's voice behind him demanding to know what was going on, and started running again.

Half a minute after he reached the beach he heard

her crash through the bushes behind him, then her feet crunched on the shingle. Of course, the wretched female would not do the ladylike thing and stay safely where he left her.

'The rowing boat has gone,' she said, staring round the tiny bay as though she might spot it hiding in the reeds. 'But I saw you tie it up properly. I saw the knot.' She was panting with the effort of keeping up with him, her face was damp and rosy and her hair was sticking to her face where it had come free from its pins. She looked a complete hoyden. She looked edible.

Will turned, kicked the sapling he had used to tie the rowing boat to, told himself that was frankly childish and managed a stiff smile of apology rather than the look of smouldering desire that was doing battle with the anger. 'I think my confounded siblings are playing a joke on us. They lured us out here with that story of a burial mound, rowed across in another boat and towed ours away.'

Miss Wingate opened her mouth, then snapped it shut on what had clearly been a frank comment on the younger Calthorpes' morals and sense of humour. With a sinking feeling he saw her expression change as she thought it through. 'Why is there fresh food in that hut? Why is there bedding? Oh, no—please tell me that I am wrong—the little devils have stranded us here, haven't they? And they do not intend on rescuing us at least until tomorrow.'

'I fear so.' Will watched warily for signs of hysteria. Any respectable young lady should be screaming or fainting or having a comprehensive fit of the vapours by now. But of course, Miss Wingate was not a conventional young lady. He doubted she had ever had the vapours in her life.

'My father will be anxious.' There was a furrow between her arching brows and he almost reached out to smooth it away.

Will clasped his hands behind his back. 'Probably.' She was too intelligent to be soothed by platitudes.

'And no one except the children has any idea where we are.'

'Unless one of the staff saw us walking down to the boathouse, then, no. I have no confidence that they did as I told them and informed my butler, or anyone else, where we had gone. Only that brood of, as you so rightly called them, little devils, can find us.'

'But *why?*' she demanded, turning to him.

That is genuine. She really has no thought of what it might mean—will mean—being stranded overnight with me. Extraordinary.

He almost smiled as Verity raised her hands to her head as though to tug at her hair in frustration, recollected herself and linked her fingers in front of her. But there was nothing to smile about. Nothing at all.

'We could light a fire. But would that be seen from the house?' She began to pace up and down the tiny beach, arguing with herself as much as him, Will suspected, so intrigued that he forgot to be angry for a moment. Ladies, his grandfather had always maintained, were incapable of sustained reasoning and the young females he had came into contact with certainly showed no inclination to think things through. An unpleasant suspicion began to creep over him that those girls had been raised to appear empty-headed. He jerked his attention back to Verity, who had passed him for the second time.

'They will launch a search eventually, I suppose, and they will look in the grounds, so they will come down to the lake and might see a fire. We could hang something up as a signal, but we do not have a sheet. Let me think… Bother these fashions, my petticoats would hardly make a small flag.' She turned again, her feet sending stones spraying out with the vehemence of the movement. 'But even a sheet will not help because the island cannot be seen from the lawns.' She stopped and addressed him directly. 'Will they search those woods?' She waved a hand towards the dense oak and beech trees crowding down to the shore.

'Not until they have exhausted the house and the gardens and the nearest areas of the park,' Will admitted. 'How likely is your father to become dangerously anxious, to leap to the conclusion that something serious will have befallen us?'

'He is a very calm person. He will assume we are together and he knows us both to be sensible adults who could cope with a misadventure. We are on your property. And Mr Hoskins will reassure him, do his best to ensure he is not agitated. He will not suffer a relapse, if that is what concerns you, his mind is too resolute. He will be concerned but, as I said, he will know you are with me—'

She broke off, spun round so abruptly that she staggered and he had to take two long strides forward to catch her by the elbows. 'Together. Oh, no. *No.*' Her hands closed over his forearms so they stood locked in place, staring at each other. 'Those little… But why? Why would they want to compromise me? I have never done anything to hurt them, surely? I hardly know them.'

'They do not want to hurt you, Verity,' Will said. 'They have taken a liking to you. They are worried that I am going to marry some exceedingly proper young lady who will be even stricter than their governess and tutor are.'

She gasped. 'They want you to marry me? Simply because they think I would not be strict with them?'

He had called her by her first name, they were standing improperly close, hands clasping arms, so close that he could feel her body heat, see the rise and fall of her breasts, the still-agitated breaths from the scrambling run, the shock of finding herself stranded. She smelled deliciously of warm woman and crushed greenery and wisteria blossom and he wanted to haul her in closer, press his lips to that indignant mouth and take the fullness gently between his teeth, taste her. *Madness.*

'You think that would be a bad idea?' he asked instead.

I have lost my mind. Marry this woman? The least suitable bride I can imagine? This rebellious, unconventional bluestocking?

'To trap a man into marriage? Any man, let alone one of the most eligible in the country? Of *course* I think it a bad idea. Do you think I have no pride? That I am desperate for a husband before I find myself on the shelf? Do you think I would be delighted that a pack of ill-disciplined children have decided to entrap me into wedlock with a man I do not even *like*?'

The realisation of what she had just said was clear in the appalled expression in those expressive brown eyes. 'I am so sorry. I did not mean that...'

'Yes, you did,' Will said calmly. It was no more than he should have expected of her after all. She was a hoyden, unbecomingly independent, outspoken and uninhibited and he had already been appallingly rude to her that day. And what was she doing to him? He should not be speaking to a lady like that. He should not be standing on a deserted island holding her like this. He should certainly not be aching to pull her down on to that patch of short turf over there—so conveniently close—and see whether he could make those intelligent eyes go blind with passion.

I am the Duke of Aylsham. I should be a perfect gentleman, a perfect nobleman, at all times. I owe it to my name, to myself. This is an unfortunate situation and not Verity's fault. So, deal with it.

Will stared at the far shore, estimated distance. 'I will swim across. It will take some time to get help to you, but I will light a fire before I go and you have shelter and food. You would not be afraid to be here alone for a few hours?'

Verity's lips compressed into a thin line and she took her hands from his forearms as though he had suddenly become slimy. 'Oh, of course, I would be *terrified*. Why, there might be dangerous frogs. Or possibly man-eating gulls. Or perhaps the place is haunted. Do not be ridiculous, Will. I would not be afraid, but that is quite beside the point. You are not going to make that swim. Have you ever swum that far before?'

'Not quite so far,' he admitted, eyeing the far shore. But he was fit, a good swimmer. He would do it because he had to do it. A gentleman did not compromise a lady, even such an unladylike one. There was no other option.

'You are not Lord Byron, swimming the Hellespont!' she flung at him. 'You are an intelligent man—or I assume you are when you are not fogging your mind with these ridiculous ideas of honour and duty. *Think*, for goodness' sake. This water is cold, you admit it is a long way, you have no idea about the currents, or dangerous patches of weed. And if I see you drowning I will not be able to do anything about it and I will be scarred for life by the experience, which would be very selfish of you.'

'You are laughing at me.' It was ridiculous how angry that made him. This impertinent chit of a female who disparaged honourable behaviour, who flatly contradicted his decisions and questioned his judgement—

'I am not laughing, believe me. I admit I was trying to find some humour in a ghastly situation to make you see how foolish you are being.'

'Miss Wingate. Will you kindly go into the hut while I remove my clothing? There is no other solution to this and I will not drown.'

Chapter Eight

'I will not let you swim.' Verity planted herself firmly in front of him, facing him down, although the top of her head only came up as far as the tip of his nose. Will had not thought that big brown eyes could seem hard and determined, but these were now. 'Never mind *my* feelings. I did not think it would be necessary to point this out to a loving brother, but do you want Basil to inherit the title knowing that it was his idiotic scheme that caused your death? Do you want him saddled with that guilt? Or with the ghastly burden of a dukedom, come to that.'

He had not thought of that. He was almost certain he could make it, but not absolutely. And if he failed, then not only Basil, but all of them, would spend the rest of their lives with his death on their consciences. And it would weigh heavy, he knew. They might seem heedless, undisciplined, wild even, but they were sensitive, intelligent children. Then the rest of what Verity had said struck him.

'You consider a dukedom to be a ghastly burden?'

'Surely it must be?' It was incredible how those eyes of hers changed with her mood. Now they were thoughtful, a little puzzled. She was thinking and he felt as though that fierce stare had turned inwards as she puzzled over his answer.

'Certainly not. It is what I was born to. It is a privilege.'

The brown gaze became sceptical and her mouth twisted into a rueful smile. 'Is it not exhausting, having to be perfect all the time in order to earn that privilege? Are the expectations of your family, your dependents, your tenants, never wearisome? Do you never wish you could simply be William Calthorpe, Esquire, an ordinary gentleman of moderate means who might live where he pleases, do as he wishes?'

'The thought has never occurred to me,' Will said firmly and truthfully. 'Very well, I will not attempt to swim. Now, let us get off this beach. You should shelter in the hut and I will see if there is some spot on the headland nearest the grounds where I can make some kind of signal.'

Verity turned obediently enough. Having got her way, presumably she was prepared to be more biddable. But that small concession to obedience did not appear to include minding her tongue. 'What exactly am I sheltering from?' she enquired sweetly. 'The weather is fine and warm, and the incidence of dangerous wildlife or marauding pirates appears to be low.'

'You have misplaced your hat,' Will pointed out, refusing to deal with her flights of fancy which were expressly designed to irritate him, he was sure. She shrugged and made a dismissive gesture towards the tangled undergrowth where it had presumably been ripped from her head in their mad scramble to reach the shore. 'Do you not wish to preserve your complexion?' he asked.

'Not at the cost of being stuck in a stuffy little hovel for hours. I will come with you.'

'Miss Wingate—' No gentleman would lay a finger on a lady, let alone raise his voice to one. He was a gentleman, so why did he have the most appalling urge to shout at Verity Wingate, say far worse things than he had already that day? Why did he want to shake her until she ceased to provoke him? And why did the thought of having his hands on those slim shoulders, pulling her close to him, produce a reaction that made him turn from her abruptly and stalk away towards the little cottage? At least with his back turned she would not notice the physical effect she was having on him.

Her feet crunched on the shingle, then the snap of a twig told him that she was following close behind.

Obedience and no argument for once—how refreshing.

'Call me Verity,' she said crisply. 'And I will call you Will. We are going to be stuck on this rock for hours— and not exactly in harmony either—and I am not going to be *Your Gracing* you the entire time.'

'Miss W—'

'We are not within hearing of the Court Chamberlain or a single Patroness of Almack's, let alone any member of the College of Arms. I believe we may use first names without provoking a scandal.' She paused and Will almost turned around to ask why she hesitated. 'Or, at least, not more of one than we already find ourselves with.'

He saw her sun hat, a frivolous disc of straw with floating yellow ribbons, hanging forlornly from a thorn bush and reached out for it. 'Here. The crown appears to have a hole in it, unfortunately.'

Verity took it, sighed audibly at the state of the thing,

and jammed it back on her head. A tuft of glossy brown hair poked through the damaged part.

'There will not be a scandal,' Will said, resisting the urge to tie the ribbons in a large bow under her chin and tickle her neck while he was at it. 'No one but my family and yours are present. I will manage this so that your good name is not compromised.'

Not that the absence of scandal was going to save him unless they were rescued very quickly indeed. She had fallen silent again, so presumably she had not realised that, scandal or no, they were not going to escape the consequences of this. A single gentleman, stranded with a young lady in a remote spot where the only shelter was a hut containing a bed, could expect only one demand from her father.

That was right and proper, of course, even if it was damnably awkward. *At least the children like her*, Will thought. And the sobering thought of an irate bishop—did they wield croziers instead of shotguns when herding sons-in-law to the altar?—had killed the last trace of that inconvenient arousal just then. But marriage to this argumentative creature?

'There, I knew you would be sensible about it once you recovered from the shock and stopped trying to be noble about it,' Miss—*Verity* said with an air of satisfaction that had him wanting to shake her all over again. And then…

'Here is the hut,' Will said, quite unnecessarily as they were standing right in front of it. He wondered if he could build a raft. If he had an axe and some strong twine… *And if wishes were horses, beggars would ride.* There was the door of the hut, of course. Would that float? He opened it and examined the hinges.

'Don't you dare think about it, Will,' Verity said firmly as he measured the thickness with finger and thumb. She appeared to be able to read minds. 'That is only one degree less dangerous than trying to swim across.'

'Does nothing ever ruffle your calm, Verity? Or do you insist on producing *sensible* advice under all circumstances?' he demanded, irritation suddenly overcoming the tattered remnants of good manners.

'Would you rather something did ruffle me?' She paused, one hand on the door frame, arrested in the act of tossing her wrecked hat inside, and smiled at him. It was not reassuring. 'I have no intention of not being sensible, or of pretending to be less intelligent than I am, even if you would prefer me to produce some tears and flutter my handkerchief. I have no idea how to have a fit of the vapours, if that is what you are expecting, Will.'

It might be easier if she did succumb to nerves, he admitted to himself. Then he could rely on his own judgement without having to give due consideration to her, undoubtedly reasonable, objections. That smile— genuine, amused, warm. He had no idea she could smile like that. And his name on her lips.

Will moved closer without consciously thinking why he was doing it. *Would you rather something did ruffle me?* she had asked.

'I expect you know what to do with tearful young ladies who cast themselves upon your manly bosom. Does it happen very often?' Verity teased.

When had been the last time someone had teased him? Male friends, of course, but not like this, certainly never with that smile that asked him to laugh with her at the joke. But it was not amusement he felt. The desire came flooding back as their gazes locked and her eyes widened with something that was not fear or apprehension but, perhaps, surprise and curiosity. *Or arousal?*

How had he come to be so close to her? Close enough to see that the brown of her eyes held darker flecks and a thin fringe of gold rimmed the irises. 'I have never had that experience,' he heard himself say, his voice husky. 'It is one I find strangely appealing.'

Had he moved again? Perhaps Verity had. Her right hand was certainly raised, the palm flat against his breastbone.

'No?' Will asked softly.

Her fingers moved slightly, not to push him away, but as though she was reading his breathing, his heartbeat, through the tips. 'Yes,' Verity murmured.

He bent his head and she lifted a little on her toes to meet him, her hands sliding up over his coatless shoulders to clasp behind his neck. The only other time Will had ever kissed a respectable young lady, a virgin, was when he had held this one on Sunday beside the pond. He thought again, with what was functioning in his brain, that this was not what he had expected. Verity was not brazen, but not shy either. She was cautious, but not tentative, following his lead, her lips parting to the pressure of his tongue, opening for him, learning fast, so that as his tongue stroked into the velvet warmth hers met it, copied his movements and then began to explore.

He tastes of coffee this time...a little, Verity thought. *But more of something else. Man, perhaps? Or just Will?*

The taste of him was familiar now, even though this was only a second kiss. His tongue caressed hers and so she answered him, almost taken aback when he let her slide between his lips, surprised by the heat of his mouth. If this was how kissing him was, so very much better than her experience nearly five years before, what would it be like to make love with him?

And then Will drew away, lifted his mouth from hers, set her back against the door frame and steadied her with his hands cupped around her shoulders.

Which is a good thing because my legs are decidedly shaky...

'I apologise,' Will said, suddenly very formal.

'Again? I thought we had discussed this by the pond.'

You enjoyed it, do not try to pretend you did not. I might not be very experienced, but I know what it meant when I felt your body change as it pressed against mine.

She did not say it and she did not let her gaze slide downwards from his face. If truth be told, it had been rather alarming in a shivery kind of way—and very arousing.

'I took advantage of you again.'

'*Oh.* You exasperating man! You asked, I said *yes*. You kissed me, I kissed you back. Then you stopped. Please define *taking advantage.*'

'You are under my protection. Under no circumstances should I have kissed you. Not then, not now. It was not the behaviour of a gentleman and as much of a mistake now as it was before.'

'Poppycock. It was the behaviour of a *man* and it is probably long past time when you allowed yourself to be one of those and not some marble statue of the perfect duke.'

Which way was the headland? Verity gave His Grace's well-muscled chest a prod with her finger, which made him sway back with a sharp intake of breath, and took advantage of his momentary loss of balance to stalk off down the overgrown path. Was this the right direction? It was of no consequence, all she wanted to do was get away from him, as far as this miniature island permitted.

Apologise? Again.

How he dared! Verity swatted a leafy twig out of the way. Will couldn't have said anything more insulting—except, possibly, *Ugh*. She was an adult, intelligent woman who had agreed to kiss him, had shown she was enjoying it clearly enough. So, was that an apology for *kissing* her or regret that he had kissed *her*?

He was following her, she could hear him pushing his way along the path, but she ignored him, tried to ignore the insinuating little pulse that beat low down in her belly and the tingle of well-kissed lips.

Think about something else. Do not let him become important.

Presumably these faint tracks through the bushes had been made by the Calthorpe children once they had discovered the island, Verity reasoned. How they must love the freedom it represented, now they had been pitchforked by the death of their father from the undisciplined life they had been used to into the formality and restraint that Will demanded.

If this was her island, she would buy a little sailing boat and she and her friends would come here every day, far from the conventions and expectations that bound them. It might be difficult to bring a pianoforte for Lucy, though.

As she came out of the scrub on to the bare rock of the low headland a snort of amusement escaped her at the thought of loading a piano on to a small boat and then sailing it across the lake.

'Something amuses you?' Will arrived at her side.

Verity shot him a rapid sideways glance. His hair was dishevelled, the immaculate fine cloth of his shirt had several small rips and even more green stains and there was a scratch on one cheekbone.

Your Grace is beginning to look like a human being. It suits you.

'I was thinking about the difficulty of transporting a pianoforte here.'

'A string quartet would be simpler and would not require a tuner to ready the instrument once it was installed,' he said, so seriously that for a moment she stared at him until she saw the faint creases at the corners of his eyes, the slight lift of his lips.

Goodness, there is that sense of humour again, ready to ambush me when I most dislike him.

At least he appeared to have accepted the change of subject, which was a relief, because if he apologised for kissing her one more time she was going to push him into the lake.

'Shall we sit and review our options?' He gestured to a smooth rock and Verity perched on the end. Will sat beside her, a good two feet away. 'There are no sheets, no tablecloth, the mattress tick is grey and the blankets are brown—none of them will make a visible signal. I suggest that you stay in the hut where at least you are sheltered and there is food and I will build a fire here on the headland. If I keep it burning, someone will see the smoke eventually. When we are returned to land we can at least assure everyone that we were not together.'

'Except up to this point, that is. Oh, and the slight matter of the fact that we kissed,' Verity pointed out. 'But if you can ignore that, I most certainly can.' *Liar.*

'I am concerned for your reputation,' Will pointed out in tones that suggested a strong desire to snap.

'Or yours?' Verity enquired sweetly. 'They used to call you Lord Appropriate, did they not? The pedestal on which you perch must be so lofty that there are probably small clouds around it. My reputation is merely a matter of the opinion of local society, where everyone knows me well. If I take a tumble off my own plinth it is a matter of hopping back on again once another local scandal distracts everyone—the quarrel between the Rector's wife and Lady Foskett over the breeding of pugs, or Miss Hutchinson cheating at the Horticultural Society's annual show, for example. Not that anyone *need* find out about this.

'You, however, have the aura of your title to keep untarnished. Even if no one but your staff, your family and Papa and Mr Hoskins know, your self-esteem must be severely bruised.'

Silence. Verity hummed nonchalantly under her breath and waited for the explosion.

'Earlier I was repressing an entirely improper desire to shake you until your teeth rattled,' Will said. He sounded as though his teeth were clamped together. 'For some demented reason I kissed you instead. At the moment I have no trouble at all deciding which impulse I wish to follow.'

'Excellent.' Verity turned her most charming smile on him.

'You are doing it on purpose, aren't you? Trying to anger me.'

'That seems to puzzle you.' Verity made herself more comfortable on the rock and tried not to worry that Papa was becoming agitated as the shadows lengthened. 'I do not care if I am compromised and I do not want to marry you.'

'In the absence of an available Prince of the Blood, single ladies appear to find the thought of marrying a duke irresistible.'

'You flatter yourself.'

'No, not at all,' Will said, quite calmly. 'I have no illusions that I am considered highly eligible for anything except my title. It would make no difference if I was one hundred years old, wildly eccentric, had two dozen irregular offspring and assorted unpleasant diseases. You saw them at church on Sunday. London would be a thousand times worse.'

'I doubt we would be in this position if you were a centenarian, let alone one weakened by unspecified diseases and a career of debauchery,' Verity pointed out. 'The rowing would have defeated you.'

There was silence from beside her.

I have pushed him too far, she thought.

Chapter Nine

Then Will laughed. He doubled up on the rock and laughed while tears streamed down his face. When he finally straightened up he swiped one hand across his eyes and demanded, 'Does nothing shock you, Verity?'

'Of course. Cruelty and ignorance and bigotry. Oh, and the current fashion for mustard yellow. And the inability of men to grasp that females have brains of equal capacity to their own.'

He gave a final gasp of amusement, produced a large handkerchief and mopped his face. 'I cannot recall when I last laughed like that.'

'I am sorry.' Verity moved a little closer, wanting to touch him and sensing he might find that an unfamiliar gesture. 'Of course you have not wanted to laugh. You lost your father and your grandfather not long ago and you have all this dreadful responsibility and the children to bring up.'

'No, I mean I cannot recall when it last seemed fitting to laugh.' The amusement had gone and his profile seemed suddenly harsh. 'Did they really call me Lord Appropriate?'

'You never heard it said? No, I suppose you would not. Who would dare risk insulting you? My cousin told me some time ago. He described you in a letter and that was why I guessed who you were so quickly when you fell into my excavation.'

'You think that a desire to be *appropriate* is something that is to be ashamed of? I have been the heir to the dukedom my entire life. I have been raised to fill that position since my grandfather removed me from my father.' There was pride in Will's voice and a complete absence of understanding of the point she had intended to make.

His title is not a burden to him, she realised. *It is what he is. Has anyone ever valued him for the human being inside or only because he was the heir to a great title? How...sad.*

'Are you cold? You shivered.' Beside her Will moved as though to take off his coat. 'Confound it. My coat is in the rowing boat.'

'No, I am not cold, thank you. It was just a goose walking over my grave.' Or the realisation that he was as trapped by being a duke as she was by being female. If Will wanted to be an artist or an explorer, if he desired nothing more than to shut himself away in a library and live the life of a scholar or to join the literary salons of London as a poet, he could not. Not without neglecting the duties he had been raised to take on.

No one could actually stop him rebelling, of course. The worst he would suffer was silent condemnation and the attentions of the satirical cartoonists. His staff would keep their mouths shut and carry on managing the land, controlling the finances, wrestling with the legal issues, even though it would be like a great ship without its captain at the helm. But if a female without substantial funds of her own took her own path through life the result would be vocal criticism, the closing of doors and a life of social isolation and genteel poverty. Even Will had been shaken out of his rigid good manners to condemn her intellectual interests and where they led her.

'We were speaking of your reputation,' Will reminded her after the silence had stretched on for several minutes, interrupted only by the strange peeping call of a pair of moorhens, the rustle of the wind in the trees, the slap of wavelets on the shore.

'I thought we had exhausted that discussion. When we eventually reach shore again it will all seem like a storm in a teacup. Papa will take my word for it that I am not compromised, Mr Hoskins will follow whatever direction Papa takes, your loyal staff will remain silent.'

And the only sound will be the rattling of the shackles you have grown up with, chaining you to proper behaviour.

'We will talk further when we are rescued,' Will said. He sounded as though he had unclenched his jaw, the better to grind his teeth. 'Now I will collect wood for a fire.'

'Very well,' Verity said, with as much meekness as she could muster. She had probably pushed him to the end of his tether. 'I will go back to the hut.'

She walked off before she could see his reaction to this act of obedience because she would probably want to push him in the lake again if he looked smug about it. Besides, she wanted a cup of tea. Needed one. If those provoking children had left any with the supplies...

There was not only tea and a pot, but a flint and

steel striker for lighting a fire. Verity picked up her hat, hitched up her skirts above her ankles and went to collect kindling and small sticks. It took her fifteen minutes, but she had a fire going, the kettle filled with water and hung over the fire on the primitive hook and chain that were fixed in the chimney, and was returning with an armful of larger pieces of wood when Will appeared.

'You have a fire.' He gestured to the trickle of smoke emerging from the chimney.

'And you have not.' Verity looked past him in the direction of the headland. No smoke. 'The striker is on the hearth.'

'You lit it?'

'Yes, all by myself. Remarkable, isn't it?' Sarcasm was unworthy, but, really, what was she supposed to do? Sit thirstily and wait on his convenience, presumably. 'Tea will be ready by the time you return.'

'Thank you.' Will strode into the hut, remembered to duck under the lintel just in time and emerged, striker in hand.

Verity indulged herself by admiring the sight of him bending to pick up a few branches she had abandoned as too heavy. Without his coat, the flex of his back muscles, the pull of his breeches over his thighs and his admirably taut buttocks, made a sight that any well-bred lady should have averted her eyes from and any female with a pulse could not help but admire.

A cat might look at a king, even if courtiers must bow so low they never see him, she thought with a smile. *And a plain miss might admire a duke, even if the wretched man has had an iron rod inserted in his spine and his brain pickled in the vinegar of duty.*

And someone had to make the tea while others stomped about being manly, she supposed, building up the fire, then peering into the basket of supplies. It was an impressive collection. Either the children had an ally in the cook or had bribed a footman or had undertaken barefaced theft, because there was certainly enough food to keep two adults well fed for at least twenty-four hours.

'What is amusing?' Will enquired from the doorway.

'Was I smiling? I was just reflecting that the world had better be braced for a shock when Araminta, Althea and Basil are let loose in it. Perhaps you should simply transfer them to the Home Office immediately and let them add the three to their roster of intelligence agents. They seem capable of cunning undercover scheming, well-executed manoeuvres and thoughtful provisioning. Look.' She gestured to the supplies set out on the table.

From the set of Will's jaw the immediate future of his brothers and sisters did not look promising. House arrest for all and a tanned backside for Basil seemed the most likely outcome.

'They are intelligent,' she ventured. 'And their unconventional upbringing seems to have made them very creative.'

'You are too tolerant. If they were cast adrift on a desert island they would be perfectly suited for the life,' Will snapped. 'As it is, somehow, I have to make them fit for society, not encourage them to behave like a pirate crew. At the moment they have no concept of common decency and they are completely self-centred and unscrupulous.'

'Shall we drink tea outside?' Verity poured it into the

two serviceable pottery mugs that stood beside the two
plates and two sets of cutlery on the table. Possibly the
combined effect of tea and her best attempt at conventional ladylike behaviour might improve Will's mood.

Not that she was averse to the effect it had on him—
that jaw, when clenched, was certainly a fine feature
and temper made the blue of his eyes deeper—but if he
was in a better frame of mind when they were eventually rescued, then it might mitigate the results for the
children. She was angry about what they had done, but
they were not to blame for their upbringing.

'Thank you. I will take it back to the fire.' He shook
his head when she offered sugar. 'I need to keep that
burning until it is hot enough to add damp vegetation.'

'To produce more smoke? What a good idea.'

Will took the mug and made his way back to the fire.
The faint pathway was now well trodden and he could
make his way without concentrating on where he was
putting his feet. As that gave him more opportunity to
think about Verity Wingate and the predicament they
found themselves in, it could hardly be said to be an
improvement.

He took an incautious gulp of hot tea and sat down on
the rock beside the fire. It was burning well and slowly
with a hot, dense, interior and he added some more of the
thicker branches, building it up ready to begin covering
it in a mantle of green foliage to make smoke.

Building a fire was calming, almost meditative, but it
could do nothing to solve the dilemma he found himself
in. He was trapped in a highly compromising situation
with a woman he found physically attractive, however
maddening her character was.

There was clearly no path open to him other than marriage. He had compromised Verity through no fault of her own and there was only one outcome to that. Of course, she was temperamentally unsuited to be a duchess, but she was an intelligent woman who would soon come to terms with the situation if he was firm enough in his directions. And, given her breeding and upbringing, she would adapt and shed those bluestocking theories about independence. A lady obeyed her husband in all things and she knew that. There was only one problem—she did not appear to want to marry him, which was baffling.

Will nudged some more dry wood into the base of the fire and tried to read some answers in the flames. Verity did not find him repellent physically, not judging by the evidence of two kisses. She did not appear to have an attachment to any other man, she liked his brothers and sisters and there could not possibly be anyone of higher rank she could aspire to marry. So, what was there to object to in him? He examined the man inside the Duke, attempting complete honesty and objectivity. His reputation was spotless, his appearance was passable, his health was good. He had no eccentric habits and his wealth was considerable.

Was she simply being coy? But that seemed unlike anything he had observed in her behaviour. Or perhaps—

Will reached for the mug and looked up as he drained it. From the beech woods on the slopes down to the lake on the far side from the house there were smudges of smoke rising in the still air. For a second his brain could make no sense of it, then he recalled his Steward saying that the charcoal burners were due to start a new cycle of coppicing and burning that week. He counted—two, no, three columns of smoke now—and calculated the angle they would be seen from the house and gardens. His own fire would be in a direct line.

'Hell and damnation.'

'What is wrong?' Verity emerged from the scrub behind him. 'Oh. The charcoal burners? Oh, no.' She sat down abruptly on the rock beside him as the realisation of what it meant hit her. 'Now what are we going to do?'

'Wait,' Will said grimly. 'Wait and hope my repellent siblings come to their senses and confess what they have done before nightfall.'

Nightfall and that tiny cottage with its one, narrow bed. Verity would be inside and he would be outside, of course. Not that that would make any difference to the situation they found themselves in, but things were bad enough without his willpower being put to the test by the proximity of a bed and an attractive young woman in it. It *would* stand the test, obviously—he was a gentleman—but he could do without the physical effects of ignoring the messages his body was sending him.

It was bad enough with her so close now, warm and relaxed, leaning on her hands braced behind her and with her head thrown back. Will risked a sideways glance and turned back to stare at the fire. The column of her throat, exposed, white, taut as though inviting a kiss, a gentle bite, a lick. What would her skin taste like?

'It is going to rain.'

The words were so at odds with his erotic musings that it took Will a second to take them in. He looked up at the sky, saw the heavy thunderheads building to the south, registered the way the air had become hotter, breathless with a quivering intensity. The birds had stopped singing and it felt as though the world was poised, waiting for the first clap of thunder.

'In fact,' Verity said prosaically, 'I do believe we are going to have a storm.'

Will stood up. The day was getting better by the minute. Now he had a wet night to look forward to. 'There is no point in persisting with this fire. I had better spend my time building a shelter for the night.'

'We have a cottage.' She stared at him as though he had said something incredibly foolish. 'Not much of one, to be sure, but there is no sign that it has let in water in the past.'

'Which means that you will be dry and warm. But, clearly, I cannot share it with you overnight.'

'Why not?'

Has the woman no modesty?

'It would be most improper.' Will knew he sounded like his grandfather, but that was what he intended.

'Could you please explain what we might do during the hours of darkness that would be more improper than what we might be doing now?' Verity enquired.

Immodest and *sarcastic.*

And, unless a miracle occurred, he was going to have to marry this stubborn woman. 'That is not the point. If we were rescued now there is some hope that the scandal might be contained and your father might accept that your reputation is untarnished. But even the most neglectful of fathers—and I refuse to believe a bishop could be such a man—would draw the line at a night spent together.'

Will got up and walked back towards the cottage, looking for some sheltered spot, some hollow tree or a patch of low-hanging foliage that might form the framework to make a rough shelter such as he had seen the Romany use.

'That is complete hypocrisy.' Verity spoke close behind him. 'You are not going to attempt to ravish me, are you?'

'Certainly not!' Will stopped so suddenly that she walked into him and grabbed at his shoulders to keep her balance. The pressure of curvaceous femininity imprinted itself on his back for a moment that was both far too long and achingly brief. He turned, steadying her with one hand under her elbow. 'Whatever can you mean, hypocrisy?'

'There are three possible scenarios,' Verity said. She held up one finger. 'Firstly, neither of us has any wish to, shall we say, misbehave. Our word as a lady and gentleman of good reputation should be adequate for any reasonable person in that case.' She held up another finger. 'Secondly, one of us wishes to, but the other doesn't. Again, as well-bred people with consciences, the wishes of the reluctant party will prevail. Or, thirdly, we both wish to…' She waved both hands as words apparently failed her.

The first time that has happened, Will thought grimly.

'Anyway, if we did, neither of us, surely, would intend merely a passing *affaire*, so we would have no reason to object to marriage as a consequence. The point I am attempting to make—'

'Is that we are not going to indulge in any untoward behaviour and a reasonable person would accept our word for it,' Will finished saying for her. One did not interrupt a lady but, as the alternative was to kiss her to stop her discussing all the things that were occupying his imagination, he was prepared to be blunt. 'Unfortunately, the truth never outweighs the assumptions of society, even in the eyes of the most reasonable persons. You will be compromised, your reputation will never recover and your chances of a respectable marriage will be severely curtailed.'

He did not wait for an answer, but he got one nevertheless, once Verity had caught up with him outside the cottage.

'Leaving aside the fact that I do not want to marry anyone, why is your word as a gentleman a cast-iron guarantee of the truth under any other circumstance but this?' she demanded. 'We both declare that you have not compromised me—but no one will accept your word, you say. Yet if they called you a liar over any other matter you would demand a duel, declare that your honour had been insulted.'

Will looked down into the indignant face raised to his. Verity was flushed, either with indignation or exercise, probably both, and her hair was coming down. If anyone had come across them in that moment they would leap to the conclusion that he had just tumbled her. He wished he had. He might as well be hanged for a sheep as a lamb… His brain felt like scrambled eggs as he sought for an explanation and for control.

'Chivalry insists that it is inconceivable that a gentleman would put a lady in such a position—I should have attempted the swim, even at the risk of drowning.' He wished he had, the cold water was very tempting just at that moment. 'And to attempt to evade marriage is an insult to the lady.'

'Even if she does not wish to marry you?'

'Opinion would be that my behaviour must have been outrageous indeed for you to refuse a duke,' he said drily. 'Which makes it even more imperative that I marry you.'

'Oh, poppycock.' Verity turned on her heel and went through the door with a swish of skirts in what was perilously close to a flounce.

Will felt a grim satisfaction. It was curiously refreshing to leave Verity Wingate without an uncomfortably intelligent riposte. He was wise enough to wipe the smirk off his lips before he ducked through the opening after her.

'What is the time?' she asked without looking up from the fire she was tending.

Will consulted his pocket watch. 'Just past six.' He glanced out of the door. 'And it is beginning to spot with rain. I must start work on a shelter.'

A low rumbling, felt through the feet rather than the ears, made both of them look out of the open door. 'Thunder,' Verity said. 'You are *not* going to spend the night in woods in a thunderstorm. It is downright dangerous.'

'I am a grown man—'

'And there is all the more of you to be struck by lightning. And you propose to leave me alone here, in a storm, while you gallantly catch your death of cold? What if the cottage is struck by lightning? Really, I had thought better of your intelligence, but it appears you are nothing more than another of these convention-bound men who cannot think for themselves. Or would you rather die than be thought less than perfect?'

Will took several long, deep breaths. Convention-bound? It was enough to make him want to behave like a savage. But under the insults was common sense. It was foolhardy to spend the night in the open in woodlands during an electrical storm and Basil would feel just as guilty if he expired of pneumonia, or a lightning strike, as by drowning.

But he did not want to find himself leg-shackled to this woman. In bed with her? Yes. Buried in her warm, soft body? Definitely. Married? Absolutely not. And he had a nasty niggle of conscience that was telling him he was doing all the right things just in case, by some miracle, they gave him a loophole to get out of this.

'I wonder whether I can arrange for Basil to be press-ganged,' he murmured and received a flash of white teeth as Verity grinned at him. She was too easy to like when his guard was down and he forgot for a second just who he was, what was expected of him. It was worrying that the Duke seemed to be melting away to reveal the fallible man beneath what he had believed, and hoped, to be an impenetrable skin.

Was everything he had learned dependent on being in the right setting and in the right clothes? How else could he account for the way he felt, standing here in his shirtsleeves, dirty and bedraggled, in front of a woman who saw only the man, not the Duke? He seemed to be like an actor who could not perform without his props and costumes and that was shameful. His grandfather had been a duke to his core.

'What is wrong?' Verity was staring at him as though he had spoken out loud. 'It will be all right, we must just be strong and not let anyone pressure us.'

She should not be reassuring him. Verity was the one who should need support and he should pull himself together and provide it. Support and leadership—and she should recognise the fact and stop this outrageous show of independence.

'Nothing is wrong. There is nothing for you to worry about. I will go and gather more wood before the rain starts.' And while he was at it, gather his wits to try to decide whether it was less honourable to refuse to marry a lady he had compromised, but who clearly did not wish to marry him, than to do what every instinct told him he must do and wed her, however much they both disliked the prospect.

Chapter Ten

So, I am not to worry my pretty little head about any-thing, am I? I suppose I could pretend that my head truly is empty of anything approaching independent thought or intelligence and then Will might be easier to deal with—provided he stops having suicidal but gallant and brave ideas about how to rescue us.

Verity shook out what bedding there was—two pil-lows and two blankets—and looked out of the door, hop-ing to find some dead bracken, but the plant did not seem to grow on the island. Will would just have to make do with the stone floor, she thought, her lips twitching at the realisation that she was not particularly sorry about that.

'What are you doing?' Will came in and dumped an armload of wood by the fire.

'Making you up a bed. You didn't think I intended to share that with you, surely? It is far too narrow. Neither of us would get a wink of sleep.'

That could have been better expressed, Verity.

Will clearly thought so, too, by the way one eyebrow lifted. She pushed away the speculation about how it would feel to be curled up against that long, hard body, what his kisses would lead to. Would he be a generous lover or a demanding, peremptory one, convinced he knew what she would want, would need? Probably dukes thought that passion in a woman was unseemly. She wondered if he had a mistress.

'I do not require a blanket.' He dealt with her blunder by simply ignoring it.

'As you say.' *And we will discuss that later.* 'Should we see what our kidnappers have packed for our supper?'

Dukes, it seemed, maintained formal dining manners even when marooned on desert islands, eating picnic dinners with cheap cutlery and earthenware plates. Will kept up a polite flow of innocuous conversation about the weather—the thunder was slowly getting closer—the latest Court gossip, the tricky issue of the replacement organist at the church, given that there were two likely candidates, both bitter rivals, and the design of mazes.

Verity preserved a ladylike propriety and responded with innocuous comments while cutting slices of veal and ham pie and fruit tart. 'Are you intending to plant your maze here rather than in the grounds of Oulton Castle?'

'This is where I intend my brothers and sisters to live and, as they requested the maze, it is better here. May I pass you the butter?'

'And the bread. Thank you. And you will reside with them here?'

'The Castle is not safe for children, not for…lively ones, that is. Can you imagine them with battlements and towers and moats and suits of armour and with sharp weapons displayed on every wall?'

'Vividly,' Verity said with feeling. 'They would love it.'

'The Dower House at the castle has a collection of elderly great-aunts and cousins already living there. The house here is far more suitable for my stepmother and, naturally, she should be close to the children.'

But not in the same house.

Although from what Verity had heard of Lady Bromhill she would be an exhausting presence at close quarters on a daily basis. She could hardly condemn the man for not wanting to live in his stepmother's pocket, even though she could only admire the lady's independence and defiance of convention.

'The last straw at Oulton was the discovery that Basil was planning to experiment with boiling oil on the battlements to see whether he could pour it over the walls on to imaginary besiegers. I decided that—'

The clap of thunder was almost deafening. Verity jumped and set her stool rocking as Will lunged to close the door just in time to prevent the sudden downpour of rain from penetrating the room. He stood with his back pressed to it, dramatically lit by the flames from the fire.

'What is amusing you, Miss Wingate? If this keeps up, we will be lucky if the roof holds.'

She got up and began to light candles from the fire. 'You look like a dramatic illustration from a Gothic novel. The hero bars the door to the raging storm while the heroine cowers before its ferocity—and your magnificence.'

For a moment she wondered if she had gone too far, then a sound that might, just possibly, have been a gasp of laughter escaped him and Will sat down abruptly on his stool. 'You will be the death of me, Verity.'

'I thought I had been working quite hard not to be the cause of your demise,' she said severely, pursing her lips to stop herself smiling, because he had sounded all too literal. 'If it were not for my common sense, you would be drowned or in the throes of developing pneumonia by now.'

For a moment she thought she was going to receive another lecture on the importance of correct behaviour, but Will picked up a candle and began to inspect the low ceiling, presumably checking for leaks. His ability to simply disregard awkwardness by changing the subject was impressive, if infuriating.

'It seems dry enough,' he said. 'I suggest we finish our meal, build up the fire and retire to our beds. No one will be searching for us in this weather.'

'That seems sensible,' Verity agreed and received a look that she had no trouble interpreting. His Grace had been issuing orders, not inviting a debate. She smiled sweetly and began to gather up the remains of their meal, closing away the uneaten food in case mice were about. 'Can mice swim?'

'I would not think so. Not this far. But they might travel on floating branches, I suppose. Are you scared of mice as well as of spiders?'

'It was not I who screamed,' she pointed out, banging the lid back on to the picnic hamper with rather too much emphasis. 'And, no, I am not frightened of mice. I do not want my food nibbled by them, though.'

Will was building up the fire, banking it in with large logs that would smoulder all night. 'Tell me, are the parents of your friends aware of what you get up to in your tower?'

'We do not *get up* to anything. We engage in rational, creative pursuits. Our parents are well aware of where we are.'

'That was not what I asked.' He pushed the last piece of wood into place and sat back on his heels. 'Do they know what you are doing?'

'No,' she admitted. 'Do you feel it to be your duty to tell them?'

'Certainly not. You appear to be doing nothing dangerous, illegal or immoral, however inappropriate it might be for ladies, and in that case it is none of my business. You seem to insist that I am a righteous killjoy, Miss Wingate. I am not a monk. I drink, I play cards, box and fence, hunt, ride and bet. I enjoy the theatre and the opera and the company of my friends.'

'But you do not approve of me, or of *my* friends, do you?'

'Approval has nothing to do with it. Your friends are none of my concern, I am glad to say.' All the *froideur* of the Duke was back in his voice, in the rigidity of his posture.

'Excellent, because neither am I your concern. You need not feel compelled to offer for me, I will most certainly refuse you if you do and we may return to mutually ignoring each other as mere neighbours.'

Is silence consent or is he simply too annoyed to speak?

Verity began to search around the sparse interior of the cottage for something she needed before she could settle for the night. A large square of wood which might once have been part of a shutter was all she could find.

'What are you doing?' Will rocked back on to his feet and stood up in one easy movement.

Horseman's thighs.

Verity blinked to regain her concentration. Miranda was wrong and indulging animal passions, even in thought and definitely in practice, led to nothing but useless distraction. *And heartbreak.* 'I am searching for an umbrella. In the absence of one, this will have to do.'

'Why on earth do you want to go outside?' He loomed, large, male, uncomprehending, in front of the door.

'Because it might surprise you to learn that ladies are not fairy creatures of such delicacy that we do not share the same bodily functions as the rest of humanity. And I have drunk several cups of tea.'

'I should have thought of that. Here.' Will took the board from her, stooped to pick up an old earthenware bowl that had been lying beside the door and handed it to her before he ducked out into the deluge, the board over his head.

Verity made use of the makeshift chamber pot and then concealed it behind a broken box in the far corner. Will was certainly resourceful. She eased her stay-laces while she had the privacy. 'Come in!' she called when there was a knock on the door. 'Thank you.'

Will dropped the board, shook himself like a large dog and raked the wet hair back from his face. 'It does not appear to be easing up.'

'Then I am going to bed.' She was *not* going to remind him to hang up his waistcoat close to the fire to dry off and certainly not going to suggest he remove his shirt. There were limits to trying to get an obstinate male to accept good sense.

She kicked off her shoes, climbed in under the blanket and pummelled the straw tick and lumpy pillow into something she might be able to sleep on. 'What are you doing?'

Will had retreated to the far corner of the hut, not that it was very far away, given the size of the place. He merely grunted.

'For goodness' sake, come and sleep in front of the fire. I am quite confident that proximity to a sleeping man will not imperil my virtue, although I may smother you with the pillow if you snore.'

'I do not snore.' He got up and moved pillow and blanket to the hearth. 'I was attempting to make you feel as comfortable as possible.'

His drive to protect and nurture was attractive, even while it was infuriating. 'I think we had established that I am not prone to maidenly shrinking, torrid imaginings.' *Oh, yes, I am.* 'Or dark suspicions about your character or motives.'

There was a sound that might have been agreement. Will punched the pillow, hauled the blanket up over his shoulders and turned on his side so that his back was to her. 'Goodnight.'

'Goodnight, Will.'

Sleep well on your hard, damp bed...

Will had not expected to sleep. The floor was cold stone, his clothes clung moistly, the pillow was lumpy and far too close for comfort was a sleeping woman in a snug bed. His imagination decided to run riot.

At least torrid fantasies were keeping him warm, he thought grimly as the storm passed slowly overhead— the thunder crashed, the rain lashed down, the cold draughts crept in from every crack and his bodily aches tormented him.

He drifted off to sleep eventually, the fantasies becoming dreams in which Verity Wingate's flow of infuriating common sense was finally reduced to moans of passion and cries of desire as she writhed beneath him.

'Will!'

'Mmm?'

Again? I will do my utmost...

'Do wake up. It is light, the rain has stopped. We should be packed and ready to leave when the rescue party arrives.'

He opened his eyes to find Verity looking infuriatingly awake, tidy and lively. Her face glowed, her hair was neatly braided and coiled around her head, her garments were, it was true, somewhat creased, but otherwise she had every appearance of having passed a restful night.

'You are awake,' he observed, redundantly.

'So will you be when you have been and washed in the lake. It is most invigorating. Did you sleep well?'

No, was the truthful answer. 'Yes, surprisingly so,' Will lied. 'Perhaps if you'd not mind going outside for one moment while I get up?'

And get my overenthusiastic body under control.

'Of course. I will put the kettle on while you are bathing.'

'Excellent.'

Icy water. Perfect.

Will stripped off on the beach and waded in, gritting his teeth against the cold, then ducked right under. He came up streaming and was standing waist-deep, shaking the water out of his eyes, when he heard the hail.

'Your Grace! Thank God!'

It was Truscott, his Steward, standing in the stern of

a large rowing boat. Judging by the width of the shoulders of the man propelling it, he had brought one of the gamekeepers with him to do the hard work.

Will waved, splashed back to shore, rubbed himself more or less dry on his shirt and was in his breeches and pulling on his boots when the boat grounded on the shingle.

'Well done, Truscott. And—Pratt, is it not? Strongly rowed. Thank you both. When did my brother admit what he had done with us?'

'After breakfast, Your Grace.' Truscott stood on the beach, a stolid figure in buckskins and good plain broadcloth, his jaw set pugnaciously. 'And I have to say, begging your pardon, Your Grace, for referring to his young lordship in such a way, but the little devil is as pleased as punch with himself over the matter.'

'I will wager he is,' Will said grimly. 'And the Bishop? I am most concerned that he has suffered a great deal of anxiety.'

'He is not happy, as you might imagine, Your Grace. But he said firmly—through Mr Hoskins, you understand—that if Miss Wingate was with you, then she would be safe and he would say a few extra prayers for you both.' His direct gaze shifted a little. 'Having another clerical gentleman with him was a great support, I am sure.' Truscott seemed positively uneasy now, Will thought, mystified. 'And is Miss Wingate safe?'

'She is perfectly well. There is a weatherproof, if very simple, cottage on the island, so she was sheltered and warm last night. If you will wait here, I will go and see if she is ready to leave. I had left her making tea.' Hopefully that gave the impression that last night Verity was in the cottage and he was not. And tea was so very innocuous and reassuring, he told himself as he made his way up to the clearing, dragging on the damp shirt as he went.

'Miss Wingate! Rescue has arrived.'

He saw that Verity had already folded the bedding and packed away everything except the makings of their breakfast. 'Oh, good. I don't suppose they want a cup of tea. No? I'll just put all this away in the basket then, if you will douse the fire. Should we take the hampers and bedding back with us?'

'No. Basil can row out and collect it,' Will said. That would be the start of the penance he was intending to inflict.

He gave Verity—*Miss Wingate*, he reminded himself— his arm down to the waterside. 'Mr Truscott, my Steward. Pratt, one of the gamekeepers and a fine rower.'

Verity greeted the men with no self-consciousness whatsoever and was helped into the boat, settled in the stern and smiled cheerfully at Will as he took the space next to her, leaving Truscott to wedge himself into the prow. 'What a lovely morning, Mr Truscott,' she remarked, setting her deplorable hat straight on her head. 'The storm seems to have left the air as clear as crystal.' She chatted on as they went, mentioning the charcoal burners, hoping that none of the staff had got wet searching for them and thanking Truscott for putting her mind at rest about her father.

'The clerical gentlemen did a lot of praying, miss. That must have been a comfort to him, to have that support.'

'Yes, Mr Hoskins is a great assistance and help to Papa.' But she frowned at Will as though puzzled. It seemed a strange way of putting it, now he came to think of it. *Gentlemen?* What other clerical support would the Bishop have? He sincerely hoped the Vicar had not called to add yet another person who knew about this. Perhaps it was Truscott's clumsy way of referring to the Almighty.

The shore was getting closer and he realised they had not had the opportunity for a calm, honest discussion about the future. He was honour-bound to offer for Miss Wingate, however little he wanted to marry her. She, it seemed, did not want to marry him. But their wishes were irrelevant if her reputation was at stake. The gossip and speculation that would swirl about a lady who had spent the night with a duke and then refused to marry him boggled the imagination. No one would believe the reason was as simple as straightforward dislike. The vulgar would be counting the months, the *ton* would cut her.

'Truscott, when we land I want you to go straight up to the house to inform the Bishop that we have arrived safely. Miss Wingate and I will follow more slowly. She must take great care not to exert herself after such an exhausting time.'

Verity whispered, 'What are you talking about?'

'We need to discuss exactly what we are to say and do,' he murmured.

'I suppose so.' She leaned sideways a little to get a clear view of the approaching boathouse round Pratt's wide back. 'Your Grace, there appears to be a welcoming party. I cannot see Papa or Mr Hoskins and who on earth is that? I cannot make it out against the dazzle on the water.'

Will squinted against the early morning sun. 'That, I very much fear, is the Bishop.'

'It cannot be. I would recognise my own father,' she protested.

'Not the retired Bishop of Elmham,' Will said, with a sinking sense of doom. 'The current incumbent.' And all his staff by the look of the small flock of black coats and fluttering white clerical bands surrounding the tall figure.

'So it is! But *we* were not expecting him—were you?'

'No. I met him at my grandfather's funeral and told him how delighted I would be if he called—not expecting him to do so without warning.'

A cold hand slipped into his. Will glanced down. Verity's face, completely exposed under the flat brim of her hat, was set and pale. For the first time he saw vulnerability there. He squeezed her hand and released it. 'We must not do anything to suggest the slightest familiarity or impropriety,' he warned, low-voiced.

'No, of course not.' She snatched away her hand and composed her features into a look of vapid blandness. 'I will take my cue from you, Your Grace. I am sure your perfect grasp of every possible social situation will carry us through this with aplomb.'

There was a tremor of anger in her meek voice.

Now what have I done to anger her? he thought.

Chapter Eleven

Foolish of me to expect some support. Even more foolish to betray my nerves, Verity thought savagely as she gripped her chilly fingers together until the nails dug into her palms. But what was Bishop Alderton doing here?

Her father had been a gentle, scholarly bishop, unwilling to judge harshly, always seeking to offer forgiveness, compromise and accord. His successor was far more energetic in the discharge of his office. Bishop Alderton's sermons were more emphatic, his tolerance of sins and errors far less elastic. The Church Militant was his ideal and he saw it as his duty to carry the light of the Church of England into every sin-infested corner of his diocese, seeking to correct even the smallest error.

The boat bumped against the landing stage before she could summon any constructive thought. Will was on his feet and on to land the moment the lines had been secured.

'Miss Wingate, may I assist you?'

'Thank you, Your Grace.'

Smile, gather up your creased skirts, step out as though alighting from a carriage at a ball.

'Why, my lord.'

Look surprised, curtsy.

'What an unexpected pleasure. Mr Carne, Mr Wellings, Mr Trafford.'

One chaplain and two curates bowed.

'My dear Miss Wingate.' Bishop Alderton advanced on her, his hands held out. 'We have prayed throughout the night for your safe return and our petitions have been answered. What a dreadful ordeal you have undergone!'

'Thank you, my lord. But it was hardly an ordeal. It was the result of a childish prank and, as I was ably protected and looked after by the Duke, I was quite safe and comfortable throughout. Shall we go up to the house? I am sure Papa will want to be reassured as soon as possible.'

'This way, my lord.' Will gestured towards the path and offered his arm to Verity. 'Have you *all* been here throughout the night? I trust my staff made you comfortable.'

'We called upon my brother Wingate yesterday afternoon. My carriage was forced to make a detour as the bridge at Little Felling was damaged by a timber wagon.' The Bishop was clearly able to discourse fluently while walking uphill. Behind him the curates were breathing heavily. 'When I was told he was here I decided to call upon you both. Only imagine my horror to discover that you and Miss Wingate had mysteriously vanished! Naturally, I felt it our duty to stay and offer what comfort and succour we could. In fact, one might think that the accident at the bridge was divine intervention to send us to Wingate's side.'

'So kind,' Verity murmured.

'Everyone in your household, under the leadership of

my dear brother Wingate, were quite remarkably calm, I must say. When one considers the hideous possibilities—assault, kidnap, the perils of the wilderness—one can only wonder at your dear father's strength of mind, my dear.'

'It is remarkable, my lord,' Verity agreed. She kept only the tips of her fingers on Will's arm and walked with a good foot of clear space between them.

'But, of course, the fact that you were with His Grace must have calmed his mind considerably.'

There was the faintest of sniggers from Mr Trafford, one of the curates. Will turned to look at him. 'Did you speak, sir?' he enquired, his voice icy.

'No, Your Grace. I merely cleared my throat. Ah, see, Miss Wingate, there is your papa.'

He had come out on to the terrace, supported by Mr Hoskins. The butler and two footmen waited a few steps back.

Verity let go of Will's arm and ran across the lawn, up the terrace steps and into his embrace. 'Papa, I am quite well, nothing at all untoward occurred and there is no need to worry about anything except keeping this foolish trick of the children's a secret.'

He hugged her to him, then held her at arm's length so she could read his lips. 'Welcome home, dear.' Then he released her and began to make signs.

'I must discuss some matters with the Duke,' Mr Hoskins interpreted. 'There is nothing for you to worry about.'

'I am not worried, not now I know you are well. And I will not marry him, Papa,' she warned, realising too late that a large male form was right behind her. 'There is absolutely no need for it,' she added with a defiant look upwards as Will came to her side.

'I cannot apologise enough for my wretched siblings and the anxiety they have caused, my lord,' Will said. 'They will be severely chastised. Naturally you will want to discuss this in private once you have assured yourself that Miss Wingate is quite well. Shall we go inside? My housekeeper can escort Miss Wingate to a chamber to refresh herself and rest and I will await your convenience in my study just as soon as I have tidied myself and said farewell to my other guests.'

Verity did not miss the compression of his lips as Will glanced towards the clerical group making their stately way up the lawn.

'I doubt they will be leaving yet,' Mr Hoskins said tartly, for once speaking on his own behalf. Her father, after a sigh, had merely looked resigned. 'They are ensconced in comfort in your best bedchambers, from what I can gather, and seem determined to interf—'

Her father cleared his throat.

'Assist,' the Chaplain finished.

'I see. Miss Wingate, here is Mrs Blagden, who will make you comfortable. Bishop, Peplow will show you and Mr Hoskins to my study.'

Verity heard no more before the tall woman in grey, whom she recalled from her arrival the previous morning, swept her towards the house.

Make me comfortable? That would be a fine trick if she can achieve it. Will looks set to martyr us both in the name of respectability, Papa is distressed, however well he hides it, the Bishop and his little flock of sycophants seem determined to interfere and even dear Mr Hoskins is reduced to snapping.

'I sent the staff to heat the water for your bath as soon as we heard you had been found, Miss Wingate.

And Miss Preston, the children's governess, appears to be similar to you in figure, so she has lent a gown and linen, which we hope will be acceptable as a temporary measure. What refreshments would you care for? Breakfast, perhaps?'

Verity pulled herself together. After a bath, clean clothes and a cup of chocolate she would be ready to face the world and she did not want to look like a ruined woman in need of rescue. 'Thank you, Mrs Blagden. That sounds delightful. A cup of chocolate and some bread and butter would be most welcome.'

And then I can do battle for my future.

The razor edge slid over the pulse of Will's jugular, up over the angle of his chin. Notley lifted the blade away, handed Will a hot towel, then leaned in to inspect the result. The *'tsk'* he produced seemed to signify approval of the shave and decided disapproval of everything else his employer had presented him with.

'The hat, Your Grace, has responded to steaming and a soft brush. The coat, I regret to say, is beyond saving. I understand that the correct term for what it was immersed in is *bilge water.*'

Will stood up and reached for one of the neckcloths laid out for him. 'You mean that my brother actually brought them to you for attention?'

'They were found here in your dressing room last night, Your Grace, laid out neatly on the chest. It added considerably to the confusion of the situation, if I may say so.'

'You may, Notley.' Presumably it also made it look as though they had been kidnapped. 'You may also establish the cost of the ruined coat for me so that it can be deducted from Lord Basil's allowance.' He frowned at his neckcloth, decided that an Oriental was a suitably subdued style for dealing with outraged bishops, and stuck in an onyx pin. A chaste choice—if that was not an unfortunate pun.

Notley eased the coat over his shoulders, handed him a handkerchief and nodded his approval. Apparently the ducal appearance passed muster.

Now what would his grandfather have done in this situation? Will paused at the turn of the stair. *Wrong question.* Firstly, his grandfather would never have got himself into such a fix and, secondly, this was Will's problem to solve. His dilemma.

The right thing, according to every tenet of correct behaviour, was to insist on marrying Miss Wingate. But she did not want to marry him and, given how eligible he was, that argued a real aversion, not simply an attack of pique. And he could not blame her. He had made no secret of his disapproval, of his dislike of her behaviour, and, by extension, his antipathy to her. He might desire her, but that was not the basis for a successful marriage.

As for himself, he owed it to his position to make a suitable and successful match. He owed it to a young lady who had been compromised, thanks to the disgraceful behaviour of his siblings, to respect her wishes. He examined his conscience. Yes, that was definitely the right decision.

'The Bishop and his Chaplain are in your study, Your Grace. I have sent in refreshments.'

'Thank you, Peplow. See that we are not disturbed.'

'My lord.' Will closed the door and took the seat behind the desk with a nod to Mr Hoskins. 'I have not yet spoken to my brothers and sisters, but I understand they concocted this outrageous incident because they have taken a liking to Miss Wingate and believed that she would make a sister-in-law who would indulge their wayward behaviour. They will, of course, present their full apologies to Miss Wingate and yourself before being suitably punished.'

The Bishop's hands moved. 'They are young,' the Chaplain translated. 'They did not mean harm.'

'Basil is old enough to know better. Lads younger than himself are serving as midshipmen or supporting their families with honest labour. That aside, I hope I do not need to assure you, sir, that Miss Wingate is unharmed in every way. In every way whatsoever.'

Mr Hoskins was blushing as he said, 'My lord fully accepts that assurance, Your Grace. No other possibility occurred to him.'

'You will expect me to offer marriage, sir,' Will said, ignoring the sudden frown on the face of the man opposite. 'And I have already done so, making the case for its necessity as strongly as I know how. But Miss Wingate is adamant that she will not marry me. She insists that, as the events are not known outside this household and ourselves, there is no scandal and, therefore, no need.'

'But—' Mr Hoskins began before the Bishop's hands could move.

'I fully understand your feelings, gentlemen. However, my lord, your daughter seems to have taken me in dislike—a feeling that predates our stranding, I should add—and maintains that our union would result only in unhappiness. I cannot square it with my conscience to attempt to force a young lady to the altar.'

'But others know,' Mr Hoskins interjected, again without waiting for the Bishop.

'The current Bishop and his attendant clergy, yes,' Will agreed. 'But they would hardly damage a lady's rep—'

The door opened and Peplow came through it as though propelled by a determined push from behind. 'Your Grace, I could not prevail upon His Lordship to wait...'

'Your butler appears to fail to grasp the nature of this crisis, Your Grace.' Bishop Alderton swept in, almost flattening the agitated butler against the door. The three junior clergymen followed him.

'Bishop Wingate and I were having a private conversation,' Will said, injecting all his grandfather's *froideur* into his voice. He did not rise and he did not offer seats, but all four sat down regardless.

The Bishop smiled, a sad and patronising expression that implied that he, the older man, knew best. Will felt his hackles rise and hung on to his temper, somehow. Losing it in front of Bishop Wingate was not going to convince the man that Will was rational and meant only the best by his daughter.

'But of course you do not comprehend the seriousness of the situation, Your Grace.' Mr Alderton pressed on, despite the reception he was receiving. 'A private settlement of the matter is impossible, given how many people know that you have spent the night with Miss Wingate.'

'Who knows?'

'Why, naturally, we had to widen the search with dusk falling. Your staff seemed reluctant to take the initiative, so I dispatched messages to the village to send out search parties.'

'You did *what*?' Will found himself on his feet, hands planted on the desk, glaring at the affronted Bishop.

'How could you, my lord?' The door was still open,

he realised, and Verity was standing there looking like an enraged, drab sparrow in a brown gown and with her hair braided into a tight coronet. 'If I was with the Duke I was, by definition, quite safe, even if…if temporarily lost,' she said. He had seen her lose her temper, but never her poise. Even after that kiss by the pond her voice had been steady.

'Miss Wingate, you are not yourself or you would not speak in that wild manner,' the Bishop said, in the tone of a man used to dealing with female hysteria.

He probably encountered it a great deal, Will thought. Any rational woman patronised by this pompous prelate would resort to the vapours.

'Calm yourself, dear lady. You must see that, for all we knew, you had been set upon by ruffians, the Duke killed or injured, yourself carried off.'

'Poppycock,' Verity retorted. '*This* man?' She made a sweeping hand gesture towards Will. 'Overcome by ruffians on his own land?'

Well, that was unexpected, Will thought, dragged out of his haze of anger by the compliments.

'No ruffian would dare to do anything so *inappropriate* as to threaten the Duke of Aylsham on his own grounds,' she swept on, her voice steadying now that her indignation was undammed.

Ah, not such a compliment then. At least he had not misjudged Verity. She did, after all, have the tongue of a scorpion. The Bishop was apparently unable to recognise sarcasm when he heard it. He merely shook his head sorrowfully. Will wondered what the penalties were for punching a bishop. Excommunication? It seemed increasingly tempting.

'The question is, not whether rousing the neighbourhood was necessary, for we have gone beyond that now,' Mr Hoskins interjected as Bishop Wingate's hands moved urgently. 'The question is, how may we mitigate the damage that has been done?'

'By marriage! There is no other possible course of action if we are to save the good name of this dear young lady.'

There was a chorus of, 'Indeed,' and solemn head-nodding from the Bishop's staff.

'I stand ready to marry the couple and I will, naturally, provide a licence. We must consider whether, in view of the circumstances, an application should be made to the Archbishop for a Special Licence. What is your opinion, Brother Wingate? The disappearance of His Grace and Miss Wingate may be truthfully presented as the result of an ill-judged boating trip just before the storm. There is no need to mention the foolish jest the young people carried out that led to this.' He sat back, looking satisfied with his solution.

And he is delighted at the prospect of presiding over the marriage of a duke, Will realised.

'You mean to create the false impression that there was already an understanding between myself and Miss Wingate? That our marriage had nothing to do with the situation that was forced upon us? To lie, in effect?' Will asked. To his surprise he found it possible to keep the anger he felt at this meddling prelate out of his voice. But Verity glanced across at him and the anxious frown that was creasing her brow faded just a little.

She trusts me to get us out of this.

'Naturally, one cannot tell an actual untruth about the matter, but if that assumption is made then there is no need to correct it and it will be far less embarrassing for Miss Wingate.'

'Miss Wingate will, I believe, find it far more embarrassing to be forced into a marriage she does not want with a man she does not care for,' Will said. 'There is no prior understanding: far from it. We have agreed that we would not suit. My family's actions have already caused Miss Wingate considerable anxiety about the effect of her disappearance on her father's health and she has had to endure the discomfort of a night spent in a primitive cottage during a thunderstorm. I fail to see why she must be made to suffer more. My staff will be discreet. The villagers are already familiar enough with the behaviour of my siblings to believe this was all a hoax on their part and they will be loyal enough, I have no doubt, to keep it to themselves.'

'You are *refusing* to marry Miss Wingate, Your Grace?' Bishop Alderton demanded. 'I am astounded.'

'I am refusing to force the hand of a lady. I am entirely at Miss Wingate's disposal.' It was curiously liberating to be doing what virtually everyone in the room clearly considered was the wrong thing. Twenty-four hours before, *he* would have thought it the wrong thing. It was totally inappropriate. *Good.*

'Papa, please?' Verity went and knelt in front of her father and Mr Hoskins lowered his voice as the three of them huddled together.

Then Verity stood up and kissed her father's cheek and Mr Hoskins announced, 'My lord is quite content that Miss Wingate's reputation is secure and that there is no necessity to consider this matter any further.'

'Excellent,' Will said. 'In that case we have no need to trouble you longer, Bishop, gentlemen. Your desire to help is much appreciated, as is your willingness to have your travel plans disrupted overnight. However, there is nothing to keep you here now.' He should extend an invitation to luncheon, he knew. He should continue to offer hospitality to this pillar of the Establishment, but he was damned if he would. 'And your absolute discretion is something I know I may rely upon.'

The Bishop bristled at him and Will smiled back, finding he was enjoying himself. He outranked a bishop, he did not like the man and he wanted him off his property. 'If His Grace the Archbishop were ever to hear of this I feel certain he would feel you have come to the correct decision.' He did not even trouble to hide the fact that this was a threat. Bishop Alderton bristled, one of the curates stared, open-mouthed. Bishop Wingate lifted one hand to his mouth and did not quite succeed in hiding his smile.

'Your Grace.' Peplow, who appeared to have recovered his poise and his dignity, opened the door and shot Will the warning look that normally preceded the revelation of yet another hideous exploit by the children. 'Lady Bromhill.'

His stepmother swept in, her sky blue skirts swishing, her waving mass of hair caught loosely into a topknot secured with a large Oriental clasp. There was a portrait miniature of her late husband pinned to her bosom. Bishop Alderton visibly winced at the sight of her.

'William, dear boy! You are both safe—I can call off the search parties, thank goodness. I should have known that darling Althea was taking too serious a view of matters when she told me that Basil had stranded you on the island in the middle of the storm. Naturally, I turned to Mr Blessington and the members of the sailing club and they put their smallest boats on carts to get here and have been scouring the lake for the past hour.'

'Mr Blessington, my lady?' Mr Hoskins asked. He was on his feet, along with every other gentleman in the room with the exception of Bishop Wingate, but his tone was hardly respectful. 'Married to Mrs Blessington, the worst gossip in the county?'

'Well, she is a trifle eager to spread news about and she is not always the most discreet of women, but that is because she has the most wonderful imagination. You should read the little pieces she writes for the newspapers...'

'I have,' the Chaplain said darkly.

Will sat down in his chair behind the desk. If he stayed on his feet he was going to lose all control over his temper and the result would be spectacular. Dukes did not lose control. Dukes stayed calm, Dukes did not tell their stepmothers that they were interfering, thoughtless baggages. Dukes solved the problem. And there was only one solution to this: marriage to a woman who disliked him before and was going to hate him now.

Chapter Twelve

'No.'

But no one was listening. Verity slipped out of the door while everyone was still talking at once. All, that is, except her father and Mr Hoskins, who must be waiting for the noise to subside, and the Duke, who sat behind his desk, stony-faced, hands palm down on the leather surface.

She wondered how long his patience would hold and was answered as she reached the door to the terrace.

'Silence!' The resulting quiet almost shuddered in the air. 'If you please,' Will added, with a savage politeness that made her wince.

Verity opened the door and went out. There was a stone bench under an arbour on the edge of the terrace, a safe distance from the house. She did not wish to hear any more, certainly did not want to listen to Will sounding every bit as formidable as his grandfather must have done.

I am not going to marry that man. I will not live with him or share his bed. I have done nothing wrong and yet I am the one they want to punish, all for going for a row on a lake.

She sat down and tried to think positive thoughts, because panicking was not going to help. There was the advantage that Will probably regarded her as the woman he least wished to wed, the eligible young lady who would nevertheless make the most disastrous duchess. On the other hand, his sense of duty and honour probably overrode his personal preferences.

Oh, drat. Verity found her handkerchief and blew her nose inelegantly.

'Why are you crying, Miss Wingate?'

Over the top of her handkerchief she could see a blurry row of heads. Verity blinked, blew her nose again and stuffed her handkerchief inelegantly up her sleeve. The wretched brats had arranged themselves in order of height, presumably because they thought it made them seem more winsome.

They need a small dog at the end for maximum impact. Basil has missed a trick there, she thought cynically.

'I am not crying. I am cross,' she retorted.

'With us?' Lord Benjamin, the youngest, asked. His face was screwed up with worry, his trouser legs were stained with grass and one pocket was inside out.

'*Of course* with you. Whatever were you thinking to do such a thing?'

'We thought you would marry Will.'

'And what if we do not want to marry each other? What if you had caused my father to suffer another stroke with the worry?'

'We asked Mr Hoskins if the Bishop was all right last night and he said he was *"bearing up with fortitude."* If he hadn't said he was all right, we'd have told, honestly.'

'But why don't you want to marry Will?' Althea asked. '*Everyone* wants to marry a duke. We saw them in the churchyard, like hounds on the scent.'

'Not everyone. I do not. I want to choose whom I will wed. Althea, you are almost old enough to marry. How would you like it if your brother announced that he was marrying you off to someone you do not like, just because they are a duke?'

'He wouldn't,' she said with absolute conviction. 'He could not anyway, because Will is the only unmarried duke under fifty at the moment. And you must like him. He's rich, there's the title and *everyone* likes Will. He has ever so many friends and they say he is a great gun.'

'They do,' Basil assured her. 'Even we like him— and he can be jolly stuffy and starched up, you know. I mean, he makes us chaps learn Latin and Greek and we all have to do this etiquette stuff and the girls have to do embroidery. And when we do something wrong he looks pained, which is pretty grim.'

'Idiot,' his twin muttered, jabbing him in the ribs. 'We don't want to put her off.'

'I had already noticed the stuffiness and the starch. It is understandable, because your brother works hard at being the perfect duke.' Whatever else she felt, she could not abuse Will to his brothers and sisters. 'I would not be a perfect duchess.'

'We like you,' Alicia, usually silent, piped up.

'Thank you for the sentiment. But as you all think it is acceptable to strand people on islands and ruin their lives I cannot say I place much value on your opinions,' she said severely. They really did expect to get away with murder, simply by adopting those expressions of wide-eyed innocence.

There was a collective sigh and shuffling of feet. 'So, *are* you going to marry Will, Miss Wingate?' Basil asked.

'Until Miss Wingate makes a decision, that is none of your business, Basil.' Verity did not turn as Will spoke behind her. 'And I suggest that all of you remove yourself from my sight. I still have to decide on what punishment is appropriate for you.'

The children fled, vanishing with almost supernatural speed. Will walked out on to the terrace and sat on the balustrade beside the arbour.

'You have got rid of them all?' Verity said wearily, too depressed to worry about her choice of words. Her nose was pink; she could see the tip of it if she squinted. Her eyes were probably red as well. She never could weep prettily, not that she made a habit of crying.

'My stepmother removed herself with some drama when I suggested that her actions, although well meant, were exceedingly badly thought out. The episcopal party departed with fulsome assurances of discretion after I became rather more forthright than I ever expected to be with a bishop. Once they had gone your father assured me that he entirely accepts that nothing untoward took place, but considers that matters have gone too far to cover up. I agreed with him and he has retired to his room. Mr Hoskins assures me he is coping well and his pulse is quite calm. We discussed sending for his doctor, but decided the fuss might only agitate him further. But if you think it best—'

'Thank goodness. I was going in to check, but I had best not disturb him now. And you are quite right about the doctor.'

So what does the perfect Duke do in these circum-

*stances? Get down on one knee? Issue a lordly an-
nouncement that we must marry? Ask me what I want?
No, that is too unlikely—not now Mrs Blessington is
spreading the news from here to John o' Groats.*

'I have a common licence,' Will said abruptly. 'The
Bishop apparently travels with stock and he and that
prune-faced cleric—Carne, is it?—saw it signed and
sealed before they left.'

'I see. So you cannot, after all, wave some ducal
wand—or sceptre, I suppose—and solve this?'

Of course he could not, she knew that even before
Will shook his head. She had best make up her mind
to it, then—she was going to be a duchess. Was she the
only woman in England who could think that sentence
and feel ill?

'Solve it according to your wishes, Verity? I am afraid
not. Not now the cat is well and truly out of the bag.'
Will met her gaze straight on. 'As I have been pointing
out from the beginning, you have no choice. We must
marry.'

Yes. The word trembled on the tip of her tongue. He
was very convincing, very used to being obeyed and,
despite everything, her treacherous body still wanted
him. Give in. Give up dreams of living her own life,
following her own interests. Stop deluding herself that
she was offering her friends anything other than a very
temporary sanctuary at the top of her tower. *Yes.*

'No,' Verity said clearly, despite her insides knotting
themselves even tighter. 'I have a choice and I say *no.*
You, Your Grace, can lay down the law and tell me what
the sensible, conventional thing to do is. You may say
I told you so when they all whisper behind my back, or
cut me to my face. But I am entirely the wrong woman

to be your duchess and you are the wrong man to be my husband.'

'You will live to regret this,' said Will—*the Duke*. It was not a threat, simply a prediction. He looked bleak. Well, that was two of them.

'I regret that I ever met you,' Verity said. 'I regret that I ever got into that boat with you. Doing the wrong thing now is not going to make any of that better.'

'You are angry with me,' he said with infuriating patience. He stepped forward and took her hand. For some reason she let him. Verity looked down, wondering, as if she was observing herself for a long way away, why she did not pull free. 'I understand that. But you cannot let that ruin the rest of your life.'

'I am angry, yes,' Verity admitted. 'Angry with those children who ought to have known better, but whose upbringing has not taught them to think of others before their own desires. Angry with your stepmother for failing to consider what damage gossip could do us. Angry with the Bishop for his patronising manner and his interference.'

Will was still holding her hand, she realised, shaken at how easily she had accepted his touch. She pulled free and walked away from him for a few steps.

You cannot run away, that will solve nothing.

She stopped and rested both hands on the balustrade, felt the roughness of stone and lichen under her palms. The gardens were developing towards their early summer glory, fresh tender green shoots everywhere, blossom on the trees, buds near to bursting on every plant.

A lovely season for a wedding.

'And angry with me?' Will asked again, close behind her.

'I do not know,' Verity said. She continued to look out over the borders to where the lawn sloped away, down to the lake. Was she? It was not his fault he was a duke, not his fault that he could not predict every wild scheme his brothers and sisters might come up with. He certainly had not invented the rules by which women were condemned to live their lives, even if he supported them.

'I wish I understood what it is about me that repels you so.'

She felt him move away, rather than heard him. His absence felt as though a void had opened up behind her when before there had been something solid, something that would support her.

'It would be idiotic of me to pretend that I do not know that I am considered an excellent match on every worldly level.' His voice came from her left now, perhaps six feet away. She did not turn. 'Humour matters to you, I know, and we have shared a joke or two, you know I am not humourless. We have shared kisses, too, and, forgive me, but you have not seemed to find them unpleasant. If it is something that I can change, tell me, and, if I can, I will.'

'You do not repel me.' It must have been hard for a man with his pride to even ask that question. 'The loss of my freedom to a man who would insist on my conformity does. I would feel a prisoner as much as if you had loaded me with chains. You do not understand why I do not want to marry you, but I understand very clearly why you do not want me as your duchess. You are wise to feel that way. It would be a disaster for both of us.'

'You want love, is that it?' Will sounded as though she was asking for something strange and slightly eccentric. 'People of our station in life do not marry for love.'

'Most often not,' Verity agreed. 'But, yes. I can live without marrying and most probably I will. But if I do, I want to marry a man who wants me. Me. Not a conformable, suitable wife. Not to fulfil an obligation, not because his honour demands it. I want a man who would make my pulse stammer and my head spin whether he was a duke or a drayman. I want a man who can look into my eyes and understand me without words being spoken. I want a man for whom the world would be well lost if he could live his life with me.'

Her hand hurt. She looked down and found she had struck the balustrade with her clenched fist as she finally found words for her dreams and the courage to speak them.

'You have hurt yourself.' Will raised her hand and opened out the fingers. There was a smear of blood from a graze and he bent and touched it with his lips. 'You have hurt your hand and you are dreaming impossible dreams. You will wake up and find that years have slipped by without this man you hope for. Years barren of kisses, of children.'

'No. I—'

Will raised his head from her hand and took her mouth. He did not hold her, except that their fingers were intertwined still, he did not do more than move his lips lightly over hers, although she could feel the tension running through him like the vibration in a violin string that has been plucked.

There is this, a voice in her head said as she fought not to simply give in to the magic he was weaving. It was an illusion, this feeling of rightness in Will's arms. But how long would it last, this flaring desire between them?

And it is only because he is a skilled lover, the cynical, hurt voice in her head told her. *It is not you, not that you are in some way special to him. He simply knows how to kiss and he knows that he must marry you.*

'Verity, listen to me.' He set her back from him and she could see no heat, no battle with his desires, in those intense blue eyes. 'Think of how your father will feel if your reputation is ruined—and it may be. What the effect could be on his health.'

Will was perfectly correct. Papa would be distressed, but she was certain that if she told him how she felt then he would support her. His health would not suffer for it—she would be there to make sure it did not.

The effects of that kiss were beginning to wear off and she could feel the resentment boiling up at the tactics of the man in front of her.

First kiss the silly female until she is dizzy, then present the arguments logically—because she is only a poor, feeble creature unused to logic so it will overwhelm her and she cannot answer back.

'When the scandal breaks your friends would be forbidden your company and be deprived of their safe haven as a result,' Will continued inexorably. 'I do not know why it is so important for them to gather together under your wing, but I can see that it matters a great deal to you.'

The impact of that must have shown on her face because his eyes narrowed, became those of a hunter who has seen his prey weakening after a long chase.

'I could only offer them room in the tower for a short while, I knew that and so do they. We hoped that with you in the district their parents would stop scheming to marry them off in the hope that one of them might catch your eye. If I married you, that shelter has gone in any case. You cannot tell me that you would tolerate your wife encouraging the neighbours' daughters to do things of which their parents disapprove.'

'Of course not. But why are you so convinced that marriage is something akin to a sacrifice? Anyone would think you were all like Andromeda, chained to a rock for a sea monster to devour, or early Christian maidens being forced to choose between marriage to a pagan Roman or the lions in the arena.' His exasperation was beginning to show in his voice now, in the taut lines of his shoulders, the thinning of his mouth.

'For some women it *is* like being thrown to the lions,' Verity said. 'For all of us, it is a gamble. Even beginning from a basis of mutual desire for the union, with a man I could love, it is a risk.'

'Life is a risk,' Will retorted.

'I choose the risks I want to run. And you?' she asked. 'Are you not going to add the reasons it is important to you to insist on this marriage?'

He shook his head, the proud, stubborn man. He was not going to use that weapon, or perhaps he gave her enough credit to understand his motives.

If she was not very careful Will could be branded as a man who had compromised an innocent lady and failed to do the right thing. His honour might be compromised.

I can rebel. I can be strong. Or will I merely be selfishly stubborn? Papa, my friends, Will...

Verity turned abruptly, walked to the steps down to the lawn and the long flower border that glowed with colour against the stone of the terrace. She felt the impulse to run again, but that would be cowardly and, besides, she could not outrun either Will or this situation.

Strong or stubborn? Determined or selfish?

She reached out and picked a half-open rose from the border.

I will, I won't, I will...

Petals showered down as she plucked at them.

I won't— An earwig crawled out of the centre of what was left of the bloom. Verity threw it from her with a violent twist of her wrist. Will was behind her, a few careful feet, leaving her space, leaving her room to think, waiting for her to realise that, twist or turn as she might, she was not going to escape.

It was strangely difficult to find enough air in her lungs to speak. She turned and faced him, brushed the petals from her skirts to give herself time. When the words came, they were surprisingly steady. 'I will not marry you, Your Grace. Not tomorrow. Not this week or next. Never.'

Chapter Thirteen

'That is a very unwise decision,' Will said. No, *the Duke* said. The man standing in front of her was not the one she had teased in the cottage in the thunderstorm, not the one whose eyes crinkled suddenly with unexpected amusement, not the one who kissed her in a woodland glade.

Unwise? Is that all you can say? Can you find no emotion? But this was who he was, the man she was refusing.

'If I marry you I will gain a great title, wealth, the preservation of my good name. And in the process I will lose myself,' she said steadily, somehow matching his calm tone.

Will closed the space between them, took her hand. 'Miss Wingate, I beg you to think again, before it is too late.'

Extraordinary, the way in which he makes it sound as though he actually wants *to marry me. A duke's manners are perfect under all circumstances, I suppose.*

How had he planned to force her into the mould of an ideal duchess? Verity shivered. This was a man who was taken from his father and schooled into near perfection by an old man whose only ambition, it seemed, was to recreate himself in his grandson when his own son failed to meet his expectations.

'You should be glad,' she said bluntly. He knew that only too well, he must do, but she wanted to shake him out of his formality, needed some sign of real feeling. Some emotion. Some thwarted passion? That was just her own pride showing, she told herself. Will had kissed her three times. Now that he was making a final attempt to persuade her to be his wife he showed no sign of wanting to do so again.

'I am sure you would make an admirable duchess, in your own style, once you had time to adjust.' There was the faintest hint of a crease between his brows now. 'There is no need to worry that you would somehow fail in any way, Verity. I will help you.'

'I am not worried. I am telling you that I will not be pressed into a mould and baked into rigidity like a gingerbread figure for you, your title or for respectability.'

'You would make a very crisp and spicy biscuit,' he remarked, with the first trace of humour Verity had seen since she had walked, uninvited, into the study where all those men had been dictating her future. He tipped his head to one side, studying her face as though he could read her true feelings if only he looked hard enough. 'Are you very upset by this?'

Upset *is such a nice, moderate word. It is so easy to settle an upset, to soothe the ruffled feathers, mop up the spilt milk.*

'I do not know how I feel about you,' Verity confessed. She could like the man behind the Duke, perhaps. But the armour that he had grown around himself was more impenetrable than a crab's shell. 'I know I do not want to marry you, that it would be a disaster for both of us. But I do not want to see you hurt by this.'

'Hurt.' He said the word as though he was trying it for taste, a bite of a strange and exotic fruit. 'I see. Then let us part as friends. I kissed you before, when I should not have done. And again just now when I suspect you were wary of my motives. But I would like to kiss you again now.' He was very close now. 'Do you wish me to?'

'Will it make this any better?' There was the somewhat humiliating awareness that, yes, it would make things better. That she wanted him in that way, if in no other. Could he tell—or would he think her simply immodest and eager for kisses, anyone's kisses? If she had married him, then, when he took her to bed, he would surely have known that she was not the inexperienced virgin he had believed her to be. Better that this was all that was between them.

'I would hope so. Kissing is generally considered to be a pleasurable activity.' His hands were on her shoulders, turning her. 'Of course, if you do not wish it, you have only to say. We could shake hands on our agreement to disagree. I would not want to presume that you would be anything but shy about such matters.'

Is he laughing at me?

'You know perfectly well that I have not been shy about it before,' Verity said crossly, although she allowed Will to turn her fully to face him.

He drew her closer in, so close that she had to tip up her face to look into his, so close that she could feel the press of his thighs through her skirts.

Verity gave a soft murmur, leaning against him just a little, answering the unspoken message of his hands.

Will's eyes narrowed and she wondered if she had

shocked him by responding like this, even now when she had so roundly rejected him. Did dukes and duchesses have passionate marriages? Perhaps one had to make an appointment with his secretary. Or one could write a note.

Her Grace the Duchess of Aylsham proposes a meeting for spontaneous mutual excitement at six of the afternoon in the Orangery...

Verity closed her eyes, because if the infuriating, baffling man did not stop calculating the precisely correct kiss to give the woman who had spurned him and actually get on with it, then she was going to kiss him herself. And then he really would be shocked.

He wished he understood Verity. Her eyes were closed, her cheeks had turned a very charming pink and she was shaking slightly. Nerves, of course. True, on those previous occasions when they had kissed she had responded without inhibition, but then it had been more in the nature of flirtation. This was, somehow, serious. This kiss was a like the signature on the bottom of a treaty. He was accepting her decision and he was undertaking—even if it had not been spoken of—to protect her reputation when the gossip mill got hold of the story of their night on the island and their scandalous failure to marry.

Mentally he was already bracing himself for the unpleasantness—and it was going to be unpleasant, he knew that. He must shoulder all the blame for her loss of reputation and that was only just. If he had controlled his siblings better, had given them a stronger example—

or had not fallen for their plot in the first place—then none of this would have happened.

But now there is this kiss. He desired Verity Wingate. He had known that from the first, had admitted it to himself. And now he had her, not as he fantasised, warm and willing in his arms, but reluctantly, because she had faced a stark choice—marry him or deal with the ruinous consequences—and had chosen the wrong path. He could have made her want him if he had been careful and then she might have agreed. But it was too late now and it was not the action of a gentleman to try to seduce her into a agreement.

Will bent his head and took the soft lips that were raised to him. He slid his hands from her shoulders to her waist and she lifted hers to clasp around his neck. Despite everything, he smiled and felt the answering movement, the warmth as her lips parted, and eased the tip of his tongue between them.

He knew her taste now, was beginning to understand the soft sounds she made as he kissed her and to have confidence that he could read the way her body responded to him, curving into his, her fingers flexing in his hair, caressing the back of his neck. She was becoming aroused and so was he. The bedchamber was surely the one place where they would have found harmony.

When he moved his hands to cup her buttocks Verity lifted, pressed closer against him and then stilled abruptly. His erection was pressed against her and, however innocent she was, he would wager that she was not ignorant. She knew what that was and she had been startled to have encountered an erection quite so blatantly. Will almost released his hold on her, but she rose on tiptoe, pressed herself tighter against him and then slid, very slowly, back down. Only then did she pull back and he released her, managing, somehow, not to groan aloud.

Verity's eyes were wide, the pupils dilated as she regarded him silently, lips slightly parted. Her nipples had peaked, all too visible through the fabric of her gown, and the sight made him growl, low in his throat. Will turned it into a cough. Growling with lust would be enough to send even the most aroused virgin fleeing down the terrace. Surely she had no idea what she had just done, the effect it had on him.

He cleared his throat.

Pull yourself together, man. She will think you are suffering from consumption if you carry on coughing.

She moved away from him, the colour high on her cheekbones. 'I will miss our kisses,' she confessed. 'That is doubtless a very shocking thing to say and only goes to show how right we are to part. I am sure duchesses do not talk about such things. I have a suspicion that duchesses do not have any human weaknesses or even bodily functions. Perhaps ducal babies are not born at all, but arrive, pink and perfect, in a satin-lined crib by some special arrangement with the College of Heralds.'

She was joking, of course, to calm her nerves. Will had the nightmare vision of his duchess discussing the delivery of babies with Garter King of Arms at some dinner party. That particular Herald was in his fifties, but as ossified in his manner and thinking as a man forty years his senior. He would never suspect that she might be teasing him. The vision was succeeded by one of a procession of Heralds with a bassinet borne aloft before them to be deposited at his feet with a flourish of trumpets.

'I believe duchesses are perfectly normal in all such

particulars,' he said repressively to cover the gasp of laughter that his ridiculous fantasy provoked. What was the matter with him? The College of Heralds was a venerable and scholarly pillar of the Establishment, not a cause for slightly *risqué* levity. Verity Wingate was infecting him with her disgraceful sense of humour, but no one made him laugh the way she did. Kisses, laughter, intelligence, those brown eyes…

'Verity. We could try. Sleep on it—'

He could see the answer in her eyes even before she spoke. 'No.' Heat flared, anger. 'I trusted you not to try to seduce me into changing my mind, Will. I was a fool to think that we could be friends…kissing friends.' She shook her head, clearly impatient with herself as much as him. He saw her straighten her shoulders, the effort it took to steady her voice and sound calm and business-like. 'I will do everything in my power to see that you are not blamed for this, Your Grace, and you have my blessing for whatever you need to say, but I do not want to see you again, or to hear from you.'

The curtsy she gave him would have not disgraced a Court presentation. As Verity Wingate turned and walked away Will thought she had never looked more like a duchess. He looked down at his hands and the smear of blood on one of them. She had pounded her fist so hard on the wall as she spoke of her hopes and her fears that she had drawn blood. He should have known then that nothing was going to change her mind about him.

'Papa, I cannot marry him. He has done nothing wrong, I do not hate him—I only know that I cannot be his wife. I could not take my marriage vows and mean them.'

Her father frowned, then began to mouth words, moving his hands slowly at the same time. As soon as they had reached the Old Palace, Verity had asked the Chaplain to leave them alone. She liked and trusted Mr Hoskins, but this was too personal. She made herself concentrate hard on understanding.

'It would be a great match, better than I could have ever hoped or dreamed for you.'

'I know, but it would be wrong for both of us.'

'The scandal…' He threw up his hands, abandoning any attempt to speak with them.

'Yes. I will just have to face it down. I did nothing wrong. The Duke did nothing wrong. I refuse to behave as though there is something to feel guilty about.'

Her father sighed, then patted her hand. 'I want you to be happy. I love you, Verity.'

'I know and I love you, too, and I am so sorry to distress you over this. Papa, I cannot see him again—but will you be seen with the Duke on good terms? Show everyone that you do not hold him responsible for this?' There was nothing better to calm the rumours, surely, than for the neighbourhood to see their much-respected Bishop treating the Duke as a friend.

Her father nodded slowly. 'Yes,' he mouthed. 'I accept that he did nothing wrong and has done all he can to make amends. He can hardly drag you to the altar and I am certainly not going to try to do so.'

They sat for a while, hand in hand, watching the shadows lengthen over the courtyard garden. Then her father stirred. 'Your aunt Caroline.'

'Yes?'

'Go to her. London. Fashionable. Knows everyone.'

'You want me to go to *London*? But the scandal—whatever you and the Duke can do here to make people realise there is nothing to the rumours, people will write to friends and relatives in town. It is too good a story not to share.'

The Bishop nodded vigorously. 'Exactly. London is where you must quash the rumours. Caroline can do it.'

And, Verity realised, she probably could. Her father's sister had married Lord Fairlie, a mere baron perhaps, but an exceptionally well-connected and very wealthy baron who had the *entrée* everywhere. His wife held a select monthly *salon* where one might find princesses mingling with artists, bankers with scientists and industrialists with Members of Parliament. Caroline was invited everywhere, including the Queen's House and St James's Palace.

'She will tell the Queen,' her father said, watching her face. 'Tell the Patronesses at Almack's. She'll know what to do to make it right.'

Verity felt slightly dizzy at the thought of the Queen contemplating her adventures, but she rather thought that she would be easier to win round than the formidable Patronesses. If she was barred from Almack's she might as well give up and return home directly, because everyone who was anyone would soon hear about it.

And Aunt Caroline, who had been known as a *dasher* in her youth, was not only influential, but blissfully unshockable, and Verity very badly needed an unshockable female confidante.

'That is a wonderful idea, Papa, but I cannot run away and leave you.'

'Why not? Not ill.' He returned her anxious look with

a bland, lopsided smile. 'Not running away. Tactical retreat and counter-attack. I'll worry less if you are with Caroline.'

'Very well, Papa. I will write to her straight away.'

Tactical retreat and counter-attack? I only hope I have the nerve for it.

Of course we understand.

Melissa's bold black handwriting scrawled across the page. Verity turned it towards the carriage window to catch the last of the evening light as the wheels rumbled across the cobblestones.

The letter, in answer to her own to her four friends, had arrived as she was leaving the day before and she had read it and re-read it in an attempt to convince herself that they did understand and that she had not blighted their lives.

Lucy cannot believe that you can turn down such a very handsome man, she says, but she defends your right to refuse him most stoutly. And Mama is all of a twitter because of the kind letter that your papa sent us, saying how he would miss you and hoping that we would continue to meet in your room to 'continue our good work' so he can benefit from our 'young company' in your absence. Is that not good of him?

The rumours and gossip are beginning to spread, but no one knows what to make of it because Mr Hoskins is telling everyone how he is going to help the Duke with his library. They are all going to be agog to see what happens on Sun-

day at church! No one is going to be listening to the sermon. They are all expecting your papa to be flourishing a shotgun at the Duke!

Do have a lovely time in London and try not to worry. It will all be a storm in a teacup, you wait and see...

Chapter Fourteen

'My dear! How lovely to see you.' Aunt Caroline swooped down the steps of the house in Bruton Street, arms outstretched, and enveloped Verity in a warm hug. 'I couldn't be happier that you have come to me and you are not to worry about a thing—we will make everything all right.'

'I am sorry to have given you no notice, but it all seemed so difficult and then Papa had the idea of asking you to help and I have to confess, it was such a relief,' she explained as Aunt Caroline ushered her up the steps and past the footmen waiting to collect the luggage.

'The notice is of no account, my dear. Besides, I would have cancelled luncheon with the Queen for you if I had to. As it is, I will have your company and all the fun of launching you properly into society. With my poor brother's illness you never did have the Season you deserved.' She steered Verity into the drawing room. 'Tea, Wethering.' As the butler left she added, 'Dinner in two hours and we dine at home. Now, you are in the Rose room as usual. I see you have brought a maid. Tell me quickly what our priorities must be while we drink

our tea. Then you can go up and change and rest a little
while I form a plan of campaign.'

'Yes, of course, thank you,' Verity agreed vaguely.
She was tired suddenly, and her mind drifted back almost five years into the past.

This room... It had been painted a soft green with silver-
grey details then and the picture over the fireplace had
been a pastoral scene. *There was a chaise in that corner and a screen that half-hid it and I was kissed there
for the very first time.*

'Do you mind if we tell Gresham and Roderick everything, dear?'

'Hmm?' Verity pulled herself back to the present
and tried to look as though she had been about to fall
asleep. 'I am sorry, Aunt. It was rather a tiring journey,
I'm afraid.'

'Stuff and nonsense. You are no more tired than I
am and I do not wonder at it. With that luxurious travelling carriage, and a leisurely overnight stop at a most
excellent inn, a young lady should be fit to dance all
night. These country ways will not suit in London, you
know. We have a great deal of work to do and much of
it will take place in the evenings. Now, did you hear
what I asked?'

'About telling Uncle Gresham and Cousin Roderick. Of course they will have to know, I quite see that.'

'Excellent. My son might pretend to be a rattlepate,
but he's bright enough and he's fond of you. He'll want to
do his bit with the younger set. Gresham will pull a long
face, but he will do his utmost.' Her smile was wicked.
'He knows the husbands of the Patronesses.'

Ah. That probably means he knows things about the

husbands of the Patronesses which might persuade them to influence their wives in my favour...

Lord Fairlie nodded at the butler. 'That will be all, Wethering. We will serve ourselves.' He waited until the butler and footmen had left and the door had closed behind them, then turned to Verity sitting at his right hand. 'So, you do not wish to marry the Duke of Aylsham? An unusual position for a young lady to adopt, one would think. What's the matter with him? Thought the man was a positive pattern card of perfection. His grandfather certainly thought so. He's been on the town, of course, moves with a fast, fashionable set and he's called out a man, but he's never attracted a whisper of scandal.' He took a sip of wine, nodded approvingly at the glass, then raised one elegant brow at Verity.

'The Duke has many good points. He is clearly a conscientious landlord and employer. He is doing his best against great odds with his brood of half-brothers and -sisters, he is intelligent, good-looking and even, occasionally, shows a sense of humour.'

'But?' Her cousin grinned at her across the table. 'He keeps a string of mistresses? He is a drunkard? He holds Black Masses at the full moon? He uses a revolting cologne?'

Verity shook her head at him reprovingly. 'None of those things. But he does not approve of me and makes no bones about it. He thinks ladies should not use their brains, he disapproves of my antiquarian interests, he hates it when I argue with him and he is absolutely determined to be perfect in all things. He would expect his wife to be perfect—his idea of perfection, that is.' She broke off to catch her breath and made herself slow down. 'I cannot face the idea of devoting myself to being a perfect duchess for a perfect duke and raising a brood of perfect children. I swear, when that man dies they will find *Always Appropriate* engraved on his heart.'

Her aunt gave a little choke of laughter. 'You want an *imperfect* man?'

'A human being would be my choice.'

Aunt Caroline passed Verity the dish of peas. 'Tell your uncle and Roderick what happened about the lake and the island.'

'I know about it already,' her cousin said with an apologetic grimace. 'At least, I know the version that is going the rounds in the clubs.'

'Oh, no. Already?'

'Apparently Aylsham has a love nest on this island, complete with a vast bed and satin sheets. You are variously supposed to have defended your virtue by hitting him with a oar and bravely rowing off into the lake where you drifted about all night until rescued by Bishop Alderton and a flotilla of curates, or you climbed a tree and sat up there all night, fending Aylsham off with pine cones until help in the form of the local boating club arrived. Or—' He broke off and took a gulp of wine.

'Or what?' Verity demanded. 'Tell me, Roderick, please. I would much rather know the worst.'

'Or…er… You were not rescued, you spent the night there, um, amicably, and either he refused to marry you or you refused to marry him. The rumours get a trifle vague at that point.'

Her uncle made a sound suspiciously like a growl, Aunt Caroline gave a hiss of displeasure and Verity told herself firmly that this was no more than she had expected.

'That settles it,' Aunt Caroline said. 'We must ensure that the Queen knows the truth, ensure that you will be received at Court and then I will deal with the Patronesses.'

'Thank you,' Verity said. 'I feel encouraged when you speak with such certainty.' She smiled at them all, cut into her roast guinea fowl and hoped that she was going to be able to swallow it, because inside everything was just one large knot of nerves.

'You are not still pining for that curate of yours, are you?' Aunt Caroline perched on the end of Verity's bed dressed in a wrapper of such frivolity that Verity feared for her uncle's blood pressure.

The thought allowed her to reply lightly, 'If you mean Thomas Harrington, he is the Vicar of a very fashionable parish in Westminster now, I believe.'

'I know. That young man was always going to do well for himself. He is too handsome by far and knows it, and he has an eye for the main chance, cleric or not. He schemes to become the youngest bishop, mark my words.'

'No doubt.' Of course Thomas did and an essential step up the clerical ladder was to find a suitable wife. He had almost achieved it, four and a half years ago, when he had wooed the Bishop of Elmham's naïve daughter. How fortunate for him that his plans had not come to fruition or he would have found himself leg-shackled to the daughter of a retired bishop in ill health with none of the influence over appointments and places that Thomas wanted so badly.

At the time, when she had found the strength to stand up to him and face down his blackmail, Thomas had been furious. Now he must give thanks daily for a lucky escape. At first, with the stinging hurt so fresh, she had wondered why he had been so ruthless, but, reading between the lines, she had concluded that a father who had granted his every wish, bolstering his sense of self-importance, in combination with early success at whatever he set his hand to, had left him convinced that he was entitled to whatever he wanted.

'And *are* you pining for him?' Aunt Caroline was nothing if not persistent.

'No.'

Giving thanks daily that I found him out in time, yes. Pining, never.

'He was not the man I thought he was and, thankfully, I discovered it before I married him.'

But not before I was foolish enough to sleep with him, unfortunately.

Verity wondered whether she could ask her aunt how likely it was that a man could detect whether or not a woman was a virgin. One day she might find this mythical creature, a man who would love and accept her for what she was, and she would have to decide what to tell him. But that was too remote a possibility to worry about, she told herself.

But the unpleasant thought occurred that Thomas might try to capitalise on the situation now. If he believed that Will might still offer for her, would he try his blackmail again? But surely not—no vicar, however well connected he was these days, would risk alienating a duke. Will could ruin him. *Would* ruin him.

'Good, I am glad to hear it.' Her aunt, who knew nothing of what had happened with Thomas, was still picking over his character. 'He appears to be courting

Lady Florence Wakefield and, frankly, given that she is not at all intelligent and very plain, poor girl, I cannot believe he is doing so for any but the most mercenary reasons. One of her uncles is an archdeacon and a cousin is attached to the Chapel Royal.' She took a sip from the cup of chocolate she held. 'And her dowry is impressive, I understand.'

'That should appeal to Thomas. If she is biddable, he will not care about how silly she is, or how plain.'

'How did you realise his true character, dear? You never said at the time and I did not like to ask.'

Verity shrugged. 'I realised that he was interested in marrying my father's daughter, not in me. When I became suspicious it opened my eyes to just how rehearsed and mechanical his protestations of affection were.' That was true as far as it went and it seemed to satisfy her aunt.

'Such a contrast to the Duke, who *is* an honourable man. But if marrying him would make you miserable, there is nothing more to be said. I know what a happy marriage can be.'

'That all seems very satisfactory, Your Grace.' George Fitcham, Will's senior secretary, put down a report from the Steward at Oulton Castle and consulted one of the lengthy lists in front of him. 'Now, if we could move on to the figures from the Home Farm...'

Four days after Verity had left for London there was an impressive pile of neglected paperwork and, for the first time since he had inherited the title, Will had needed to force himself to send for the patient secretary and tackle it.

Will let him talk. If there was something he needed

to do, or make a decision about, Fitcham would tell him. Like the neglect of the work for several days, this was untypical of him and, while his conscience nagged him about it, something else told him that it was not important, that he had other things to worry about.

Why has she gone to London? Why is Bishop Wingate being so vague about it? I cannot protect her there. The rumours will be vicious...

The clock struck three, there was a tap at the study door, then it opened to admit his siblings, all clean—scrubbed and polished, by the look of it—dressed neatly and looking decidedly miserable. He had deliberately delayed announcing his decision on their punishment to give them time to think over just what they had done.

He waited while they lined up in front of the desk. Fitcham stood up to leave, but Will waved him back to his seat. They could have the added discomfort of an audience.

'You behaved with unconscionable discourtesy to a guest, to a lady. You lied to me. You put both of us in a situation that was uncomfortable, embarrassing and compromising. Miss Wingate has decided that she cannot bring herself to marry me, which is exceedingly honourable of her, even if her decision probably has a great deal to do with her unwillingness to find herself in a family containing you. And, Basil, if I see one more smirk on your face, you will spend the summer without access to your pony, your fishing rod, your cricket bat and any books other than your school texts.'

Basil's expression of dismay at least showed a gratifying belief in his brother's willingness to carry out the threats.

'Althea, Araminta and Basil will all receive no allowance for the next four weeks. Alicia, Bertrand and Benjamin will receive half their usual allowance. And if I find you lending any of it to your older siblings, then you will lose that as well. Your schoolroom hours have been doubled for a month. In addition, the boys will spend an hour every day assisting in the vegetable garden and the girls in the kitchen. If I do not see signs of improved behaviour and genuine regret by the end of that period, then it will be extended. Is that clear?'

They stared back at him. If he had not been so angry with them then it would have been laughable, the way they all had the same open-mouthed expression.

'You are just saying that, aren't you, Will?' Althea quavered. 'You don't really mean it, do you? Not for four whole *weeks*?'

'You seriously distressed a lady who had done nothing to deserve it,' Will said. 'You have compromised my position, made this family, as well as hers, a butt for vulgar gossip and speculation. If you do not know what is due to your name, then I do.'

He had not meant to extend the punishment beyond the first couple of weeks, just give them all a good scare, but now he realised he did mean it. He kept seeing the despair in Verity's eyes, the anger and her refusal to compromise, even in the face of the ruin of her reputation. It seemed that the children had ruined the life of the only woman in the country who hated the idea of wedding a duke and he found that upset him more than the besmirching of his own name, the intrusion of tasteless gossip into his privacy and the danger that the tale might have an impact on his own future marriage plans.

'And I still see no sign that you have any idea of the seriousness of what you have done or that you are sorry about anything but the fact that you are being punished,' he added. 'You may go.'

He picked up the topmost list in front of him and stared at it unseeing while six pairs of feet shuffled out of the door and Fitcham cleared his throat and blotted a note.

Why had she gone? Because she thought he would continue to press her to marry him? Because she misguidedly thought that in London she would attract less attention? That might have worked if the man who had compromised her had not been a duke. Damn it, he missed her. Missed her spiky independence, missed seeing her pace up and down while she argued a problem out with herself. Missed her kisses. If Verity came back they could be...friends?

That was ridiculous. Unmarried ladies did not become friends with single men. Men and women were different. They might be passionately involved, sexually attracted or form contented marriages based on duty and family life. But friends? Was that what his father had found with his stepmother? Could that have been what held their improbable marriage together? He had assumed his father had been ensnared by a strong woman with undeniable physical appeal, but he was beginning to have an uneasy feeling that there had been more to it than that. That he had misjudged them both. His father had adopted extreme ideas without question, but that did not undermine the basis of what must have been a happy marriage.

Did he owe it to Claudia to try to be more understanding? Should he re-evaluate his picture of her children's upbringing? Had they actually been happy and secure in an environment that had made him unhappy and confused? There was no one he could talk to about this, no one except the woman he had driven away.

'The first post, Your Grace.'

He had not heard Peplow come in. 'Thank you.' Will gestured to the desk and picked up the pile of letters before Fitcham could. He sifted through as though dealing cards. Most landed in front of the secretary, but five, clearly personal letters, stayed with him.

Would Verity have written to him if she needed his help? He doubted it, but he had only seen her handwriting once and would not recognise it.

He opened the letters. One from his godmother in Kent, one from a tenant at Oulton, disputing a decision over leases. He tossed that to Fitcham. One from Jack Hendry, asking if he was interested in buying a promising young hunter of his… A friend suggesting the making up of a shooting party later in the year… And a scrawled sheet from Chris Bancroft, Marquess of Dalesford, old friend, sportsman and notorious rake.

What the devil's going on, Will? The word in the clubs is that you seduced a bishop's daughter on some island, or that she kidnapped you and had her wicked way with you—you lucky devil—or half-a-dozen other even more improbable stories, all culminating in—nothing. Certainly not orange blossom and wedding bells.

And the jest is, the damsel in question has arrived in London—bold as you please, the hussy. The old biddies are sharpening their hatpins and the bucks are laying wagers on who will have her first.

Yours truly wants to know the real story, you dark horse!

'I am going to London.' Will pushed back his chair, the letter crushed in his hand. 'First thing tomorrow morning.' He tugged at the bell-pull. 'Peplow, send my valet to pack, tell the stables to ready my travelling chaise.'

Whatever she wanted, whatever she was to him, he was damned if he was going to leave Verity Wingate to the wolves.

Chapter Fifteen

'That went very well, I thought,' Aunt Caroline said as the carriage pulled away from the Queen's House and began to skirt Green Park on its way back to the Bruton Street townhouse.

'Her Majesty was very gracious.' Verity still felt as unreal as when they had been ushered through the long corridors to the Queen's private sitting room. She had made her curtsy at St James's Palace, of course, swamped in hoops and ostrich feathers and in the company of dozens of other young ladies. But that had been in her first Season, cut short by her father's illness, and she had been too miserable over Thomas Harrington's treachery to be overawed.

Coming face-to-face with the Consort over the tea-cups was quite another matter. 'I had not known what to expect, but she is very intelligent, isn't she?'

It was one thing to read that the Queen was a keen amateur botanist, much involved with the gardens at Kew, and quite another to actually hold a discussion with her about Mr Banks's discoveries and the voyages of Captain James Cook. 'And she is interested in the education of women. I had not known that.'

'That is one reason why I thought she would be sympathetic to you when she realised that you are an intelligent, well-informed young lady and not some fast, wilful girl who has thrown over a duke on a petulant whim. And she has kept her daughters close to her—when I wrote I implied that it was mainly duty to your father that has made you turn away from marriage. She sympathises with that and approves.'

'Will she help me? Does she ever interfere in such a way?' Verity found she was fidgeting with her skirts and clasped her hands in her lap before she twisted indelible creases into the silk.

'You will be invited to a Drawing Room which will signal approval and the fact that we have been received will soon be widely known—and in the Court Circular. That in itself will not be the final word for the Patronesses. Which reminds me, that must be my next concern, to secure you vouchers.'

'How may I help?' The prospect of actually being able to do something to help herself was invigorating.

'What we need is a party, one where we may be sure of influential ladies being present. I will see what invitations I have when we are home.'

They went straight to the drawing room. 'Now, let me see.' Aunt Caroline took a stack of invitations from her little writing desk and fanned them out. 'Not a ball, you do not have a suitable gown yet. Not a masquerade, too much of a romp which is not the impression we want to give. Ah, the very thing—Lady Notting's musical evening. Good food, pleasant music, but not too much of it and the very best of company, for she only invites interesting people.'

'That sounds perfect,' Verity said. 'A chance to dress up, meet new people—I cannot wait.'

It might be an ordeal if the visit to the Queen had failed to work its magic and she was cut, but she had to be optimistic and it was a long time since she had enjoyed social events in London, not since her father's illness. Not that she resented their quiet life or the company of her close friends, but even so, country society did tend to dinner parties and small dances where the same people met over and over again.

'And tomorrow we will embark upon some serious shopping. You have a few pretty gowns—the one you are wearing is charming—and the half-dress gown you showed me will be very suitable for this evening, but you need a complete new wardrobe, my dear, and all the accessories. No one will think you have anything to hide if you dress in the first stare of fashion. Modestly hiding yourself among the wallflowers will not serve our purpose at all.'

'But my allowance—'

'Your papa sent me a draft on his bank, Verity. He wants this belated Season to succeed as much as we do.'

'Aylsham! What a pleasure, I had no idea you were in town.'

Will bowed over Lady Notting's hand and then kissed her cheek. 'Aunt Julia. I am hoping that if you had known, you would have invited me and, as it is, I am presuming on the forgiveness of my favourite godmother and honorary aunt not to have me thrown out as a gatecrasher. My coming to London was in the nature of a last-minute decision or I would have called.'

'You have, if I recall rightly, six godmothers and you

call all of them *aunt*, so do not think I will fall for your outrageous flattery, young man.' Lady Notting dealt him a painful rap over the knuckles with her fan, but she was smiling, as he had known she would. 'I am glad to see you out and about. Dreadful business with your father and then to lose your grandfather so soon afterwards— enough to cast anyone into the dismals. But you can enjoy yourself this evening, even if you are as much a stickler for form as the old Duke. It is all very decorous and respectable. No dancing, no light music—perfectly acceptable for a man in mourning.'

'Ma'am, you are very gracious, but I am holding up the line. Perhaps we may talk later.'

Will walked through into the first of the reception rooms, his progress impeded by having to stop and speak to virtually everyone he passed. When he had merely been Lord Calthorpe he would have exchanged bows with most of the older ladies and gentlemen; now his rank overcame the disparity in ages and everyone wanted to chat. And, he realised, they wanted favours, however subtle they were about it. Some had sons and wanted his advice on where they might find useful occupation—he filed a few names away as possible librarians for Stane Hall. One had a younger brother in holy orders, looking for a living. Any number of hopeful mamas were too subtle to thrust their daughters at him directly but murmured of this or that select gathering at which they hoped they might see him.

He reached the second room, congratulating himself on not having committed to anything or anybody, and took a glass of champagne from a proffered tray with the sense of having earned it. No wonder his grandfather had developed that air of cool distance. It had not been an exaggerated sense of his own position, but sheer self-defence.

He had arrived in the early morning after travelling through the night with his valet and the essential baggage. His groom, following with his riding horses and the travelling coach to carry the rest of the luggage, had arrived in the early evening.

His townhouse in Grosvenor Square had, naturally, been ready to receive him even though there had been no time to send ahead. It did no harm to keep the staff on their toes in case they began to be complacent and think his standards were lower than his grandfather's had been, he had thought as he handed Gustav, the butler, his hat and gloves.

The footman he had sent out to discover what engagements the ladies from Bruton Street had accepted returned within the hour with the information that had brought him here to Lady Notting's musicale. Convenient that she was his godmother, but he sincerely doubted that he would have been unwelcome wherever he had turned up.

Will looked around as he sipped his champagne. The company in this room was rather livelier, perhaps because the number of footmen with trays of drinks seemed more numerous here or perhaps because the strains of the string quartet were penetrating more loudly which made everyone speak up.

After a while his ears became used to the noise and he began to pick up conversations. There was no sign of Verity or her aunt, which was perhaps why he could hear nothing about her, he thought. Then Lady Marchmont turned from a cluster of matrons in the opposite corner, saw him, raised both eyeglass and eyebrows and favoured him with a stiff inclination of her head. Will responded with a bow. Colour high, she turned back and all the ladies in her group glanced in his direction. Will bowed again and strolled away.

Interesting. They had heard the gossip, clearly. But where was Miss Wingate? Or had they run her off already with their sharp tongues?

Over in the far corner a group of younger men were clustered around one of the window seats. The object of their attention must be sitting down, because Will could not see what was amusing them so, but then he heard a peal of laughter and knew. Verity was in the middle of whatever was going on. He strolled up to the group and listened, relieved that she sounded happy and that she had found some friends, at least. Although he would have preferred respectable matrons to young bucks.

'Miss Wingate, you are teasing us! I cannot believe that such a catalogue of disasters could have happened,' one gentleman protested.

'But I assure you, every word is true,' Verity said earnestly. 'The church doors were open because of the heat, the choristers were right in the middle of rehearsing a new anthem and a swarm of bees from Widow Fawcett's hives encountered Farmer Partington's herd of pigs being moved from one field to another. The pigs stampeded, followed by the bees, right into the church, upset the buckets of flowers that the ladies were arranging for Sunday and Mr Partington's prize sow was last seen careering across the village green with a garland of roses around her neck. The choir boys were stung, the organist fainted and Mrs Norris refused to do the flowers again.'

'I had no idea life in the country was so entertaining.' That was Viscount Sedgley, one of the worst flirts in London in Will's opinion.

'It often is,' Verity said. 'I expect it is because everyone mixes so much more.'

'But you are not so enamoured of it that you are going to rush back to your village and abandon us, are you, Miss Wingate?' The Viscount's voice had become a deep purr.

'I do not know, Lord Sedgley.' Verity gave him a look of wide-eyed innocence. 'It all depends on how diverting I find London.'

Sedgley was clearly expected to read that as an invitation to help her find entertainment. Will, admiring the technique but far from amused, stepped forward. That was dangerous and it would be fatal for her prospects if she was thought to be fast.

As he thought it, one wag said, with a laugh, 'How about boating on the lake, Miss Wingate?'

Will touched the man in front of him on the shoulder and moved into the gap as Verity said, 'Now that is very unkind, sir. As if I have not already been given a dislike of lakes after those impossible children stranded me on an island!' Her laugh was a little shaky now.

'You and Ayl—' the man began, then saw Will and melted back into the crowd with a muttered, 'Oh, hell.'

'Miss Wingate. How charming to meet a neighbour so far from home. I trust I find you well?'

She was pale, although smiling bravely. When she saw him all the remaining colour fled. He put out one hand, ready to catch her if she fainted, but Verity stood and dipped a curtsy, an exaggerated acknowledgement of his rank in the circumstances. 'Your Grace. I am very well, thank you. And, as you say, it's so delightful to meet and *so* unexpected.' Will was conscious of the rest of the group, their attention riveted on the interaction and on Verity's pale cheeks.

'I had unexpected urgent business in town. I hope I may call on you—you are staying with Lady Fairlie, I imagine?'

'Yes, I am,' she said, her colour coming back and her eyes sending him a message he had no trouble interpreting. She resented him coming to town, thought he was making things even more difficult for her. If she was falling into company with the likes of Sedgley she was making complications all of her own. 'I am sure my aunt will be delighted to receive you.'

But you will not.

'I am the bearer of the abject apologies of my scapegrace siblings, who are smarting under their various punishments,' he said lightly. If they spoke of what had happened on the lake openly it could only help to establish her innocence.

'I do hope they are not punished too severely, Your Grace. It was youthful high spirits, not malice, as I observed to Her Majesty only this afternoon.'

That was a well-placed bombshell, Will thought appreciatively as a whisper of speculation ran round the group. Lady Fairlie was a skilled player.

Verity was learning fast, too, he realised. Just when the interest in the two of them was becoming oppressive she turned back to Sedgley. 'What do you think I might find diverting, my lord? My aunt is threatening me with a positively tyrannous schedule of shopping and fittings. My entire wardrobe is too provincial for words, apparently and I long for escape.'

'A drive in the park, perhaps, Miss Wingate?'

'*Not* behind your famous matched greys, Lord Sedgley?'

'But of course, Miss Wingate. Nothing else would be worthy of you.'

Now how did you hear about those? Will wondered, trampling firmly on the instinct to rush off to Tatt's the next morning and buy an even more spectacular pair to put the Viscount's nose out of joint. Surely Verity was not trying to provoke him into showing possessiveness, or, worse, jealousy? She was going to be sorely disappointed if that was the case.

On the other hand, Sedgley had a certain reputation that she could have no idea about. Will was in no position to forbid her to drive with the man—that would either provoke her into rebellion or reveal more about their acquaintance than was healthy, or possibly both. But he needed to keep an eye on her. Intelligent and courageous she might be, but he doubted Verity had the experience to extricate herself from a lecherous buck in one of London's parks' quieter corners when she was trapped feet above the ground on a high-perch phaeton.

Will let an expression of faint *ennui* cross his face and sketched a bow. 'Miss Wingate. I do trust you have a pleasant stay.' He turned and strolled away before she had a chance to react, moved behind a gaggle of betoqued dowagers who stopped talking so fast that they must have been deep in speculation about him and sidestepped from there to a bank of potted ferns and lilies which brought him neatly round behind Sedgley's welltailored shoulders, just visible through the fronds.

'Tomorrow is not convenient? Well then, shall we say the day after at two? Not the fashionable hour, but we will find Hyde Park far less crowded. So much more pleasant, do you not agree? Excellent.'

Will moved back into the room. He did not have his

phaeton and team in town, and his own riding horses must be rested after their long journey, but he did have friends with saddle horses who would be glad to lend him a mount. And their company.

Her aunt had lent her a magnificent amber necklace, bracelets and earbobs, her maid had gone out and purchased silk stockings with delicate gold clocking on the ankles and a pair of the finest kid gloves and her own newest gown—an elegantly simple affair in dark brown silk with an amber gauze overskirt—looked even better than she had hoped as a result.

Stepping out of the carriage into the crowd of arrivals at Lady Notting's house had been an ordeal, one that continued after she had been kindly received and had braved the reception rooms. Aunt Caroline had introduced her to so many people that she soon lost track of names and faces. Her approach was the same for all of them. 'The poor child has come to me to escape from foolish provincial gossip. Have you heard about her adventures? Of course you have. Really, those half-brothers and -sisters of Aylsham's, quite out of control by all accounts. But thank heavens dear Verity was with the Duke, otherwise the poor Bishop's nerves would have been shredded. And Bishop Alderton was there also, with his staff, so that was a great help…'

Aunt Caroline prattled on until they were all dizzy, Verity thought. Dizzy and left with the impression that so much frankness meant that there could be nothing to hide. And that it would be inexcusably *provincial* to gossip about it.

Verity sensed that to behave as though she had something to be ashamed of would only confirm their suspicions, so she smiled and chatted and, when she found herself in the middle of a group that she suspected might be rather fast, had responded to their sly questions with a lively account of the excitements of rural life.

But what had Will been doing? Sudden urgent business? She could not believe it. Dukes sent minions on urgent business; they did not come hurrying up to London themselves. For a dreadful moment she feared he had come to break bad news about Papa, but a second's thought told her that he would have spoken to Aunt Caroline first, not walked up to her in the middle of a musicale.

For the life of her she could not imagine what he was doing there, as she said to her aunt as they drove back after the party. 'I do wish he had stayed away. Surely it will only make things worse?'

'It might not. To see the pair of you exhibiting nothing but neighbourly good manners with no hint of awkwardness can only confirm that nothing shocking occurred.'

'Will has come up to London to keep an eye on me,' Verity said. 'I do not believe that he needs to attend to anything personally at all—he simply summons people when he wants them.'

'Then it is rather charming of him, don't you think?' Aunt Caroline's voice held a hint of teasing. '*Will* is clearly concerned about you.'

'Nonsense. He is just used to being in charge of everything and cannot let well enough alone. I hope he goes home soon.'

Very soon.

Chapter Sixteen

'The Duke of Aylsham, my lady.' The Fairlies' butler did not, apparently, think it necessary to enquire first if the ladies were At Home to a duke.

Aunt Caroline stood up and went to shake Will's hand. 'What a pleasant surprise, Your Grace. I glimpsed you last night, but did not have the opportunity for a conversation. And so pleasant for Verity to have a neighbour from the country here.'

'I do hope so.' Will turned those beautiful blue eyes on her, but she could not interpret their expression. It was not disapproval, for once, she decided.

Will sat down at a gesture from Aunt Caroline, taking an armchair at an angle to Verity. 'I found I could more easily transact some necessary business in person and I wanted to reassure you that your father's health is good. May I escort you ladies anywhere today?'

'Thank you, no. There is absolutely no need to delay your own meetings.' Try as she might, she could not keep the scepticism out of her voice. What was he doing in London? She had told her aunt it was to keep an eye on her, but was he really that concerned about her? Then she realised that perhaps he wanted to face down the gossip on his own account. It did seem sensible, now she thought about it, for them both to be seen to be on amiable, but distant, terms. 'Aunt and I will be taking her carriage with her dresser and a footman to assist us,' she added with a smile that, to her surprise, he returned. 'You would find our shopping a complete bore, I imagine.'

'Then I hope you can both join me for dinner tomorrow evening? I am at the Grosvenor Square house.' That was more in his usual style—it sounded like an order, for all the pleasant tone.

'So kind of you, but I have no idea if we have any commitments,' Verity said, turning to Caroline.

'No, we have none.' There was more warmth in her voice than the acceptance of a dinner invitation merited, Verity thought. Perhaps her aunt had noticed a constraint between the two of them and was compensating. 'It would be delightful to dine with you, Aylsham.'

'Fairlie is free to accompany you, I hope? Excellent. It is quite some time since I have had the pleasure of speaking with him.' Will carried on talking with her aunt about mutual friends, about Lord Fairlie's charitable interests and how Roderick Fairlie was finding life at Oxford.

Verity assumed a sweet, meaningless smile and sat silently listening, watching Will's profile. After five minutes he looked across at her. 'I have very little news from home to convey. As I said, your father is well and sends his love. Mr Hoskins begs to be remembered to you. The children are undergoing their month's penance with good grace, for the moment. Whether that will last in my absence is not something I would like to wager on. My gamekeepers have been experiencing trouble with poachers which is annoying.' He smiled without humour. 'I dislike anyone encroaching on what is mine.'

In other words, he is going to take exception to me even conversing with other men, because he feels obliged to watch over me, she thought resentfully.

Last night she had thought she read a challenge in his attitude to Lord Sedgley and had been surprised—and relieved—when he had left the group without making it more apparent. But she was not his to watch over, simply a neighbour he had become entangled with.

I can look after myself, she thought, meeting his eyes, hoping he could read the message.

'I am keeping you ladies from your shopping,' Will said, getting to his feet without any sign of having understood her unspoken message. 'I look forward to tomorrow evening.' He shook hands with Aunt Caroline, then took Verity's right hand in his and bent to drop a chaste—very chaste, she thought resentfully—kiss on her cheek.

The butler came at the ring of the bell to show him out. 'That was thoughtful of him to call with messages from home,' Caroline remarked. 'The Duke—oh, bother, he has dropped a fob from his watch chain, he must have knocked it when he stood up. See?'

Verity bent to pick up the golden disc. 'I will see if I can catch him.' Wethering had left the hall when she reached it. She opened the front door to find Will three strides along the pavement in the direction of Berkeley Square. 'Your Grace!'

He turned, came back. 'Miss Wingate?'

'Your fob.' She held it out on the palm of her hand

and, as he came up the steps to her, she stepped back so he could enter the hallway.

'Thank you. The hook must be weak.' He pushed back the sides of his coat to pull out the chain.

'Let me see, clasps are always so tricky when you fasten them yourself upside down.' She did not think until her fingers were around the gold links, their backs pressed against the smooth silk of his waistcoat, feeling the solidity and warmth of his stomach muscles beneath, and then it was too late to pull back, not without betraying her agitation.

The clasp that must have secured the fob swung free, its hook distorted. She caught the tiny thing between thumb and forefinger, head bent, conscious of the familiar scent of him, of her pulse kicking up. 'It is broken. You had better put the fob in your pocket.'

'Put it with the watch.' As she slid it into the tight space in the little waistcoat pocket Will leaned back against the door, his shoulders pushing it shut. 'Verity. Why did you come to London?'

'Why?' She looked up, confused by the question. 'To face it out, of course. Everyone at home knows me, they are loyal, it will all die down. But it will not here, not unless they can see it is all nonsense, that I am not some seductress out to snare a duke, or some poor little victim of your wicked wiles or whatever other nonsense it amuses them to believe.'

'Aren't you a seductress, Verity?' he asked, his eyes dark and intent. 'I don't understand this otherwise.'

'This?'

'What am I doing here? Your aunt knows what she is about. I have no idea whether I am making things better or worse. My head rules my emotions, it always has, it is how I have been raised. You were right, we would be a disaster together and yet I still want this.'

'This?' she repeated. Somehow she was in his arms, close, tight against his heart. She looked up and he kissed her.

Kissed her hungrily, angrily, as though he was fighting himself. His hands were tight on her waist, lifting her against his chest, bringing her up to rub intimately against his aroused body, and Verity knew she wanted it, *this*, as much as he did.

Will shifted and one arm lashed her against him while the other hand found her breast, his thumb rubbing against the nipple under its modest covering of linen and fine cloth. The darkness behind her closed lids became the fireworks at Vauxhall, explosions of light and heat against velvety blackness. It was all part of the inferno when there was a crash. Will's head jerked up and she found she had her leg raised, her knee at his hip, her skirts sliding upwards. His hand was on her garter and hers was crushed between them at his falls—

'Oh.' Verity recoiled backwards and sat down on one of the hard hall chairs with a thud.

'What—what was that bang?' She dragged her skirts into some kind of order, tugged at her bodice.

Will looked round, picked up his hat, his gloves and cane where they lay scattered at his feet. 'Your butler slamming a door, I think.' He was breathing hard. 'That was beyond apology, that was insanity.'

'It was desire,' Verity managed to say. Whoever had slammed the door had not opened it again to see what was happening. Yet. She didn't know whether to fix her eyes on it or look at Will. She looked at Will. 'Melissa says that is a natural animal instinct.'

'I sincerely hope Melissa knows nothing about it.' Will was still leaning back against the door, eyes closed.

'I think it is theory,' Verity murmured and he smiled and straightened up, tugged at his waistcoat, grimaced.

Verity glanced down at his falls and rapidly away. 'You had better go.'

'I had better make my apologies to your aunt,' he said, rather grimly.

'Goodness, no! Just go. It doesn't matter, doesn't mean anything…important. And we will not be alone again.' She stood up and went upstairs, not running, not looking back. After a few moments the front door closed with a soft bang.

Verity tied her bonnet ribbons with a sharp tug. Linton, her aunt's dresser, made a soft clucking noise with her tongue and darted forward to rescue the bow.

With Linton following them into the town coach and sitting on the seat opposite, Verity could hardly begin explaining that her aunt's butler had found her and the Duke of Aylsham locked together and virtually…virtually *rutting* against the front door.

Had Wethering said anything? Or was he truly the perfect butler and would keep silent? Or perhaps it was one of the other staff. That was an unsettling thought. Was she going to receive a far-from-subtle request for payment to keep it quiet?

Aunt Caroline was not going to be happy if she did find out about that explosion of desire. She might start pressuring Verity to accept Will. Could she persuade her that the only thing they had in common was the experience of an uncomfortable night on a storm-lashed island, the pleasure of five kisses, mutual and inconvenient desire and an occasional, very occasional, shared flicker of humour?

But the pleasure of those kisses, of his caresses, the warmth of those moments when their eyes met and his mouth twitched in acknowledgement of a joke that only they knew… So many awkward parts of her body were tingling, her mind was all over the place…

'Corsets,' Aunt Caroline said, making her jump. 'They must be our next priority. Your gowns will not hang well if you do not have stays made to flatter the latest fashions.'

'I had forgotten about corsets. They will take some time to make which will delay my dress fittings, I suppose.'

Linton produced a faint smirk, as though young ladies from the country could not be expected to understand about such vital things. 'We are going to Mrs Clark in St James's Street, Miss Wingate. She has them partly made so they can be adjusted to fit very quickly.'

'Although why on earth she has to set up shop in a street full of gentlemen's clubs and outfitters, I do not know,' Aunt Caroline grumbled as they drew up outside Number Fifty-Six. 'Put down your veil, dear. One would not wish to be stared at by idlers and pavement-saunterers as we go in.'

Verity would quite like to have stared herself. St James's Street was not somewhere a young lady would normally go, although Pall Mall, Piccadilly and, of course, King Street where Almack's was were all entirely acceptable if one had a footman in attendance. But St James's Street was the focus of the clubs, their windows a perfect vantage point for bucks and rakes to ogle any female foolish enough to pass by. She wondered which clubs Will belonged to.

There was no space for the carriage to pull up immediately outside the shop so they had to walk up the road a little. Verity dawdled after her aunt with Linton making small flapping motions with her hands as though to shoo a flock of chickens safely past a fox's den.

'Is that Brooks's club down there?' And what a very elegant pair of gentlemen who had just come down the steps and turned up the hill towards them. Glossy tall hats, tight, biscuit-coloured pantaloons, Hessian boots with silver tassels.

The shorter of the two dropped a glove. A pity he had no chin, poor chap, Verity thought as she reached the threshold of the shop and gave one last glance to her left. His companion, dark and tall, swung his cane idly as he waited for him to catch up. Then he turned and Verity shot into the shop so fast that she collided with Aunt Caroline.

'I am sorry, Aunt.'

Linton shut the door behind them. 'Are you all right, Miss Wingate?'

'Yes, quite—thank you. I tripped on the mat. I do hope I didn't hurt you, Aunt?' She glanced around, but the window, which held nothing other than a length of draped satin and flowers in a vase, was backed by heavy gauze curtains. She could see only vague shapes passing by and anyone outside could not see in at all.

'Not in the slightest, dear. Ah, Mrs Clark. I have brought my niece, Miss Wingate, to you to be fitted. She will be acquiring an entire new wardrobe.'

Verity smiled and submitted to being borne off and undressed and measured and laced and all the while could think of nothing but the tall, dark man who had walked out of the club.

Thomas Harrington. The Reverend Thomas Harrington. Now Vicar of St Wulfram's, but once, when she had been very innocent, very romantic, her lover.

'Oh, I am sorry, Miss Wingate. Did I prick you?'

'No, not at all. It was my fault. I moved.'

Thomas. So handsome, so earnest, so very attentive, both to her and to Papa. Apparently modest, but clearly intelligent, he was the second, favoured, son of a country baronet, well bred but not well connected in ecclesiastical circles or in society. He had to work hard to secure advancement, he explained, not that he was ambitious for himself, of course. What he wanted was to do good, to find a parish where, by self-sacrifice and spiritual leadership, he could effect change for the better.

Verity had never been quite certain how he had done it, but little by little Thomas became a regular visitor to the Bishop's household, helping Papa with references for his studies, copying out sermons in his fine, clear hand, squiring her about to modest, unexceptional social events. Mutely gazing into her eyes with an intensity and a humble worship that was intoxicating.

She fell for him so hard she had felt stunned. She had certainly lost all her critical faculties, she told herself bitterly afterwards. But that moonlit evening, with the nightingales pouring their heart-aching magic into the soft air, she had let him make love to her in the summer house. There had been kisses before—shy, tentative ones, like those he had pressed on her in Aunt Caroline's drawing room—but this had been something else altogether.

Verity had not enjoyed it very much. It had hurt and had been hurried and sticky and, frankly, embarrassing. Looking back now, she realised that Will's kisses had excited her more than the totality of Thomas's lovemaking. But Thomas had been so apologetic, so frank about how he had been carried away by passion. It would be so much better when they were married, he promised. He would go and ask for her hand immediately.

But Papa had said only a few days before that he did not want her to marry until she had a London Season and an opportunity to look around her a little. So she had begged Thomas to wait for a week or so while she brought Papa round to the idea that she might have already fallen in love. It would not do to hurry things and turn him against Thomas, but, given time, what could his objection be to such a promising curate?

Thank heavens she had waited. The good angel who looked after innocent young ladies might have slept through her seduction, but she had certainly been alert two evenings later when Verity had strayed down to the river's edge at Lady Heskith's party. Thomas had not been there when she arrived and the rooms were overheated and the music too loud, so she had strolled out on to the lawns down the path to the seat beside the weeping willow where she could dream about married life.

No sooner had she sat down than she realised from the fragrant drifting smoke that two men on the far side of the tree were taking advantage of the garden to smoke cheroots. She stood and began to tiptoe away when one spoke. Thomas.

'It's a triumph, old chap. She's as sheltered as a nun and besotted with me. With the Bishop as a father-in-law I'll be set for life—a rich, fashionable, parish and then, who knows where I'll finish up. And she's not bad-looking. With a bit of practice she'll be quite good in bed, too. But if not, well… What matter, eh?'

What Verity should have done, of course—being a well brought-up young lady—was to take herself off, nurse her broken heart in silence and send the swine a note next morning informing him in dignified terms that she had no desire to see him ever again.

What she did—and it still gave her a warm glow of satisfaction to recall it—was duck under the overhanging branches, march up to the pair of them and push her startled lover into the water.

As he had flailed around in an attempt to sit up in the muddy shallows she had turned to his companion. 'Do drag him out, sir. If he drowns it will pollute the river. And perhaps you would pass on a message,' she had added as the young man gawped at her. 'Tell him that I am no nun and not besotted. I am vengeful. Mr Harrington may whistle for his advancement.'

Two days later she had received a note.

If you try to ruin me, think what tales I can tell of you and the pretty little birthmark on your right thigh. T.H.

It was stalemate and then she'd had a fortnight of deepening anxiety because her courses were late. They'd come at last and with them the realisation of what a narrow escape she'd had. The only small mercy was that Thomas Harrington had found himself a position as tutor to the son of an earl in the north of England and vanished from the district. Her father had appointed Mr Hoskins as his Chaplain and secretary and rarely mentioned his occasional assistant Thomas again.

It had been a painful lesson. The heart could not be trusted and, it seemed, neither could the head, because Papa had sensed nothing wrong with the ambitious young curate. She could have been tied for life to a lying, unscrupulous, unkind man who regarded his faith and his calling as merely the means to influence and wealth and she could have done nothing about it.

'Breathe in, please, Miss Wingate. Oh, excellent, such a deep breath... Now, let me just tie the ribbons and we will see. Is that comfortable?'

'If comfortable implies being able to breath or move, I am afraid not,' Verity said, too immersed in her black thoughts to be tactful. 'Oh, yes, that is much better.'

But nothing would make the fact of Thomas Harrington's presence in London any better. All she could do was hope and pray that he was too busy on church business, or in his clubs, to be found anywhere she might encounter him.

Chapter Seventeen

'Whatever is the matter, dear?' Aunt Caroline gave her a very beady stare across the breakfast table next morning. 'You will get lines if you frown like that.'

'Nothing, Aunt. Just a momentary thought about something of no importance.'

Actually it had been a prolonged thought about something of pressing importance. What was she going to do about Will? *Try to avoid being alone with him.* And what to do about Thomas Harrington. *Avoid him at all costs.* And there was a third man to think about now.

'I did tell you last night that Lord Sedgley is taking me driving this afternoon?'

If Will had not arrived so unexpectedly at the musical reception then she would not have been provoked into flirting outrageously with Lord Sedgley—Verity stopped fretting and examined her conscience for a moment. Well, not exactly *provoked*, she had to admit. Will had stood there, looking self-assured and ridiculously handsome, just as usual. It was enough to drive any woman to commit an indiscretion. And he had not seemed at all put out by it, which was inexplicably provoking of him.

She had known about Sedgley's greys because Roderick had rhapsodised about them in one of his letters and anyone would want the opportunity to ride behind those. But, despite offering what any red-blooded duke would surely consider provocation, the infuriating man had merely bowed and taken himself off in a dignified manner.

Not that she wanted him to be provoked. Merely to have his perfectly straight nose put a trifle out of joint, display an emotion.

'Yes, you did tell me. I suppose it is all right, provided you do not leave the park and he has his groom up behind at all times. Although he does have a slightly warm reputation.'

'I will be careful,' Verity promised.

'Oh, well, in that case there is no problem. Hyde Park is always so full of people—make sure he goes there, not Green Park or St James's Park. And we are dining with Aylsham tonight. Fairlie, you haven't forgotten, have you?' she demanded of her husband, who was silently demolishing ham and eggs at the head of the table.

'Forgotten? This evening? No, of course not,' he said with all the emphasis of a man who had done just that. 'Aylsham, you said? Should be an excellent dinner, always keeps a good table, does the Duke.'

'That was his grandfather,' Aunt Caroline said with a roll of her eyes towards Verity, who suppressed a smile.

'I don't suppose you would consider selling, would you?' Will asked Malcolm Shipley as they drew rein after a long gallop across the further reaches of Hyde Park and turned to canter back to the small group of other riders waiting for them near the head of the Serpentine.

'I would be mad to,' his friend said frankly. 'That's the best young horse I've had my hands on in years and I got him for a song. I'm holding on to Galaxy no matter what I'm offered.'

'I appreciate the loan,' Will said. As he had hoped, Shipley had not been able to resist showing off his latest acquisition and had been meeting friends to ride out in any case. They would provide excellent cover from which to observe Sedgley and ensure that Verity came to no harm without Will making his interest too obvious.

'That's him now. You can't mistake those greys.' Shipley pointed towards one of the rides leading to a stand of mature trees and shrubs. Will had confided that he wanted to keep an eye on the daughter of his neighbour, the retired Bishop, and his friend had immediately grasped the necessity. 'Perfectly good fellow in all kinds of ways, Sedgley, great sportsman, but I wouldn't want him squiring my sister about.'

'There's no groom up behind,' Will said.

Damn it, what was Verity thinking of, to agree to get into the vehicle with no groom?

'Dashed bad form.' Shipley gestured to his two friends who had ridden out with them. 'Shall we go that way? Not too crowded with confounded matrons in barouches.'

'Good idea,' Captain Wainfleet called back and the group cantered towards the distant copse on a course converging with the phaeton, its high perch swaying over the big wheels, the four greys stepping out strongly in the traces. Two more riders were trotting along the track in the opposite direction, but otherwise they had the area to themselves.

Sedgley must think he would have no trouble snatching a kiss or two once the riders had passed, Will thought grimly. The knack would be falling in with the phaeton *accidentally* and then demonstrating a complete lack of tact by failing to leave Sedgley alone with his fair passenger.

At least I had the sense to wear a good stout hatpin in my bonnet, Verity thought.

She admitted to herself that she had underestimated Lord Sedgley, who was showing excellent tactics in keeping up a flow of lively chatter while sweeping her off to the most deserted area of the park with, she was sure, decidedly dubious motives. The fact that he had sent his groom off on some errand the moment they had entered Hyde Park had been indication enough of his motives. It was reassuring to think that a hatpin in the thigh and an elbow in the ribs would put paid to any nonsense. She had her guinea purse in her reticule— the application of that to the falls of his natty buckskin breeches might also be called for.

'There is the most charming prospect over Kensington Palace Gardens from just the other side of that copse,' the Viscount said with a casual air that did not deceive Verity for a moment. Although the park was as busy as her aunt had expected, the far side of the trees would shield the phaeton from the main area and from the two groups of riders who were converging on them.

She put up a hand to her bonnet as though to check it was secure, slid out the pin and held it concealed in the folds of her skirt.

They passed into the shadows. 'Alone at last,' Sedgley remarked, with what she could not help but feel was a shocking lack of originality as he reined in the greys and tied the reins to the whip handle. Well trained, the horses stood quite still.

It was all very well to be prepared and armed with a sharp hatpin, Verity discovered, but the way the trees shut off the rest of the park was more comprehensive than she had imagined. There might not have been another person for miles around.

'I cannot see a view of the Gardens. We should drive on.'

'I must have mistaken this for a different clump of trees,' Sedgley said. 'But never mind. This gives us a charming opportunity to get to know each other better, don't you think?'

His arm went around her waist before she could reply and his lips met her cheek. Head turned away, Verity whipped out the hatpin and stabbed blindly at the thigh now pressed against hers on the narrow seat. Sedgley swore and jerked away and must, she realised, have knocked against the whip in its holder, pulling the reins.

The team of greys snorted and backed, the phaeton, swaying on its high springs, lurched and Verity, off balance as she recoiled from the Viscount, went over the low side rail.

Nothing actually hurt too much, which was a relief, although she had no desire to get up, or open her eyes, especially as a pair of strong arms was holding her against what felt like an impressively solid chest and a male voice was murmuring reassurances into her hair.

Will. He does care... How...how wonderful.

Wonderful? Verity dragged herself out of an increasingly warm, fuzzy daydream and back to reality. Whoever was holding her did not smell like Will, did not sound like Will and what on earth was she doing *wanting* it to be Will?

She opened her eyes, blinked. *'Thomas Harrington?'*

'Kindly lay the lady down, sir.'

Now, that is *Will.*

'I am a friend of the family and will take care of her.'

'I am also well acquainted with Miss Wingate,' Thomas began as Verity sat up abruptly. 'And as a man of the cloth—'

'It has been a long time, Mr Harrington,' she said as coolly as she could manage with her hair coming down, her skirts twisted around her knees and a growing sense of panic choking the words. Then a groan made her look beyond Thomas's shoulder to where Lord Sedgley was hauling himself to his feet by means of a carriage wheel. 'What happened to the Viscount?'

'I hit him,' Will said.

'Good.' She pulled her skirts down to cover her legs. 'Thank you.'

Will came down on one knee beside her on the other side to Thomas, whom he ignored. 'Are you much hurt, Miss Wingate?'

'A little bruised. Luckily I did not land on the trackway, but on the turf.' The trees and the grass and the sky were still not quite steady or in their right place and she rubbed at her eyes. 'I did not faint. I think I must have been disorientated by the fall.'

'Rest a little, Verity—Miss Wingate,' Thomas said. 'Then when you feel strong enough I will take you up before me on my horse.'

'Certainly not,' Verity said, her words colliding with Will's.

'You will do no such thing, sir.'

'I am Thomas Harrington, a minister in holy orders,' Thomas said, getting to his feet.

Will merely rocked back on his heels and looked up dismissively. Despite herself, Verity could not help being impressed both by the sheer arrogance with which he ignored the implicit threat of the large, fit man towering over him and the lightly reined strength and anger she could feel emanating from him.

'I do not care if you are the Archbishop of Canterbury, sir.' If he had held up a placard over her head reading, *Mine*, Verity thought he could have hardly made his attitude clearer.

'I fear you have the advantage of me, sir.' There was a hint of doubt in Harrington's voice now and something else, an interest that made Verity look from him to Will with a sinking sense of dread.

Don't tell him who you are. She almost said it aloud.

Will stood. 'I am Aylsham.'

'The Duke?'

'I am not aware of another.'

She could not decide whether Will wanted to provoke a fight or simply cow the other man, but whichever it was, he was reinforcing the idea in Harrington's nimble mind that she mattered to the Duke and that gave him an advantage in a game that he clearly expected to play according to his rules.

'My apologies, Your Grace. I did not recognise you.'

Will shrugged. 'Why should you? I doubt we move in the same circles.'

It was clearly a rhetorical question and Harrington's

jaw clenched before he managed to accept the snub with a smile. 'Miss Wingate, if an old friend can be of no further assistance I will leave you in the capable hands of the Duke. I will call at the earliest opportunity, as I am sure you would expect. Good day.'

His companion, who had been sitting astride his horse, the reins of Harrington's mount in one hand, raised his hat and the two turned and rode away.

As I am sure you would expect.

That had been a threat. Thomas would call and make clear his demands for keeping quiet about their past. He thought she had, by some miracle, hooked a duke and would be entirely at his mercy. If he revealed that he had taken her virginity, then he could expect Will to break off the connection instantly.

But what could he hope to gain? Verity wondered as Will bent and drew her to her feet. She had little money of her own, her father no longer had influence over appointments and advancement. Was it simply revenge for the loss of his dignity?

'Thank you,' she said to Will, who took her elbow, walked her slowly to a bench under a tree, gave her a look which promised a lengthy discussion to come and turned on his heel to stalk across to the phaeton.

One of his companions hauled the Viscount upright to face Will. There was an exchange of words that she could not hear, then both men walked towards her. Sedgley stopped a few feet away. 'Miss Wingate. I trust you are not hurt. I must apologise for the actions of mine which led to the accident.'

Verity inclined her head. It made her jarred neck ache, but that was worth enduring for the appearance of dignity. 'I accept your apology, my lord. And I apologise for stabbing you in the thigh with my hatpin, causing you to lose control of your team.'

Everyone looked with interest at the Viscount's tight buff pantaloons, now much begrimed, then back at Verity.

'I do not suppose anyone has seen my hatpin?' Verity asked sweetly.

'I am certain Lord Sedgley will replace it,' Will said. 'Just as I am certain that he will find himself refreshed by walking home after he has kindly loaned me his vehicle to convey you, Miss Wingate. You will not mind leading my mount, Shipley?'

Will waited until he had assured himself that the four greys were uninjured and calm enough to carry on, had her seated comfortably beside him and the others had ridden off, before he spoke. 'Whatever possessed you?'

How does he know?

'He seemed perfectly respectable. Papa thought highly of his intellect—'

'The Bishop knows Sedgley?'

'Oh. No. I mistook your meaning. No, Papa does not know the Viscount. Driving with him was an error of judgement on my part. I had heard about his famous greys and I thought I could manage him. And the hatpin worked exceedingly well.'

'So well that you almost broke your neck,' Will said. The team, that had been walking sedately, tossed their heads. 'You had set out to flirt, set out to make me jealous.'

'I had no idea you would be at the musicale. I was merely enjoying myself.' She was sounding defensive now. Verity swallowed the urge to excuse herself and went on the attack. 'And you have no cause to be jealous of me. You have absolutely no claim on me.' One sideways glance at his profile made her add, disastrously, 'It is just your pride and possessiveness, your feelings are not engaged in the slightest.'

The team came to a plunging halt, dust and gravel spurting around their hooves. Will brought them under control one-handed. 'You have no idea of my feelings,' he said, his gaze still fixed over the heads of the leaders. 'None at all.'

'I see what you allow me to see.' She was not going to let him put her in the wrong over this. 'What you allow the world to see. Even when you were speaking of marrying me it was clear you would reveal nothing of yourself, that you want your wife to see no more than the mask you wear for the world.'

They were still in the shadow of the grove, the only signs of life nearby the diminishing figures of Will's companions cantering away and the trudging figure of Lord Sedgley making for the Uxbridge Road gate. Will jumped down from the high perch, led the horses into the trees and tethered the leaders to a low oak bough.

'Come down.' He held up his hands to her.

'Why?' If Will was going to shout at her, or lecture her, he could do it while he was driving and could not focus all his attention on her.

'Because I wish to discuss feelings.' His voice dropped to a growl. 'Demonstrate feelings.'

She leaned down, put her hands on his shoulders and closed her eyes as he took her by the waist. He felt so strong, so steady and, despite her skittering pulse, she felt so very safe. He would not drop her.

That safety proved to be a delusion, because Will lifted her from the seat, but not to the ground. Instead he swung her into his arms and strode into the cover of the trees where one, falling, had opened up a tiny clearing and the park keepers had set a rustic bench.

He sat, with her on his knee. Verity wriggled, pushed at his chest.

'Are you afraid of me?' He was no longer holding her, she realised.

'No.' She heard the hesitation in her own voice. 'No, of course not.'

'But you want to be free?'

'Here, now?' A moment ago the answer would have been *yes*. She had wanted a safe distance of six feet or so. 'No.'

'Good.' Will's arms came around her again.

'But I should. There is no butler to bring us to our senses here.'

'True. But I am not an exhibitionist by design, Verity. I have no desire to be caught in a passionate embrace by a barouche full of dowagers, believe me.' He put his hat on the bench and began to nuzzle her neck above the high collar of her pelisse.

'What do you call that?' she demanded, twisting a little to give him better access.

'If I hear carriage wheels or hoofbeats,' Will said, his voice somewhat muffled, 'you will be sitting demurely next to me in seconds.'

'Will!' It was difficult, but a firm hand on his chest made him stop. 'That is not proper behaviour for a perfect duke and you know it.'

'No,' he agreed and set her on the seat although there was no sign of anyone approaching their copse. 'I desire you and that is something I find hard to resist. I like you. I would like to be your friend. I want to protect you.

That is why I came to London. Those are feelings—
desire and liking and protectiveness.'

Verity swallowed. 'Unmarried ladies are not supposed to be friends with gentlemen.'

'And there I was thinking that the unconventional
Miss Wingate does not care about society's strictures
on what she should, or should not, be doing.'

'And I thought you cared too much about how the perfect Duke should or should not behave,' she shot back.

'Perhaps we were both wrong,' he said lightly, lifting
her hand and beginning to play with the tassels on the
cuffs of her gloves. 'Perhaps you are more conventional
and I am more of a rebel than we believed.'

'Friends, then,' she said. 'But friends do not kiss like
we have been kissing.'

Chapter Eighteen

'No,' Will agreed, his face still hidden as he untangled the dangling leather glove-trim that had been knotted by her fall. 'Friends do not kiss like that.'

'Perhaps that is why unmarried men and women are rarely friends,' Verity pointed out. 'Married couples often are, I have observed. Those in happy marriages.'

Will made a sound suspiciously like a grunt. 'I have good friends already, male friends. I know what we talk about—and it is not feelings. I know what we rely upon each other for: loyalty, support, to have each other's backs in a fight. What does a woman look for in her friends?'

'Loyalty, listening, sharing, talking about feelings.' Will looked up and grimaced and she laughed at him, just a little. 'I rely on my friends to tell me if a bonnet I passionately desire makes me look a fright and to lend me their last pair of silk stockings because I have been invited to a very special ball. I rely on them to listen and sympathise when I am breaking my heart over some ridiculous man, or I have just been snubbed by an antiquarian who thinks that ladies are only fit to write out labels for his collection of stone arrowheads, not venture an opinion about their origins. I rely on them for comfortable gossip, for bracing lectures when I am feeling sorry for myself, for laughter and shared happiness.'

'Feelings, then,' Will said ruefully. 'Who was the ridiculous man who broke your heart? Not the pretty cleric I just met, surely?'

'No, certainly not.' Why had she lied so instantly, so vehemently? Why couldn't she have admitted it? All she needed to say was that she had been disillusioned when she had discovered that he was using her to gain her father's patronage. There was no need to tell Will that they had been lovers.

'He really did not matter,' she went on, even though she suspected that she was over-explaining. 'I was very young—but love hurts, doesn't it? Even when it is only foolish first love.'

'I do not know,' Will admitted. 'I have never been in love, do not look for it in marriage.'

'Never? Not even some foolish calf-love?' He shook his head. 'And it is very sad that you do not hope to love your bride. Surely that would be preferable to some sensible, chilly, *suitable* arrangement?'

'Is that one reason why you would not marry me? Because you want declarations of love?' The familiar wry twist of his lips was back.

'Of course not. I mean…' Verity searched for the right words. 'Yes, I would not marry without love, but, no, I would hate it if you had made some pretence of love just to get me to agree.'

'I can understand that, but surely affection would develop with time in a marriage where everything else is right—liking, suitability, mutual respect. Desire…?

But love… Love seems to me to be as dangerous to happiness as dislike.' The warmth that had come into his voice when he spoke of affection seemed to evaporate, leaving her chilled.

'The example of your father and stepmother was not a happy one?' Verity suggested. That must be the marriage Will would have been closest to. He was very young when his own mother died, perhaps too young to be aware of the relationship between his parents. 'I thought theirs was a match based on an instant, great love.'

'Instant, yes. One reads about a *coup de foudre* in novels, but I had never believed in such a thing until I looked back on that marriage. It was all consuming, obsessive perhaps. It certainly excluded everything and everybody.'

'It must have been very difficult for you,' she said. 'How old were you?'

Will shrugged. 'Nine. I suppose I was like any other child in a household such as ours—I saw more of my nanny and tutors than my parents and I had been an only child. But when my father remarried he and my stepmother spent all their time together and it was strange to see how absorbed they were. I think I might have been jealous.' He said it almost as a question, as though he either did not believe he might legitimately feel like that or as though he did not understand why he might be so. Verity was not certain which was worse, but she stayed quiet, let him talk.

'But then my half-brothers and -sisters began to be born, the first four, and that was…good.'

'Your father and stepmother were closer to them than your parents had been with you? That must have been your stepmother's influence, I suppose. She must love her children.'

'Love? I do not know,' Will said. 'Is that how parents love their children? They were the outward symbol of the marriage, they were the means by which she could express her educational theories, they were a focus for her intense emotions. Is that love?'

'I do not know. I have never seen her with them. They appear to love her and, surely, every family is different.' She recalled the stilted confidence he had made to her in the centre of the maze and ventured, 'The death of your half-sister must have been very difficult for all of them.'

Will closed his eyes, leaned back on the bench, but his fingers remained loosely around her wrist as though keeping contact with her heartbeat. 'Yes, it was devastating. I blamed them for it; Claudia, my stepmother, most of all. She believes that willpower, fresh air and exercise will overcome most bodily ills. One of her most strongly held theories is that it takes strength of will to succeed with all things and that if you try hard enough you will find that strength. She did not recognise how ill Bella was and Bella wanted to be brave, to be strong, to please her. She collapsed, but by then it was too late.'

'Oh, the poor child. And you loved her. You must have been heartbroken.'

And his stepmother must have been devastated, would have blamed herself. How utterly ghastly.

'She was my sister, I was her older brother, it was my duty to protect her. I was angry,' Will said. His voice was quite steady, his gaze apparently fixed on the phaeton. 'I had not been able to do anything, they wouldn't listen, said I was exaggerating. They both seemed blind. But I was thirteen and I should have known enough, have had enough strength to make my father send for the doctor at least. Or I should have taken a horse and gone myself. But I did not. I failed her.

'The night she died I wrote to my grandfather. He and my father had been on very distant terms since the marriage. I said that my stepmother was an unfit mother. I accused her of responsibility for Arabella's death, I stated that my father was too weak to see beyond his feelings for his wife.'

He stopped abruptly, as though recollecting who he was, where he was.

'Go on,' Verity murmured. 'What happened then?'

When Will spoke again it was as though he had re-placed the mask of the Duke and pushed away the nat-ural emotions of sadness and anger and frustration. 'Naturally I should have expressed myself more mod-erately. I should have taken into account my stepmother's good intentions and I should have had the determina-tion to have protected my sister. I saw that later. As it was, my grandfather removed me from my father's con-trol as a direct result and it made the breach impossi-ble to heal, which was entirely my fault. My behaviour was inappropriate and my other brothers and sisters lost their elder brother and what support I could have been to them then.'

It seemed to Verity that by writing he had acted swiftly and decisively to protect his younger half-siblings and that it had been a brave thing for a thirteen-year-old boy to do. He had been hardly more than a child himself; how could he have stood up to an infatuated man who believed his wife could do no wrong? But Will clearly blamed himself for the total estrangement between the old Duke and his heir as well as failing to secure help for Arabella in time.

She could point out that the children seemed bursting with good health and spirits now, so perhaps their upbringing had not been so very bad, that perhaps their parents had learned from that tragic loss, but somehow she did not think that Will was looking for reassurances. His instinct to protect, his sense of responsibility, were both very strong and he thought he had failed. To heal he had to forgive himself and Verity had no idea how to help him do that.

If I could teach him to love, then perhaps he could judge himself less harshly. But I do not love him, so how can I hope to do that? Can it really be possible to be his friend?

She made some inarticulate sound of frustration and he looked down at her. 'Verity?'

'Imagine if the same thing happened now, but it was Basil in your shoes and Alicia died.'

'Basil has not had my upbringing.' Will was frowning.

'No, he has not. He has grown up with all those brothers and sister, like a litter of puppies. They love each other, their mother loves them, their father loved them. He has the confidence to speak his mind, demand what he wants. Ill mannered and naughty sometimes, yes, but he would yell the place down until someone sent for a doctor. You were brought up alone, raised to obey, be dutiful and *proper* and defer to those who knew best—and that was before your grandfather got his ice-cold hands on you. The two things they did not train you in was disobedience, which is a very useful skill, and loving. For you to have rebelled at all was incredible.'

'You know how to speak your mind as well, that is clear.' Will stood, took three angry paces away from her, then spun round. 'Is this what you and your female friends do? Pick each other to pieces?'

'We help each other see the truth. It was not your fault and, even if it had been, whipping yourself for it does no good now. You love those children and you are doing your absolute best for them. I just wish you would be as kind and loving to yourself.'

'That sounds somewhat self-indulgent.'

'It is no such thing.' Verity refused to back down, even in the face of his most imperious expression. 'You can learn from what has gone wrong, celebrate successes. It makes you stronger, happier, kinder, I think. It makes you see things in a truer light and helps you see what it is you truly want. What you need. That isn't selfish.' She let herself smile. 'It makes you more pleasant to be with, too.'

'What I need,' Will said slowly, walking away from her towards the horses. He stopped, back turned.

Now what is he thinking about? Some other duty he must add to the load he carries around? Some objection to being happy?

She watched him—no hardship when he made such an attractive study standing there, beautifully cut coat emphasising broad shoulders and tight waist above a length of leg shown off by breeches and boots.

I could draw him.

But it would probably lack life and emotion—she was used to drawing bones and broken pottery, not flesh and blood.

Then Will turned and walked back. Strode back, as though time was of the essence. 'Verity, will you—'

He broke off as a group of riders swept into view at a canter, calling to one another. 'Not fair!' a young woman in a dark blue habit called. 'You had a lead, you beasts!'

The four men in front of her and her three companions reined in, swinging their mounts around towards the ladies, making the greys in the phaeton snort and back up.

Will ran to the team, caught the bridle of one of the leaders. While everyone was looking at the phaeton, Verity sat quite still, her moss-green walking dress, she thought, must merge quite well with the bushes behind her. One of the men rode up to Will, greeted him. She caught snatches of their conversation. 'Apologies, Aylsham…didn't realise anyone was here… Cousin Thea…race…'

No one glanced towards the bench. Will walked over to the others, raising his hand as though to doff the hat he had left on the bench. There were introductions, some laughter, then the group rode off and he came back to her.

'I do not think they saw me, did they?' she asked as he came closer. 'What a relief.'

'A relief?'

'Well, yes. The whole point of me being in London is to kill the rumours about us and sitting on benches in secluded groves with you is hardly likely to help with that, is it?'

'No.' His smile was the cool ducal social smile that she had learned to mistrust. 'No, we need to avoid speculation at all costs, do we not? The sooner I return you to Lady Fairlie the better, in fact.'

Now what have I said to put him in a temper? Verity thought as she followed Will back to the phaeton.

Because a temper that was, however beautifully he disguised it. *He doesn't want to marry me. I do not want to marry him. Neither of us wants vulgar gossip and speculation about our relationship.*

She was lifted up to the high seat by strong hands that lingered not a second too long, she noted, even as she was wondering why about her own choice of words. *Relationship? Do we have one?*

Will seemed to have all his attention on the horses. Verity studied the severe profile, softened by a sweep of dark lashes, the unexpected fullness of his bottom lip, the tilt of his head as he concentrated. Then he turned, caught her watching him and smiled. Smiled—and a trace of colour came up over his cheekbones before he looked back at the path ahead.

The realisation swept through her, the sudden solution to a puzzle. *I love him. I love Will. Oh, no. No.*

She clutched at the curling metal guard rail beside her. The fine kid of her glove split across the palm and she bit her lip to stop the exclamation of pain as the thin metal dug into her hand. He did not love her; she would make him a terrible wife, a comprehensively unsuitable duchess. They would fight over everything— and Thomas Harrington would either spend a lifetime blackmailing her or she could defy him and have another scandal added to the name of the Duchess of Aylsham.

Because Will would insist on marriage if he discovered the slightest weakness in her determination not to accept him. She had held out against his insistence when her feelings for him had wavered between physical attraction and dislike of everything he seemed to stand for. But now, how could she refuse him when it would break her heart? *Was* breaking her heart.

* * *

'Verity?'

She turned to him with a jerk of her head, so unlike her usual grace. 'Yes?' A moment ago she had been looking at him, looking as though she had to close her eyes and describe him in detail. He had felt the beginnings of a blush, not of embarrassment, he realised with surprise, but of pleasure.

'Yes?' No encouragement there, all her barriers were up again.

Lord, but she was the most provoking female.

'Nothing.'

Very smooth, Will. Very sophisticated conversation. Well up to standard of a bashful youth confronting the object of his first half-innocent love, in fact. He had lied when Verity had asked him whether he had ever had an attack of adolescent calf-love. There had been the Squire's daughter in the next parish. She had been eighteen, just out, lovely with all the feminine assurance that left adolescent males floundering like landed fish in her wake. He had been sixteen, uncertain about what he was feeling except that it had been overwhelming. In retrospect she had been much kinder than he had deserved.

Since then Will had become confident he knew what he was about in the bedchamber. But those other emotions, that breathless sense of anticipation, that intensity of focus whenever the beloved object was near—that was something he had never thought to feel again.

Until now.

He stopped breathing. The sounds of the park, the birdsong, the distant voices, the crunch of stone under wheel and hoof all vanished. Then, within a second it came back and he was breathing normally and his hand was steady on the reins and the woman beside him showed no sign that he had said or done anything out of the normal. Certainly not that he had said, *I love you.*

He was in love with Verity Wingate, the one unmarried woman in England who did not want to catch a duke. Verity, who wanted her freedom of thought and action. Verity, who expected him to conspire with her to give other unmarried women theirs. Miss Wingate, the argumentative antiquarian who handled human skulls without a single maidenly quiver of distaste.

Verity Wingate, who was sympathetic and bracingly kind about his childhood, whose kisses inflamed him, who turned to supple fire in his arms. Who would face ruin rather than marry him.

Chapter Nineteen

'Are you still convinced you did the right thing in refusing to marry me?' Will asked. Incredibly, his voice was quite steady. 'The reception you have received in London has not changed your mind?'

'It has been far better than I dared hope,' Verity said. If she was surprised by the change of subject, she did not show it. 'The Queen's acceptance has been a great help, of course. There have been some snubs, some cuts, but not too many. There is a Drawing Room at St James's Palace in a week's time. My aunt is certain I will receive a card for it and then even the stuffiest matron should decide that it is all a storm in a teacup.'

So, she had not heard about the whispers in the clubs that he had got her with child. Or, alternatively, that she had humiliated him, thrown him in the lake and he was plotting his subtle revenge on her. Some gossip had her as a clever, heartless wanton, others as a frigid prude. He could only pray she did not hear before it died down and a new scandal became the talk of the town. If he could put a name to the whisperers or if he found a wager in the betting books, then he would be issuing challenges.

'And your decision?' he pressed, his voice neutral as though this only concerned him as a matter of right or wrong.

'Of course it was the right thing. How can you doubt it? My goodness, can you imagine the two of us married?'

Yes, I can.

There was a strained edge to her laughter, he had obviously embarrassed her by raising the subject.

'Friends, then,' Will said. He turned the horses on the track towards the Stanhope Gate and willed his rebellious body, stirring at the thought of Verity's embrace, into submission. He had been trained to hide his emotions. Now, for the first time, that restraint was going to be tested to the utmost.

'Whatever have you done to your walking dress? Thank goodness it is not one of your new ones.' Her aunt had followed her into her bedchamber to hear all about the drive.

'Are these grass stains, Miss Wingate?' The maid stood ready, clothes brush poised. 'Only I had best take it now and sponge them before they set, if they are.'

'Yes, I fell from the phaeton,' Verity said. 'The horses pecked, I was off balance. You know what those high-perch phaetons are like. There is absolutely nothing to worry about, Aunt. I landed on the grass, as you can see.'

The maid helped her out of the dress and into a wrapper and hurried off to work whatever magic happened to stains below stairs.

'You are not hurt?' Aunt Caroline asked, tugging at the bell-pull. 'Tea and *sal volatile*, I think. Now, should we send for Dr Tancroft? What Lord Sedgley was think-

ing of, I cannot imagine. It is definitely the last time you
go driving with him. He might at least have escorted you
in to make his apologies for his bad driving.'

'No need for the doctor. I am just a little bruised and
sore.' Verity sat down with a wince. 'And Lord Sedgley
did not bring me home. The Duke did.' There would be
no hiding it, the footman and the butler had both seen
him.

'Aylsham? But what was he doing there? Oh, there
you are, Wethering. Tea, if you please, and ask my
woman to bring *sal volatile* and something for bruises.'

'The Duke was riding in the park with friends. He
saw the accident and, um, was displeased with Lord
Sedgley for not driving carefully enough. He suggested
that it would be better if he drove me here himself in the
Viscount's carriage.'

'And Sedgley?'

'He walked home.'

Her aunt blinked once. 'Verity, am I to understand
that Aylsham struck Sedgley?'

'I believe so. I was momentarily stunned and I did not
see it.' She braced herself for the explosion.

'How wonderful!' Aunt Caroline clapped her hands
together. 'So romantic.'

'It was nothing of the kind,' Verity said, wishing that
Will had been inspired by love, not by gallantry.

'If you say so, dear.' Her aunt bit her lip in thought.
'Perhaps it would be best to cancel the dinner engage-
ment. You are bound to be a trifle stiff after that fall and
I would not wish you to appear anything but graceful.'

And I would like a little respite before I have to face
him again… 'Yes, I think that would be for the best,'
Verity agreed.

* * *

Will normally slept well. It was a matter of composing oneself to sleep and having the discipline not to allow disturbing thoughts to intrude. As he sat up in bed at five in the morning the day after the incident in Hyde Park he admitted to himself that he had obviously never had sufficiently agitating reflections to truly put that to the test. Except, of course, for that wakeful night spent in extreme discomfort on the floor of the island hut.

Being in love as an adult was not the state of idiotic, rose-coloured happiness he had always assumed it was. It was painful and the physical pain of unsatisfied arousal was the least of it.

A month ago, faced with a reluctant young lady, Will would simply have exerted his powers to charm her and would have relied on her own self-interest and her parents' pressure to secure her acceptance of his suit. But Verity had made him see things from the woman's point of view and he realised that was simply a form of bullying, with his rank and wealth as the weapon.

Verity did not want him, other than for kisses against her better judgement. She had even been dubious about his offer of friendship. It was not false modesty that held him back from trying to change her mind. Will knew his own worth. His mirror told him that he was acceptable-looking. His fencing master, a hard critic, assured him he was in fine physical shape. He knew himself to be intelligent and hard-working, believed that he was fair and loyal. His bed partners always seemed more than content. If there were aspects of his personality or life that a wife objected to he would do his best, within reason, to modify them. No, what stopped him was that Verity knew her own mind, had her fair share of pride and pushing her would only make her either dig in her heels or retreat.

If she could come to like him and trust him, then he could build on that. He had almost a year before he was out of mourning and would be expected to make a public show of seeking a wife. Months to show Verity the man behind the title, to build on what they had. And if that was not enough, then he at least knew how to hide pain.

Will pushed aside a pile of paperwork sent through by Fitcham and managed a rueful smile for his secretary's choice of phrase. No, he had not found the tangled tale of an ancient lease *of considerable interest.* Of any interest at all, in fact, although his concentration was not helped by an internal battle over whether or not to call on Verity that afternoon. It was too soon and she had said she was shopping for a new wardrobe, which would mean time-consuming fittings, he told himself. He would leave it for a few more days.

'Your Grace. A Reverend Harrington has called.' One of the footmen proffered a silver salver with one card in the centre. 'He is waiting in the Jade Room as I was unsure whether Your Grace is receiving.'

'Harrington?' Will picked up the card.

The Reverend Thomas Harrington, B.D. Cantab.
Vicar, St Wulfram's Church, Chelsea

Ah, yes, the large, dark, self-assured specimen who had behaved so possessively towards Verity in the park. Now what did he want?

'Your Grace?'

Will realised that he was tapping the rectangle of

pasteboard against the edge of the salver. 'Show him into here, John.' It might be more courteous to go to the visitor in the reception room and offer him refreshments, but instinct kept Will in the study. *My cave*, he thought with an inward smile.

'The Reverend Mr Harrington, Your Grace.'

They shook hands, Harrington took a seat, shot his cuffs, crossed his legs and smiled, displaying a fine set of white teeth. Will decided that he did not like the man and that he had no grounds other than Verity's impatience with him the day before and his own instincts.

'To what do I owe the pleasure of this call?' he asked, taking the other seat on the visitor's side of the desk. No need for displays of dominance. Yet.

'As you may have gathered yesterday, Your Grace, I have the pleasure of Miss Wingate's acquaintance.'

'Yes, I observed that Miss Wingate knew you.'

'And I observed that you had an admirably protective attitude to the young lady. Almost, I might venture, proprietary.'

Will narrowed his eyes at the cleric, whose smile hardened.

'As a man of the cloth I feel it my duty to come to you on a most delicate matter, one I feel bound to mention, as it touches the honour of your great house and name.'

'I find it extraordinary that you might concern yourself with something so personal to me. It might be best, Mr Harrington, if you were to come to the point directly.'

'As you say, Your Grace. Miss Wingate is a most attractive, lively and charming young lady, but—'

'Do have a care, Mr Harrington.' Will did not move.

'But she is not what she seems. Miss Wingate, I must

tell you with great sorrow, is a young lady of experience, if you follow me. I— *Aagh!*'

Will stood toe to toe with the man he had dragged from his chair by his neckcloth. 'I did tell you to have a care, Mr Harrington.' He let go and the clergyman sat down with a thump.

Will resumed his seat, crossed his legs. 'Continue, sir. Carefully.'

Harrington tugged at his neckcloth, cleared his throat. He had gone pale, but he hung on to his composure. 'Some years ago Miss Wingate and I were…close. I was on the verge of offering for her hand. I was young and, as a theological student, inexperienced in carnal matters.'

And I'll believe that when the Prince Regent takes holy orders.

Will wanted to strangle the bastard, but he needed to discover just how much venom this particular viper contained.

'A chaste kiss one evening by the summer house be- came… I tried to be strong, tried to resist, but her at- tractions overcame me, her wantonness—'

'So you ate the apple,' Will said. 'This certainly has a theological theme to it. Genesis three, if I am not mis- taken.' He stood up and Harrington shot to his feet. 'I should call you out, of course, for slandering a lady, but duels are for settling matters of honour between gentle- men and you are a worm, sir. I think I will adjust your features until you are ready to apologise for your sor- did accusations.'

'If you lay another finger on me I will make certain that all of London knows that Verity Wingate is no vir- gin,' Harrington said breathlessly. 'I can describe the mole on her thigh, I can repeat what she says in the throes of passion—' He slid rapidly around the desk when Will took a step forward. 'I will not fight a duel with you, even if you offer one. It is beneath the dignity of my cloth.' He eyed Will warily. 'And I do not think that such a perfect gentleman as yourself, a premier nobleman, will stoop to murder.'

For Verity I might.

But there was more that Harrington wanted to say, he could tell. He would not have risked a beating just to spread his trail of slime over Verity's good name.

'So you paid me a call out of the goodness of your heart to tell me the touching tale of how an innocent young cleric was debauched by a wanton and all to protect my good name?'

'You should be forewarned if you are interested in the lady. I mean only a friendly warning in exchange for a small favour.' Harrington's confidence was returning with every second that Will kept his hands by his sides, but he could smell the nervous sweat, see the tremor in his hands.

'Yes?'

'The deanery in the diocese of Elmham is about to become vacant, the present Dean is unwell and unlikely to recover. The influence of a duke—*your* influence— will secure it for me.'

'Now, why did you not marry Miss Wingate? I wonder. Do not give me any nonsense about being repelled by her falling prey to your seduction. Could it be that her father's illness meant there were no favours to be got from your prospective father-in-law? Yes, it must be that. And now you believe you can use her again because you have picked up the gossip about the two of us being stranded overnight on an island and assume that Miss

Wingate will become my bride.' He moved a little closer, smiled. 'You should make certain of your facts before you show your hand, Vicar. The lady has refused me.'

The colour ebbed and flowed in Harrington's face before he recovered himself. 'But you care for her, she is your neighbour.'

Will told himself to tread warily. Short of murder, he could not be certain of shutting Harrington's mouth. There had been something Will could not quite identify in the other man's tone when he spoke of Verity: anger, perhaps? Certainly, spite. Somehow she had wounded him, because this was not merely disappointed hopes of a marriage schemed for and foiled when the Bishop had been forced to retire. Now he was determined to secure his prize or damage Verity as a reprisal.

There were a number of possibilities for drawing Harrington's teeth, more or less within the law, but he needed to make certain he knew precisely what was at hazard before he showed his hand. 'That is true,' he conceded.

Harrington had edged his way right around the desk and Will reached the great carved chair behind it, the chair that had been his grandfather's. He sat down and took a moment to recall the old man and his teaching. With a wave of his hand towards the seat opposite he steepled his fingers together, bent his head as though in thought and waited until the Vicar had seated himself, rather more warily this time.

'The lady's welfare and good name are important to me,' Will admitted, his gaze still on his fingertips. The urge to fling Harrington through the window was almost overpowering and that might show in his eyes. Let the man think he had the upper hand for a while; it might dent Will's pride, but that was a small concern now. 'I have no influence with the present Bishop of Elmham, who was present when Miss Wingate and I returned from the island and severely displeased him by failing to marry. However—' he raised his eyes and looked directly at Harrington '—the Archbishop of Canterbury is one of my godfathers.'

Greed, triumph, calculation—they were all there in the other man's dark eyes. He thought he had won the lottery. This was far better than he had imagined, Will could see. 'I would have to proceed carefully,' he pointed out. 'He has many requests and this must seem perfectly genuine if it is to succeed. We must allow a little time to pass for it to appear that I am becoming well acquainted with your virtues.'

Harrington smirked. 'Of course. I could allow a month, given the state of the present incumbent's health.'

A man is dying and you calculate how many days he has left so you can step into his still-warm choir stall. I am going to destroy you, Vicar.

Will reached out for the bell-pull. 'Come back in one week, unless I send for you sooner.' The door opened. 'John, see Mr Harrington out.'

Now, the important thing was to deal with this without letting Verity find out. She had enough to deal with as it was, she did not need to know that her treacherous lover was using her as a bargaining chip. Will picked up a pen and scrawled an urgent note to Fitcham.

'The Reverend Mr Harrington, my lady,' Wethering announced.

Aunt Caroline broke off from her conversation with Lady Godwin. 'Thank you, Wethering, another cup, if you please. Mr Harrington, good afternoon. It is quite some time since we have met, is it not?'

The shortbread finger that Verity had just picked up crumbled over her skirt and she brushed frantically at the mess while Miss Yarrow, sitting next to her, flapped with her handkerchief.

What was Thomas doing here? She looked around, but there was no possibility of escape. This was one of her aunt's regular days for receiving; the drawing room was crowded with ladies, two elderly gentlemen and one awkward youth dragged along by his doting mama. She had actually been relaxing after a morning's shopping, relieved to find that no one was tactless enough to refer to the scandal or the Duke.

For the first night after their encounter she had hardly been able to sleep, worrying over Thomas's promise to call *at the earliest opportunity*, but daylight had made that seem like no more than a passing jibe. He could gain nothing from her and, surely, no one could hold a grudge over lost dignity for so long. When four days had passed she had begun to relax.

Now her stomach felt as though she had swallowed too many of Gunther's ices and her hands were unsteady as she put down her plate and thanked Miss Yarrow for her help.

Aunt Caroline was introducing Thomas and he, with all the skill of a cleric used to a fashionable parish, was responding with appropriate suavity. Perhaps he was only baiting her, giving her a shock by appearing.

'I see a place free by Miss Wingate,' he said. 'Excuse me, ladies, thank you so much.' Balancing cup and plate, he wove his way between chairs and chaises and sat down beside Verity as the volume of conversation picked up. 'And here I am, as I promised. I do hope you have suffered no ill effects from your fall in the park?'

She turned, creating a private space where, low-voiced, they would not be overheard. 'None, other than the unpleasant sight of you.'

Thomas raised his eyebrows. 'Tut, tut, Miss Wingate. That is no way to speak to someone who can ruin your reputation.'

'Have you not heard? It is already besmirched and through no fault of my own. I am, as you can see, surviving that scandal. I am invited to Court. I am received and acknowledged.'

'And you have a good friend in the Duke of Aylsham.' His smile was smug, his eyes, spiteful.

'The Duke is a good neighbour.'

'Whose name is now linked with yours. You have already made society look at him twice for failing to marry the daughter of the so very respectable Bishop of Elmham after your island romp. Now just think how he will appear if it is revealed that he is still entangled with her and that she is not the virtuous young lady who has been receiving all this sympathy for the unfortunate stranding, but a wanton who seduces innocent young clerics? Lord Appropriate, the model of virtuous nobility, revealed as a fool and a shirker. Delicious.'

Verity put down her cup, the rattle of the saucer on the little side table seeming as loud as a church bell. No one took the slightest notice. 'It would ruin your reputation as well. And you have more to lose.' Somehow she kept her voice steady.

'Goodness, I wouldn't be spreading the tale myself and the poor young man would not be named, you silly chit.' Now the venom was clear in his voice. 'You cannot accuse me without confirming the story is true, now can you?'

No, she could not. But surely he could see the weakness in his threats? 'What would be the point? I have nothing you want—no money, no influence.'

'I do not want anything from you, Verity my sweet. All I desire is payment for your little jest by the river, for being made to look a fool. And your ruin and your knowledge that you have tarnished the name of the Duke of Aylsham will be quite sufficient.' He put down his untouched cup of tea and stood up. 'Now, delightful though it was to see you again, my dear Miss Wingate, I must bring this visit to an end and allow room for more of Lady Fairlie's many important guests.'

Chapter Twenty

I must tell him. I cannot tell him.

Verity paced up and down beside the reservoir at the north-eastern corner of Green Park, her long-suffering maid trailing a few steps behind her. The occasional sound of a stifled yawn was audible above birdsong, the sound of early morning traffic along Piccadilly and the distant lowing of the park's herd of dairy cows being gathered together for their morning milking.

If I tell him he will call Thomas out.

Which Harrington richly deserved, of course. But what if Will killed him? Surely a duke was powerful enough to escape the worst consequences of that, but how would Will feel with a death on his conscience, to say nothing of the resulting talk?

If I tell him he will despise me for being a fool and for my weakness in allowing myself to be seduced.

He might even think her wanton and suspect that she had slept with more men than Thomas. Will had never allowed the passion he so clearly felt overcome him, he had never tried to make love to her.

Because he believes me to be a virgin and a respectable lady and now he is going to discover that I am not.

She gave herself a little shake. What did that matter? What mattered was that none of this was Will's fault and so she must tell him, as soon as possible, because then he might be able to prevent Thomas spreading his horrible smears.

I love him and he is going to hate me.

Verity turned the corner of the reservoir and stopped to allow three nursemaids taking their charges out for some fresh air to walk across to one of the benches. But what did that matter? Will did not want to marry her, had never *wanted* to marry her. He certainly did not love her. He already thought her behaviour unseemly, her interests faintly shocking and her willingness to speak her mind, outrageous.

But he had wanted to be her friend and, somehow, that brought the tears to her eyes for the first time. She shocked, baffled and annoyed him, even if he did desire her, yet he had still wanted to be her friend. One of the babies let out a howl and began to sob. And why was she letting that upset her? She had known the possibility of ever finding someone who would want to marry her, and whom she wanted to marry, was tiny. But the children of that marriage were theoretical, yet those she might have had with Will were, somehow, very real.

Verity turned abruptly. 'Logic.'

'Miss?' The maid, side-stepping to avoid running into her, blinked in confusion.

'Nothing. I'm sorry, I was talking to myself.'

You pride yourself on your intellect, so think logically. Firstly, you love Will, but he does not love you. Therefore, secondly, you are not going to marry him. Thirdly,

*his good name is more important than any shame your
own bad judgement brings down on you, therefore,
fourthly, you must tell him about Thomas Harrington
and, somehow, stop him calling the man out.*

Things were bad enough without that.

Fifthly: and then tell Papa.

Clarity, she was almost surprised to discover, did
not make the prospect in front of her any easier. If you
dreamed there was a monster in the dark of your bedchamber, and you lit a candle and discovered that there
really was something with fangs in the wardrobe…

'Molly.' She waited for the maid to catch up. 'We are
going home now.'

'Yes, miss.'

'And after breakfast I will change into my new walking dress and pelisse. I will be paying a call.' Not that
looking her best was going to be the slightest help in the
interview ahead of her.

'Yes, miss.'

'And I will require you to come with me.' Visiting
a gentleman's home alone, or with a maid, was outrageous. But what was one more social transgression on
the negative side of the scales weighing her reputation?

'There is a young lady to see you, Your Grace.'

Will looked up from the papers he and Fitcham had
spread out before them and saw his secretary's startled expression. He probably looked as disconcerted. 'A
young lady, at this hour, alone?'

'With her maid, Your Grace. She declined to give
me a card.'

There was only one young lady so reckless as to call
on a man in broad daylight in the heart of fashionable

London. At least Verity had retained discretion enough not to hand over a card for the servants to read. 'Where is she? You did not leave her on the doorstep?'

The footman's lips tightened, as near to a retort as a well-trained servant would go.

'No, of course you didn't. Is she veiled?'

'Yes, Your Grace. I have asked the young lady to sit in the Painted Room, with her maid.'

'Thank you. Tell her that I will be with her directly.'

'Small mercies,' he said to Fitcham as the door closed behind the man. 'A maid and a veil. I can only pray that she did not arrive in her aunt's carriage with the crest on the doors.'

'Miss Wi— Er…the young lady must have a matter of some urgency.' Fitcham tapped one bony finger on the open atlas in front of him. 'Surely the gentleman whose future we are arranging has not made a move already?'

'I sincerely hope not,' Will said as he went out. What was he going to do with Verity? How was he going to keep her safe if she did these reckless things? Medieval visions of banishing awkward females to locked towers occurred to him. Tempting…

Verity stood up as he opened the door, as did the little dab of a female sitting in the corner. Much good she would be if anyone offered her mistress any insult or threat—she wouldn't be able to deal with a six-year-old pickpocket, let alone some buck on the prowl.

'Your maid can wait outside.' Will held the door open and the girl, after one glance at her mistress, scuttled out. He closed it with a certain emphasis and was annoyed that Verity did not so much as start nervously. 'What in blazes are you doing here?' And what in blazes had happened to his manners? Was this what love did to you—reduced a gentleman to some sort of primitive?

'Good morning to you, too, Your Grace.' Verity dipped a mocking curtsy as she flipped back her veil. She looked as though she had not slept for days, he thought. There were dark shadows under her eyes, despite some expert powdering. Her poise seemed to be maintained through tense muscles, not natural grace, and her voice had a brittle edge.

'You look ill,' Will said. He wanted to hold her, kiss her until she forgot how tired and anxious she was, tell her he loved her. 'Verity, there is something—'

Her chin came up. 'You certainly know how to make a woman feel special. I apologise if I have dragged you away from some riveting entertainment.'

It was enough to stop that self-indulgent urge to pour out his feelings. She needed his protection, his friendship. She did not want anything else, not yet. He had months to build her trust, her…affection. 'I was working with Fitcham. That is rarely entertaining. Did you drive here in your aunt's carriage?'

'Am I so totty-headed that I remember a veil but forget the crests on the doors, you mean? No, I did not. I walked.' She ignored the exasperated sound he made and swept on. 'There is something important I have to tell you, Will.' She hesitated. 'Two things. Roderick—'

So that air-headed cousin of hers had opened his big mouth, had he? This situation went from bad to worse. 'I do not want to hear them, Verity. I want you out of here, safely at home. I am dealing with this.'

For a second he thought that she was going to sit down, then that she was going to faint. 'Dealing with what?'

'The talk in the clubs.'

'*What* talk in the clubs? I thought… The ladies all seem to accept that I was blameless. That we were both the victims of an accident and there is nothing scandalous.'

Hell and damnation. 'Nothing. I was speaking of something else.'

'No, you were not. Tell me.' She swept up to him, toe to toe, took his upper arms and tried to shake him. Will stood stock-still, feeling like a bull terrier being threatened by a mouse. A very fierce, brave mouse. '*Tell me.* Or I swear I'll ask Roderick, because it is something he knows, isn't it? You thought he had told me something.'

'You said his name.' Will was playing for time and they both knew it.

'I was going to say I would have asked for his escort, but he is away for a few days.' She did not move and the force of her grip on his arms was almost painful.

Now he was so close he could see those signs of strain far more clearly. Was it possible that she had lost weight in the few days since he had seen her? He wanted to kiss her, hold her, sweep her up in his arms and take her away from all this. Verity should be cherished, nurtured—and argued with.

'The sensible ladies have taken their lead from Lady Fairlie and Her Majesty. The clubs…the clubs are full of men who enjoy scandal, especially sexual scandal. They have been talking, speculating. There are no wagers in the betting books, none of them would risk me calling them out, I think. But I will put a stop to the talk.'

'I see.' Verity released his arms, turned and walked away. 'I had no idea. What a…nuisance I am to you. But there is something else I must tell you about. Thomas Harrington—'

'I do not want to hear it from you,' he said harshly, cutting her off. Verity should not have to mention that man, should not have to confess her past to him as though she owed him an explanation, required his forgiveness.

She turned slowly, her face as white as paper now. 'Why not? What do you know?'

'It is disgraceful,' Will said, hearing all the banked anger he was feeling for the man harshen his voice. He stamped down on it, forced it back. Letting his fury loose now would affect his judgement and he needed to handle this delicately if he was to draw Harrington's teeth. 'Thoroughly sordid. We will not speak of it.'

'And yet you will deal with the talk in the clubs for me.' There was as little colour in her voice as her face now.

'I promised I would help you.'

'Because you were my friend. Yes. I understand. I will go now.' She turned, picked up her reticule from the chair.

Will opened the door to the hall. 'Escort this lady wherever she wishes to go. Good day, Ver— ma'am.'

'Good day.'

So he knew. Knew about her *affaire*, knew about Thomas. And it had made him angry and disgusted. To the man she loved she was a disgrace, her story a sordid one.

She was not going to cry, not here on the street. Not anywhere. If she gave way to tears and shame and lamentations she would be worse than useless and she still had to deal with Thomas before she escaped back to Dorset and the Old Palace and Papa.

'Thank you,' she said to the footman when they were within a hundred yards of the turning. 'I am almost home now.'

He hesitated, but Will had worded his orders carefully. This was where the lady wished to go. The man bowed and set off back the way he had come. Verity waited until he was out of sight, then continued on her way, the maid silent at her heels.

How could she deal with Thomas before he caused damage to Will, untold distress to her father? Her own reputation, Verity realised, hardly mattered now. She loved Will and she was not going to marry him, so there would never be anyone else.

Murder, bribery… No, even if she had the slightest idea how one secured the services of an assassin, she knew she could not kill. To save a life, perhaps—although she hoped if it ever came to that it would not result in anyone's death—but not in cold blood, even if the victim was a cold-blooded reptile himself.

Bribery. Verity considered that as she climbed the stairs to her bedchamber. Thomas was greedy and venal. He would certainly be tempted from vengeance by a large enough bribe, but it would be like paying blackmail. One payment would never be enough, he would come back for more, again and again.

She let Molly take her pelisse and hat and changed her shoes, put her hair in order, all the time thinking about Thomas. If she let herself think about Will, then she was going to throw herself on the bed and howl, and there would be more than enough time for that later.

Thomas was a bully and bullies backed down if they

were confronted because they were cowards, so Papa always said. Cowards were fearful, so, what was Thomas afraid of? Who was he afraid of?

He should be afraid of Will, but he clearly thought that she would not tell him or, that if she did, he was such a pattern card of respectability that he would not fight over one disgraced and disgraceful young woman.

There was Bishop Alderton, but he was not Thomas's superior and, besides, he already thought Verity was at best a hoyden and, at worst, all that Thomas would accuse her of being. The thought of appealing to him for help was rather less attractive than the idea of walking down St James's Street with a placard announcing that she was a trollop.

She ought to know which parishes the Bishop of London was responsible for... But why stop at a mere bishop? She had met the Archbishop of Canterbury on three occasions and he had seemed a very fair and reasonable man, not a prig like Bishop Alderton. He respected her father and she felt certain—almost certain—that if she was completely frank with him, he would help her and deal with Thomas.

Although I would much prefer not to have to.

The thought of confessing her youthful mistakes to a venerable churchman made her toes curl. She would give Thomas one chance to withdraw his threats, admit that they should forget the past and then, if he would not, she would go to the Archbishop.

Her reticule bumping against her thigh was satisfyingly heavy. Verity mounted the steps to Thomas's front door and pulled the bell, looking around while she waited. The vicar's house was on one side of the little square with the church of St Wulfram opposite. A very nice neighbourhood and very nice house. He would not want to lose this.

All very genteel and, although she was alone with no maid, no one was staring in a vulgar manner. Presumably well-dressed, veiled women were a common sight on the Vicar's front steps. Were they all calling to discuss one of the welfare committees this parish doubtless abounded in or, knowing Thomas, were some of them visiting the handsome Vicar for other reasons altogether?

'Yes, ma'am? How may I help you?' A very superior footman in livery was waiting respectfully for her to stop air-dreaming.

'I am here to see the Vicar. I do not have an appointment. Please tell him it relates to the effectiveness of cold bathing.'

'Cold… Yes, ma'am. Would you be so good as to step into the drawing room and I will ascertain whether Mr Harrington is free to receive you.'

The drawing room was located at the back of the house. It was furnished with good taste, nothing was vulgar or ostentatious, but money had been spent wisely to create just the right image. A clergyman who was 'one of us' as far as the parishioners of this fashionable parish were concerned—undoubtedly a vicar who was going to rise up the social scale still further.

Verity sat down with her back to the door. She had no desire to find Thomas between her and the way out if she needed to leave in a hurry.

He came in more quickly than she had imagined and from his raised colour she guessed that her unexpected arrival had disconcerted him. 'What are you doing here?'

'I came to discuss your threats,' she said, hoping she

sounded bored and disdainful. Keeping her gaze on his face, she loosened the drawstring on her reticule and slipped her right hand inside until her fingers closed over the butt of her uncle's duelling pistol.

'They were not threats, Verity. I was making promises.' He took the seat opposite her, crossed his legs and smiled.

'I see. In that case there is only one thing I can do.'

'Go home to your papa and wave goodbye to your Duke and to respectable society.'

'Give up and let you win? Good gracious, whatever made you think that I was such a feeble creature, Thomas? I shall go and see the Archbishop of Canterbury and tell him the entire story.'

'It would ruin you.'

'But I will be ruined anyway if you carry out our threats. This way I will have the great satisfaction of knowing that I have brought you down into the bargain. You must see the attraction of that.'

He stood up. 'Who knows you are here?'

Verity slid the pistol out into plain view and lifted it. 'I am able to use this. I taught myself to shoot in the country. Target practice, you know—I am accounted quite a good shot with a pistol and bow and arrow, although a bow might have caused raised eyebrows on the streets of Chelsea.'

'You wouldn't dare.'

The hair on the nape of her neck stirred as though in a cool breeze, but she told herself to keep calm, that his expression was frustrated fury, not killing rage. Thomas's gaze was darting from her face to the door and then to the far corners of the room and his mouth was half-open, as though he was about to rage at her.

'This is one of my uncle's Mantons. Hair trigger, of course. And, yes, I would dare. Dare to shoot you if you threaten me, dare to confess all to the Archbishop. You see, I love William Calthorpe, my Duke, and I will not have him punished for my follies. He does not love me, but then I would not expect him to. I have been nothing but a trouble to him from the moment we met and I am the most unsuitable woman for him to marry. But there it is and there is nothing to be done about it.'

'I would not say that,' Will remarked from behind her, his voice husky.

Chapter Twenty-One

Verity jerked round, her finger tightened on the trigger and the gun fired. There was a splintering crash, Thomas screamed and Will took the pistol out of her hand.

'A pleasant enough Chinese bowl, but not of the best period,' he remarked, gesturing towards the shattered remains in the hearth.

'You could have killed me! I'll have the law on you—'

'And I shall tell the constable that I entered the room just as Miss Wingate was defending her virtue from your cowardly attack. Most fortunately I had this weapon on me, fired a warning shot—and so on and so forth. Mr Fitcham here was witness to the entire incident, weren't you, Fitcham?'

'Indeed, Your Grace. A most disgraceful affair.' The secretary turned and faced the footman who was trying to push his way into the room. 'Nothing to worry about, my man. All under control and nobody hurt. Is that not so, Vicar?'

'Er... Yes. Yes, just an accident, Simon. You may go.'

Fitcham came into the room, closed the door behind him and sat at the table in the corner. Verity glanced at him, but he was calmly removing papers and a portable ink well from a small case.

'My dear.' Will took her hand, still trembling from recoil and shock, and kissed it. 'My very dear Verity.'

'When—when did you come in?' He had heard her, of course. The door opening silently behind her was what had caused that draught. She pulled her hand away.

He looked very serious. 'You were telling the Vicar all about hair triggers.'

Will had heard her confess that she loved him. So had Fitcham. There was nowhere to hide, the floor was not going to open up. She could feel the blood heating her cheeks, knew she could not meet his gaze.

At least he heard me acknowledge how unsuitable I am. At least they know I have no hopes, no expectations.

That was not particularly consoling.

'Why not sit down over here?' Will took her elbow and she went, unresisting, to the armchair at the side of the room. When he turned back she saw he was smiling, that false, dangerous social smile. 'Now, Mr Harrington. There is absolutely no need for Miss Wingate to visit the Archbishop or to write to him.' He must have heard her gasp of protest, because he glanced towards her, shook his head. 'I have already been to Lambeth Palace and called on His Grace, my godfather, and secured an appointment for you, one he feels is most appropriate to your character and talents.'

'Thank God someone has some sense.' Thomas shot her a look of hatred mingled with triumph.

'Indeed. You will be setting sail within the week to take up the post of Assistant Chaplain to the head of the Anglican Mission to Seamen based in English Harbour on the island of Antigua. Regrettably the previous incumbent died of yellow fever, but that does open up this fascinating opportunity for service to you. It is the main anchorage for His Majesty's Navy in the Caribbean, as you doubtless know. The scope for doing good and bringing lost souls to redemption is enormous, so the Archbishop says, and the head of the Mission is a most rigorously devout man.'

'It is a fever pit, a notorious fever pit!' Thomas gabbled. 'You promised me preferment. You promised me—'

'I promised I would speak to my godfather and secure you a position. I did not promise not to tell him that you were blackmailing me and a young lady whose only fault was to fall victim to a plausible seducer, a wolf in clerical robes. The Archbishop has placed you where he feels you would benefit most.'

'It will kill me. I won't go.'

'Now that is a pity, because your berth is all arranged.' Will studied the weapon in his hand for a moment, then looked back at the white-faced Vicar, who was clutching at the mantelpiece. 'My cousin, Vice-Commodore Lord Anstruther, is sailing tomorrow and he has sent two of his larger seamen along to help you pack and find your way to the ship. He will also ensure that, should you start slandering Miss Wingate, or anyone else for that matter, you will find an ocean voyage even less healthy than English Harbour. Unhealthy, short and very wet.'

Through the fog of her own embarrassment and relief Verity saw the realisation come over Thomas that he had nowhere to escape. She wondered if he had ever failed to get what he wanted before. When she had pushed him into the river, of course... Otherwise he must have thought himself invincible, his rise unstoppable. 'But—my parish, my possessions…'

'A most excellent young clergyman has kindly agreed to step in at short notice,' Fitcham said, looking up from his notes. 'If you will give me written authorisation to your solicitor and banker, I will see your possessions safely stored and your affairs taken care of. Your will is up to date, I trust? Always wise before a sea voyage, I feel.'

Thomas subsided into a chair, his hands to his face. Verity felt a twinge of pity, then recalled the young lady he had been courting, Lady Florence Wakefield. Plain, not at all intelligent, doubtless being pressed by her relatives to marry this rising young cleric. She must think he loved her. Perhaps, after all, he did.

'Do you want to write to Lady Florence?' she asked.

Thomas lifted his head from his hands and stared at her. 'What for? The silly chit can't help me now.'

I must seek her out and tell her that she has had a narrow escape.

It was bad enough breaking your heart over a man who merited it. To be cast into despair by the loss of an unscrupulous climber was a waste of tears, Verity thought bleakly. She removed her handkerchief from her reticule, discovered that she had no tears to shed into it and sat twisting it into a knot.

She had been brooding, she realised when she came back to herself and found Thomas gone, the sound of deep voices in the hallway, the footman protesting that he had received no notice and Mr Fitcham assuring him that he, and the other staff, would be no worse off.

The room was empty. She could slip out through the

kitchen area if necessary, hail a hackney. Escape. She stuffed her handkerchief away, stood up.

'Are you ready to go back to your aunt?' Will rose from the deep wing chair beside the fireplace.

'*Will.* You made me jump, I thought you had gone. I will just go and find a cab. I am so glad you have dealt with Thomas... Goodbye.'

He caught her to him as she tried to reach the door, held her away from his chest at arm's length. 'Verity, you are positively gibbering. What is the matter?'

'Nothing. I really must go. Oh, and I must take the pistol with me. I borrowed it without asking.'

'I doubt your uncle is going to fight any duels today. It can wait. Verity, I heard you, very clearly, say you loved me. Why are you running away?'

'Because that is neither here nor there,' she told his neckcloth firmly. 'I mean, I like you very well and I am quite used to your being perfect in every way and I can even forgive you being a duke, but you have kindly said you will deal with any gossip in the clubs and all the influential matrons accept me and Thomas cannot spread his poison about either of us now. So I can go home and next time I come to London it will all be forgotten.'

'Do you not want to marry me, Verity?' Will asked.

'You don't love me and I would be a most unsuitable duchess, so I would be unhappy and you would be, too.'

'Do you think you could bear to stop talking to my top waistcoat button and look at me?'

'No.'

'Why not?'

'Because if I look at you I want to kiss you and that would not help in the slightest.' If he did not let her go,

she was going to weep and that would be even less help-
ful, she thought shakily.

'But it would cheer me up considerably,' Will said.
He switched his hold from her arms to her waist, picked
her up, deposited her on the edge of the table in a swirl
of Mr Fitcham's papers and bent to kiss her.

Verity kissed him back, curled her arms around him
and held him to her as, with lips and tongue, he pro-
ceeded to reduce her to helpless longing. Something
crackled beneath her, a long-fingered hand came to cra-
dle the back of her head and Verity blinked her eyes open
to find herself staring up at the ceiling and Will lying
beside her on the table.

'Will, we can't!'

'I can make love to my wife-to-be anywhere,' he said.
'Now, how does this charming garment unfasten?'

She was beyond coherent reply—even if she had been
able to remember how the gown did up. Will had worked
it out, she realised, as his hand slid, warm and gentle,
over her breast. She arched into his palm as he caressed
the swell of flesh above the edge of her corset with one
hand and the other slid up under her skirts, over the edge
of her garter, on to the bare skin.

This was Will and she loved him and she wanted him
and her whole body was screaming for him as his thumb
found her nipple and his fingers caressed over intimate
folds that she could feel were already wet for him.

He desired her, she had known that from their first
kiss, could tell it now from the rasp of his breathing and
the hard thrust of his body against her thigh. 'Verity. You
will be mine. Not here, not now, but soon.' One finger
found a point of aching sensitivity, moved and she cried
out at the exquisite pleasure of it.

So good. Seducing me as though he knows my body inside and out... Seducing...

Verity twisted away, found the edge of the table and staggered to her feet. 'No. Will, you are trying to seduce me into doing what you think is right and I will not, because I know it would be wrong.' She was weeping now, at last, feeling the moisture slipping down her face. She pulled up the neckline of her walking dress—goodness knew where her pelisse had gone—shook out her skirts, saw her reticule and grabbed for it.

'You might *want* me, but you do not need me and you have said yourself, over and over, that I would be a disaster of a duchess. Do you think I want to be tied to a man who does not love me? Who married me because he felt he had to and because he would quite like to get me into bed? If I did not love you, it would be bad enough, but now, it would break my heart.'

He stood stock-still, his clothing disordered, his hair across his brow, as dishevelled as he had been on the island where she had come to know him, perhaps where she had learned to love him. For once he seemed to be lost for words. Verity took her chance and ran, out of the door, down the hall, dodging between two burly men with straw hats and tarred pigtails who were ordering the footman to fetch his master's trunk, out of the front door and into the street. And there, just rounding the corner, was a hackney carriage.

What had just happened? Other than him losing his mind and his self-control and attempting to make love to Verity on a vicarage table and then standing like a lightning-struck tree when he should have been reassuring her. From the window Will saw Verity scramble into a hackney and drive off.

She loved him, she had said so, not only to Harrington, but again just now. He loved her and that was what she wanted, so why... Oh, hell. He hadn't told her, had he? He had demanded that she marry him, attempted to ravish her in conditions of extreme discomfort with strange men just the other side of an unlocked door, but he had not said those three simple words. Verity had many talents, but mind reading was not one of them, he told himself ruefully.

'Your Grace?' Fitcham stood just inside the door staring from the floor, where his paperwork was strewn, to his dishevelled employer and back again.

'Carry on, Fitcham,' Will said, with a sweep of his hand to encompass papers, errant vicars and hard-jawed sailors. He tugged his neckcloth into some semblance of order, scooped up his hat from the hall table and strode out of the house. Simply turning up on Lady Fairlie's doorstep with declarations of undying love was not going to convince Verity, he knew her well enough for that. She would assume that he was telling her he loved her because he was determined to do the right thing and marry her.

Will stopped dead in the middle of the pavement. A stout woman with a small dog on a leash swerved round him with a loud comment about young bucks with no manners. He lifted his hat automatically and she sniffed and walked on.

Verity believed that the most important thing in his life was being the perfect duke but, somehow, he had to convince her that she was what mattered most to him, perfection be damned. He saw a hackney and hailed it.

'Grosvenor Square.' As he settled back against the worn old squabs without a care for his coat he told himself that Verity would not simply run for home. Her aunt had accepted invitations for them over the next few days, including one to a Drawing Room at St James's Palace. Verity would not want to let Lady Fairlie down, he had to believe that.

'But what if he is there?' Verity said, for perhaps the sixth time that day. She was sitting in extreme discomfort on the backwards-facing seat of the Fairlies' town coach, her hooped skirt tilting up at an absurd angle and forbidden by her aunt to hold it down in case she creased the fabric. Her head was bent forward to avoid bending the three ostrich plumes in her headdress and she had to keep them to one side to avoid them tangling with those of her aunt opposite. Her uncle was barely visible to one side, his wife's bell-shaped skirt draped across the satin breeches of his Court suit. His dress sword and *chapeau bras* were held by straps in the roof of the coach and his expression beneath his powdered wig was one of stoical discomfort.

'If the Duke is present, which no doubt he will be, he will behave with the utmost decorum. If he bows and exchanges a few words of greeting, that will be all,' Lord Fairlie said, with rather more patience than his wife had been showing in response to the previous five queries. 'You should curtsy and merely respond with some platitude.'

Will had given up on her, that was clear. It was three days since the incident in Chelsea and a short note from Mr Fitcham informing her that a gentleman of their acquaintance had taken ship for the West Indies was the closest thing to a message from the Duke that she had received.

He must have finally accepted that it was futile, that his sense of honour—and his physical desires—weighed nothing in the balance against her complete unsuitability to be a duchess. And her declarations of love must have helped tip the balance, too, because what man wanted a wife pathetically loving him when he felt no such emotion for her?

The clock struck two as the crawling queue of carriages finally reached the door and there was the business of disentangling the ladies with their hoops and feathers, yards of train and fans without anyone treading on a hem, impaling themselves on the sword or knocking Lord Fairlie's wig askew. One last chance to wish silently that one had paid a visit to the privy, to discreetly blow one's nose and clear one's throat—it was preferable to choke silently to death than to cough or sneeze, apparently—then the slow progress along the corridors, nodding carefully to acquaintances, everyone keeping their voices low, their expressions dignified.

At least there were no disapproving glances from the matrons and, if there were some sideways looks from the younger men, that was no more than they were giving any of the other young ladies. Will must have trodden very firmly on the salacious club gossip. Perhaps, next year, she would feel comfortable coming back to London. Next year seemed a very long way away.

Then they were through the double doors, their names announced. To the left were rows of tall windows, to the right, unlit fireplaces and paintings in heavy gilded frames and ahead the Cloth and Canopy of State rising to the high ceiling, marking the position of the empty throne. The Queen, invisible behind a wall of hoops, plumes and wigs, would be seated on a slightly less impressive chair a step below.

As they edged forward, marshalled into a receiving line by men in Court uniforms encrusted with silver lace, Verity did her best not to stare around her too obviously. There were a number of young ladies being presented, all looking as terrified as she had once felt in their place, a cluster of naval and army officers, be-medalled and in their dress uniforms, all waiting to be congratulated on some engagement or another, diplomats, laden with foreign honours and colourful sashes but no familiar tall figure looking down his perfect ducal nose at the common herd.

Only he doesn't, she told herself. *Will doesn't look down on anyone, he merely holds himself to a higher standard as though an extra weight had been laid on his shoulders at birth and he is braced to bear it, convinced that if he relaxes for a moment it will all come crashing down and he will fail everyone whose welfare he holds himself responsible for.*

'Lord and Lady Fairlie, Miss Wingate, Your Majesty.'

Verity swept into a low Court curtsy, her back straight to balance the plumes, knees braced to support the weight of her skirts. She took a steadying breath to rise without a stumble and there, on the lowest step of the dais, was Will.

She had no idea how she managed to stand or how she kept her eyes fixed on the Queen, who spoke to her aunt as an old friend, smiled graciously at her uncle and then condescended to speak to Verity.

'I understand that you are to leave us, Miss Wingate.'

'Yes, Your Majesty. My father will be missing me.'

'Do give the Bishop my good wishes for his health. One found his sermons very enlightening.'

'Thank you, ma'am. He will be most gratified.'

'I trust, ma'am, that Bishop Wingate will also be gratified by the news of his daughter's betrothal, if I have your permission to put the question here and now.' Will spoke as though interrupting the Queen in the middle of a Drawing Room was a mere trifle. Around them there was the sound of sharp indrawn breaths, the flutter of fans. Out of the corner of her eye Verity saw the Chamberlain's head swivel to stare at Will.

'"Put the question," Your Grace?' The Queen's tone could have frozen the ratafia in the refreshment room.

'I crave your indulgence, ma'am. But Miss Wingate believes that I am so wedded to correct behaviour that I will never allow my true sentiments to show. I hope to convince her that my desire to marry her is so heartfelt, so real and founded on my deep love and affection for her that I would risk dismissal from Court in order to express it.'

Chapter Twenty-Two

She was asleep and dreaming, of course, Verity reasoned. No one interrupted the Queen. No one even initiated a change of subject in her presence. This was one of those ghastly dreams where one was dancing naked at Almack's or driving a curricle pulled by geese along Rotten Row at the fashionable promenade hour. Or perhaps she was ill, feverish. That must be it. She was in bed and this was a delirium.

'Well, Miss Wingate?' That could not be right. The Queen was addressing her. No one was naked and there were no geese to be seen, only Her Majesty looking at her, unsmiling, outwardly severe and yet with just the hint of a twinkle in those tired, faded, blue eyes. 'The Duke can leave or you may retire to a private room with your aunt. Or you may give him your answer now.'

With an effort she dragged her gaze from the Queen and looked at Will. He was smiling at her; he seemed unconscious of the fact that every person in that crowded room was staring at him, agog, but what she could see, and they could not, was that William Xavier Cosmo de Whitham Calthorpe, Fourth Duke of Aylsham, was nervous, that her answer mattered to him, that the love and affection for her that he had just professed, without hesitation, were real.

Verity took a deep breath and looked back at the Queen. 'Thank you, ma'am. You are very gracious. I have no need to withdraw because I have an answer for His Grace.' She curtsied again, not the deep obeisance that Court etiquette required, but as low as her shaky legs would let her. Then she stepped to the side and held out her hand to Will. 'Yes.'

She said it clearly, loud enough for everyone four ranks back to hear, but the room was suddenly filled with a buzz of conversation and shocked exclamations as he took her hand in his and raised it to his lips.

'You have our permission to retire, Miss Wingate. Lord and Lady Fairlie will doubtless wish to accompany you. Aylsham, I suggest you also retire. Doubtless you will need time to prepare for an immediate journey.' She inclined her head, a half-inch of cool acknowledgement. Will bowed, stepped down and backed away towards a side door. Verity and her aunt and uncle followed, made their way out as the throng parted to let them through.

'This way, my lord, my lady.' Someone, a very senior official by the weight of silver on his coat, ushered them into a room where Will was standing alone except for an elderly man with thinning hair who was speaking earnestly to him.

'Yes, I know,' Will said as they came in. 'Most irregular, enough to have me clapped in the Tower, I have no doubt, Edgerton. I will write a grovelling apology to Her Majesty, but it appears she is letting me off without threat of the headsman's axe. Now, if you will excuse us, I believe my betrothed wishes to have words with me.'

It could have been her imagination, but Mr Edgerton, whoever he was, muttered, 'I cannot say I blame her,' as he gave a stiff bow and stalked out.

Verity looked around, but she and Will were alone in the room, its heavy red-velvet hangings muffling all sound from outside. She should say something, but she had no idea what and, besides, how could words escape? She felt as though she had inhaled a great cloud of happiness and her lungs could not cope with anything as prosaic as words.

'Did you mean it?' Will asked, his gaze dark and intent over the few feet that separated them.

'Of course. Did you?' she said.

'I would never lie to you, Verity.' Then somehow they closed the gap between them and she was in his arms, hers tight around him, the hooped skirt tilting up and the metallic embroidery edging his formal coat scratching her cheek. The *chapeau bras* dropped to the floor unheeded from beneath his elbow. 'These damned feathers,' he growled, batting at them. 'How is a man supposed to kiss you?'

'I have no idea.' She took a step back, her skirts swinging like a bell. 'Will, that was the most—'

'Embarrassing? Ridiculous? Shocking?' he suggested, the side of his mouth tilting into that faint smile she found so irresistible.

'The most romantic thing I ever heard of. Will, do you think we will be banished from Court?'

'It would be a saving in ostrich plumes,' he said. 'Come here, my darling, turn around.' When she did, he flipped up her skirts, caught hold of the strings that fastened the ludicrous cage of hoops, gave them a tug and they fell to her feet.

'Will!' But her shriek was muffled by her three feathers as they were tweaked from her hair, slid down her nose and fell to the floor.

'Now that's better,' he said as he pulled her tight against him. 'Verity Wingate, I love you. I have been in love with you ever since I fell into your excavation and you set your Druid on me. I just did not realise it until that day in the park.'

'The day I fell out of the phaeton? But that is when I realised I loved you, too.' She stood on tiptoe and pressed her mouth to the corner of his lips. 'Why didn't you say so, you provoking man?'

'Would you have believed me? I decided I would woo you patiently over all the months of my mourning, hoping that eventually you would realise that I wanted to marry you.'

'And I was supposed to just guess that you loved me?' she demanded, indignant now. 'We have wasted *days.*'

'My only excuse is that I am new to being in love. We could make up for it now,' he offered.

'We are in St James's Palace,' Verity said with a faint shriek, making a despairing grab at some kind of restraint.

'My darling, are you going to prove to be a boringly conventional duchess?' Will enquired, looking up from his determined assault on her neckline.

'No. No, I promise to be an absolute disgrace—but may I work up to it? Oh, that is...not start by being discovered *in flagrante* by the Chamberlain? *Oh*, Will, kiss me like that again. Don't stop.'

Eventually he did and they clung together, laughing, shaking, trembling with frustrated desire.

'If you can forgive me for stopping, how soon can

we be married?' Will asked as they struggled to return their clothing to some kind of order. Verity stepped into her hoops and he tied them, smoothed out her yards of skirt and train like the most competent of lady's maids. 'You must forgive me, I have bent a feather.'

'Never mind.' She took them, threw the damaged one aside and pushed the remaining two into her coiffure. 'I can only hope you know a way out of the Palace, Will. And I would like to be married just as soon as possible, because I do not think I can stand stopping and behaving respectably much longer.'

'I do know a way out. And I have an idea for a wedding that will be exactly right, considering that we are both in disgrace and I am in mourning. I will take you back to Bruton Street and then call on my godfather again and hope I have not exhausted his good will.'

'The Archbishop?' she asked as Will opened a door, looked out and gestured for her to follow out into a deserted corridor. 'For a special licence?'

'For a very special licence,' he agreed. 'For a very special wedding.'

The dozen musicians were managing remarkably well, Will thought, considering that one of the violinists had fallen in the lake getting into the rowing boat and they were all crammed into a hastily made clearing behind the tiny cottage. He had been tempted to try moving the piano across, but Verity had explained that Miss Lambert would not have been able to play because she wanted her to be a bridesmaid.

He only hoped that none of the bridesmaids had fallen in. They must be on their way now.

'Stop looking at your watch,' his best man said.

Will looked down and grinned. Most people would have said that he should have asked one of his adult friends to stand as groomsman, but he had wanted Basil, the little wretch who had started this. Basil had risen to the occasion. He was neat as a new pin, scrubbed painfully pink and swore faithfully that not a single live creature was about his person. 'Is the ring safe?'

'Of course. It is on a ribbon pinned to my pocket, just like it was last time you asked. Listen! Something's happening.'

The musicians, who had arranged signals with a footman, stopped playing vaguely twiddly music and launched into something more positive. The dozen guests—all that could be fitted into the space in front of the cottage—sat up, stopped surreptitiously flapping at the insect life and fell silent then stood as the music changed to the 'Arrival of the Queen of Sheba.'

Will's stomach swooped, he felt the blood draining out of his face and wondered vaguely if he was going to faint. He never had, so it was only guesswork. Verity would never forgive him so he took a steadying breath and turned to face the temporary altar that the Reverend Mr Hoskins had set up. The Chaplain stood before it, smiling encouragement, and then the little congregation drew a collective sharp breath.

I can turn now, he thought as Basil gasped. Verity was walking very slowly out of the trees. Benjamin and Bertrand in front, strewing rose petals under the supervision of Alicia in her first grown-up, full-length dress.

The Bishop, stick in one hand, a beaming smile on his lips, had his daughter's hand on his arm and behind them Will glimpsed Verity's four friends with Araminta and Althea, the rest of the bridesmaids.

But they were a blur. Only one figure, the veiled bride, was in focus. She stopped, called to Alicia, gave her the bouquet of roses and myrtle that she was carrying and threw back her veil. And then she smiled and the world tilted on its axis.

He is so white, Verity had thought as she came into the clearing.

She had assumed that she would be the nervous one, that Will would negotiate the wedding with as much lofty ducal poise as he managed everything else. But she felt quite calm, buoyed up on clouds of happiness and the conviction that this was so perfectly right that nothing could go wrong now. She stopped and gave her flowers to Alicia, put back her veil and smiled at him and Will smiled back and raised his hand to his lips, then held it out to her.

'The Bishop's supposed to give her to you,' Basil said bossily, but her father extended his own arm so Will could take her hand before Mr Hoskins could say the words.

She turned and kissed her father and waited while a footman came and helped him to a chair at the side, then looked at her bridegroom, saw the love in his eyes and stood beside him as the Chaplain began to speak.

'Dearly beloved—'

'Dearly beloved,' Will said, tucking her hand under his arm as they stood on the beach and waved as the last of the little fleet of rowing boats pulled away and the voices and laughter of the guests became fainter over the water. There had been a great deal of good wine at what Will had insisted on calling the Wedding Picnic and now they were heading back to a more substantial meal at the Old Palace presided over by the Bishop and Will's stepmother, who had struck up an unlikely alliance during the preparations for the ceremony.

'I do love you,' he added, looking down at her. 'Are you very tired now?'

'Is that a polite husbandly way of asking whether I want to go to bed and sleep or go to bed and make mad, passionate love?' Verity asked. Her heart was doing very strange things and she was not at all certain it was designed to flutter quite like that, but if Will could control himself, so could she. Duchesses probably did not drag their husbands through the undergrowth in their eagerness.

'It was,' he agreed, very serious.

'Perhaps I should go and lie down and see how I feel?'

'An excellent idea. Allow me to carry you in case you feel faint on the way.'

'If I hadn't before, I am now,' Verity said against his neck as Will adjusted his grip on her and began to walk back to the cottage along the path that the gardeners had scythed the day before. 'This is quite indecently romantic, Your Grace.'

He made a very satisfactory growling sound as he ducked and carried her through the doorway into the cottage, then set her down on the bed. The staff had worked miracles with the tiny building. The walls were whitewashed, the windows clean with gay cotton curtains. The bed had a feather mattress and heaps of pillows, there was a rug on the floor and hampers of food, some on ice. There was even a discreet tent with commode and washstand and the fire was made up so that they could heat water or make tea.

'I find I am wide awake,' Verity said and stood up. 'And now I am going to take all your clothes off because I want to inspect my new husband *very* thoroughly.'

It was unkind to tease him, but perhaps Will was enjoying it, she thought, seeing his blue eyes turn indigo, his lips part, as she unbuttoned and untied, removed his stickpin and neckcloth, slid off his coat and waistcoat, pulled his shirt from the waistband. He did nothing to help her, but nor did he hinder, letting her hands go where she willed, holding his own away from his sides and not touching.

When she dropped to her knees and began to roll down his stockings he kicked them and his shoes away, then went very still when she stayed where she was, studying the evidence of his arousal through the fine cloth of his breeches.

Would he stay still if she continued to explore? Verity began to undo the buttons fastening his falls, then slipped her hands inside to touch.

Will said something under his breath, moved abruptly, then stood stock-still as she began to caress the hard heated flesh. She flipped the final button open, drew him out, stared, at the beautiful raw masculinity of desire.

I want to kiss him there.

Was that allowed? She had no idea, but she was now a disgraceful duchess, so she could try to see.

Under her lips he was smooth and hot.

'Dear God. *Verity.*'

His hands closed around her head, she could feel him fighting the urge to move against her mouth. 'You shouldn't.'

'You don't like it?' She looked up.

'I shouldn't ask it of you,' he ground out.

'But you aren't asking and I want to.' And when she bent her head and began to lick he stood there and let her.

Smooth and hot and hard and musky with the scent of man, of her lover. Of Will. Impatient, Verity pushed at his breeches, pulled them down over his narrow hips, closed her hands over his taut buttocks and took him into her mouth.

It lasted one dizzying moment of discovery, then he pulled her to her feet, kicking his breeches away. 'I can't... Too good... Not this time. *Verity.*'

She sank into the feather mattress under his weight, his mouth sealing in her whimpers of need as he caressed her, palms skimming over peaking nipples, down over her belly, down to push her legs gently apart and tease his way between the folds that were wet for him already.

'Let me,' he murmured, lifting on one elbow as his fingers continued to work wicked magic. 'I won't hurt you, tell me if you want me to stop.'

'You won't. I won't.' The words were wrenched out of her as he slid two fingers into her and her whole body convulsed into pleasure. *'Will.'*

'Yes, my love,' he said, and shifted over her. 'I'm here.'

And he was, filling her, possessing her. He was true to his word, it didn't hurt, not like it had with Thomas, but it was overwhelming, even so. But she trusted him and her body wanted him and adjusted and welcomed him in. She rose up to meet him, dug her fingers into his back and wrapped her legs around his waist and cried out her encouragement, urging him on when he would have held back, learning to move so he gasped out his own pleasure with each thrust and she lost herself, not sure where she stopped and Will began.

She opened her eyes and found his were intent on her, every line of his face taut and racked as though in pain. 'Yes,' she said and the world unravelled as he shouted her name and shuddered in her arms and the world swirled around her.

'How long can we stay here?' Verity asked after they had made love twice and were lying in a tangle of limbs.

'Like this?' Will heaved himself up on one elbow and began to toy with her left nipple, making her squeak. 'About another ten minutes, then we will feel sweaty and sticky and I will light the fire so you have hot water to wash. Then we will eat something and come back to bed.'

'That is not what I meant.' Verity pushed his hand away, rolled over and began to play with the hair on his chest in revenge. 'Here, on our island.'

'For two days. Then the food will run out and I'll hoist the flag on our new flagpole to summon the rowing boat.'

'Can we come back whenever we want?'

'Of course. Why?'

'Because I intend to be a very respectable, dignified, dutiful duchess. But I want to be able to escape with you to be an absolutely disgraceful one on a regular basis.'

'That sounds an excellent scheme.' Will sounded as though he rather doubted her ability to be dignified and dutiful for very long at a time and had no objections to that. 'I think I will love both my duchesses equally, but so far you haven't been *absolutely* disgraceful.'

'Have you any suggestions, Your Grace?'

'I have.' Will stood up, pulled her to her feet and led her outside.

'My love, we have no clothes on.'

'Darling, I cannot see as much as a sparrow to be scandalised. I think we shall have to go and shock some trout.' He scooped her up and marched purposefully towards the beach.

'Will? Will! Don't you dare! Will—'

The splash as they hit the lake was loud, the cold shocking, the feel of the water on her bare skin, delicious. 'You beast,' Verity said as she surfaced, splashing. 'I adore you. This feels almost as good as your lovemaking.'

'Nothing is as good as my lovemaking,' Will said, diving under. He came up in front of her, lifted her. 'Put your legs around my waist and slide down.'

'Oh!'

Perhaps the water isn't so cold after all.

'You, Verity Calthorpe, are the light of my life, the delight of my days, the wickedness of my nights and the most deliciously unsuitable duchess in England. I don't know what I did to deserve you, but I never mean to let you go.'

'And you, William Calthorpe, are the most perfect Duke in England and I love you for it.'

Verity had a whole speech ready about how much she adored him, but he kissed her and they overbalanced and then they were far too busy showing each other how much in love they were to be able to find any words at all.

* * * * *